SLAVIC SU1
AN ANTHOLOGY OF SLAVIC-INSPIRED
SPECULATIVE FICTION

Slavic Supernatural: An Anthology of Slavic-Inspired Speculative Fiction
Publisher: Shtriga
ISBN
ebook 978-953-8360-25-1
paperback 978-953-8360-26-8

EDITORS
Vesna Kurilić and Antonija Mežnarić
COVER DESIGN
Antonio Filipović

shtriga.com
shtrigabooks@gmail.com

SLAVIC SUPERNATURAL

AN ANTHOLOGY OF SLAVIC-INSPIRED SPECULATIVE FICTION

Rijeka, 2023

TABLE OF CONTENTS

FOREWORD
by Karmen Fodrek
host of the podcast Mythoslavic

Mythology, in its marvelous essence, has been an important part of most cultures for thousands of years, enriching each and every one of them.

It can help by giving meaning to people's lives—explaining the origin of natural phenomena and ideas, revealing ancient beliefs and customs, the purpose of cultural rituals and ceremonies, understanding our elders and ancestors, and, most importantly—it has provided endless inspiration for many magical stories throughout the centuries.

The Slavic mythology is certainly no exception.

It includes the polytheistic beliefs and rituals of the various Slavic nations, and it is a home to numerous mythical beings, those that people respected and feared, as well as the Gods the ancient Slavs worshipped.

There are a number of mythical creatures from folklore in Slavic Mythology that have paved their way into pop culture and it has embraced them in full. They are featured not only in the form of books, comics, television shows, and movies but also in music, art, theater, even cartoons. Nowadays, it's almost impossible to find a medium where Slavic mythology is not represented.

Today, in the modern age, everyone has their own version of every mythology. Slavic mythology certainly came from the past, but it has become a part of life for many people.

You've probably heard about the Slavic pantheon that includes thousands of deities and creatures, however, what do we really know about it?

Throughout their history, the Slavs have believed in many Gods, monsters and legends, that's for sure. They have always lived on the frontiers of Europe, interacting with other cultures, which gave them a rich mythology to call upon.

Having all that in mind, Slavic mythology is undoubtedly an ever-growing archive of stories handed down through the centuries, through many generations and families, each story more intriguing and captivating than the next.

Float into the far reaches of Slavic mythology with these eleven short stories inspired by Slavic mythology, ranging across secrets, love and loss, fear and friendship, darkness and light. All in all, eleven mystical tales that will take you to a world you never knew existed.

So, buckle up and embark on a journey full of pure Slavic magic, raging werewolves, mighty dragons, deceitful fairies, divine Gods and terrifying witches with the Slavic Supernatural anthology.

INTRODUCTION

As a micro publishing house (which we lovingly call a 'publishing cottage') from a small South Slavic country only rich people know about—if a certain show is to be believed—we were floored by the reactions and interest shown for our first anthology. Not to mention, incredibly happy that people trusted us to share their stories with the world. This book collects a variety of authors, from newcomers making their debut here, to professional writers with plenty of published books, and those with literary awards under their belt. It's a small book, as is our cottage, but it's a product of love.

The cover was illustrated and designed by the amazing Antonio Filipović, who always knows what to do with our ideas, takes in the atmosphere of the stories, and turns it into a visual sensation. In this case, it's Morana, with her beautiful young face, an eerie look in her shining eyes, and with shriveled, old hands, against the background of a winter forest, with only a hint of spring at the back.

The symbolism in the cover was drawn directly from the creativity of our authors, who found their inspiration in winter and the seasonal changes, the coming of spring, the goddess Morana, and death. Many of these elements found their place in these stories. A dark atmosphere abounds in these tales of revenge, tragedies, trauma, oppression, and repression of love.

But there's also hope in here, adventure, and humor, spanning over the centuries written into the history of the Slavic nations. It's truly a combination of inspiration which arose from different Slavic cultures, folklore and mythology, but also a way of life.

Thank you all for being a part of this book, from our

Foreword author Karmen Fodrek—who shares Slavic tales on her podcast Mythoslavic—to the eleven authors whose hard work you have in your hands, and the cover artist who gave our book a face.

And in the end, thank you, dear reader, for picking it up and giving it a chance. May your days with these stories be filled with bittersweet joy, a sense of pride, and a dash of Slavic supernatural.

From a rainy Rijeka, 'The City That Flows',
Antonija and Vesna
February 2023

THE DEEP WOODS

JOSH REYNOLDS

BARON PALMAN VORDENBURG SITUATED himself on the wooden stool and reached into his coat for his cigarette case. Outside the hut, the sun was setting over the forested slopes of the Northern Urals, and the labourers were setting aside their tools as their overseers called them back into camp for the night. "Tell me," Vordenburg said, selecting a cigarette from the case.

"It comes in the night," replied the man standing in the doorway. He claimed his name was Andris Karole. He and his men had escorted Vordenburg from the train station at Chelyabinsk and into the Urals. They had spoken little, but that suited Vordenburg fine. He hadn't journeyed all this way to make idle chitchat.

Karole was nondescript in his shapeless brown military coat and his battered officer's cap. He had a pair of steel-rimmed spectacles in his hand, and was methodically wiping the lenses with a patched handkerchief as he stared out at the forest of dense Siberian pine. His only weapon was a Nagant revolver belted around his waist. The grips were worn smooth, denoting a weapon that had seen a fair amount of use, though he did not strike Vordenburg as a man who'd seen much combat.

"In my experience, these things usually do," Vordenburg said, lighting a cigarette. He hadn't bothered to offer one to Karole, who claimed a distaste for the social niceties of the bourgeoise.

11

Whether that extended to tobacco, Vordenburg couldn't say and didn't particularly care. "What does it look like?" Karole paused. "I have not seen it myself. I have only second-hand reports." He slid his spectacles on.. "The loggers say it is bigger than a man. Hairy and strong."

Vordenburg frowned at the vagueness of the description. Hairy and strong could be anything. "I am told there are bears in the Urals," he pointed out.

Karole turned to Vordenburg. "It is not a bear. If it were a bear, we would not require one such as you, Comrade Vordenburg." He did not sound pleased by this admission. Neither did he sound displeased. It was as if he were commenting on the weather. "You will forgive me if I do not use your title. The legitimacy of the hereditary aristocracy is not recognized by the Soviet state."

Vordenburg grunted. His title was largely theoretical these days. His lands were gone, confiscated in the aftermath of the war. Styria was no longer home; indeed, it was no longer anything at all. Since the dissolution of his homeland, he had lived in many places.

But while he might have lacked a place to call his own, he was still possessed of a purpose. Hardly glorious, but necessary all the same. "I do not care what you call me, only that your masters pay me in a timely fashion."

"My superiors have agreed to your fee." Karole grimaced as he said it, as if the thought pained him. Perhaps it did. Karole was a true believer, Vordenburg thought. For Karole, the glorious workers' paradise was just that—a utopia. That many, including the forced labourers who inhabited this very camp, might disagree with him was not something he likely considered. But Vordenburg was neither a politician nor a revolutionary and left such matters to those who were best suited to them. The world had plenty of both after all, but it only had one of him.

"They always do." Vordenburg pushed himself to his feet. He was taller than Karole, and rawboned. His long face was marked by a surfeit of scars, some small, some large. Each attested to the righteousness of his chosen path. Or so he often prayed, in the sleepless hours before dawn. "What else do you know?"

The questions were mere formality. A way to fill the time. Before journeying to Chelyabinsk, he had taken the liberty of searching the records of the old Imperial Russian Forestry Corps for similar occurrences in the region. He was surprised that Karole had not done it himself. Maybe he had, and simply not mentioned it.

Regardless, what he had learned was that the pine forests of the Urals were home to many strange things—all of them duly reported and catalogued on behalf of superiors who would never read said reports. Numerous encounters with a foul-smelling, shaggy giant had been recorded in the years prior to the war. *Borovoi*, the loggers called it—'he of the pine barrens.' Most Russians just called it 'Leshy', or 'he of the forest'. The reports had tapered off as logging efforts dwindled to almost nothing. But now the logging had started up again, and the Leshy had returned to make his displeasure known.

Karole looked back at the forest. His fingers tapped nervously at the pistol on his hip. "The deeper our people push into the forest, the more aggressive it becomes," he replied, finally. "Like an animal defending its territory. Only it is no animal. No animal can uproot and hurl a tree the way a man might toss a javelin. They lost a wagon of good timber the day before we arrived. The day before that, it dropped a boulder onto the paddock and killed their horses. It even dragged one of them off—to eat, presumably."

"Hopefully," Vordenburg said. He joined Karole at the door and peered out at the forest. He had seen many forests in his life, all over the world. No two were ever the same. It was the shadows. The shadows were always different. "Have you lost many of your men to the beast?"

Another hesitation. Or, perhaps, a moment of calculation. "Fifteen. Just labourers, thankfully."

Vordenburg raised an eyebrow. "So many, then?" He'd come to the conclusion early on that Karole wasn't telling him everything. He didn't know whether that was simply because Karole didn't know much of value, or because Vordenburg was a foreigner.

Karole shrugged. "There are more where they came from."

Vordenburg blew a plume of smoke into the air. It twisted like a snake and dispersed. The temperature was dropping. It got cold in the mountains at night. "I am sure they were only too glad to give their lives for the Soviet state."

Karole looked at him, the light of the setting sun reflecting off of the lenses of his spectacles. He adjusted them. "You were not hired to make vague criticisms, Styrian. You were hired to kill an unsanctioned abnatural entity."

"You are paying me to kill it. The criticisms are free."

Before Karole could reply, a bellicose cry rose from the darkening forest like sudden thunder. Vordenburg knew instinctively that the cry had originated from no human throat. It was a sound full of fury and what might have been sorrow. It echoed among the huts of the logging camp and men froze in place, their eyes searching the trees.

His hand fell to the Mauser C78 holstered beneath his arm. The revolver was outdated, but still serviceable. Much like himself. But he didn't draw it. There was no panic on the faces of the labourers—only a dull, resigned apprehension. They had endured too much these past weeks. Terror had been burnt out of them, leaving only a sort of hollow acceptance. The Borovoi would come; men would die; the sun would rise.

Vordenburg himself felt no fear at the sound. Instead, he felt only an atavistic anticipation. His family had hunted the unnatural on behalf of the Habsburgs for generations. Now he hunted on behalf of anyone who could pay him, as well as for his own pleasure.

The echo of the cry faded and the night became still once more. "It is here," Karole murmured. He'd half-drawn his sidearm, and his eyes were wide. He didn't seem startled or frightened, but simply uneasy. Perhaps he was made of sterner stuff than he looked.

"Yes." Vordenburg went back to his stool, where a heavy duffel bag sat on the dirt floor. He opened the bag and began to pull things out. "Have you done as I suggested?" He'd advised Karole to stretch tripwires between certain of the camp huts. The wires were connected to a number of *stielhandgranate*—stick grenades.

Karole looked away from the forest. "Yes, though I do not think blowing up the camp is what my superiors had in mind when they hired you."

Vordenburg strapped on a gun belt holding a Mauser C96. "Their expectations are not my concern. I was hired to do a job, and this is the most efficient way to do it. Get your men ready. We must confront it as soon as it arrives."

"We?" Karole asked, with a startled expression.

"You and your men seem competent enough. And many hands make for swift work." Besides the second pistol, Vordenburg also armed himself with a basket-hilted sabre and a katana. Both blades were heirlooms of a sort, and both had seen much use over the past century. Finally, he slid a thin, silver-edged knife into his boot.

"That is an obscene amount of weaponry," Karole said, eyeing the swords with obvious displeasure. He gestured at the weapons. "Why does a man need two swords?"

Vordenburg shrugged. "Why does a chef need more than one knife?"

"You are not a chef." Karole checked the cylinder of his revolver.

"Much to the shame of my mother," Vordenburg said. He brushed past Karole and stepped out into the night.

The air was cool—cold, even. He barely noticed. The pines rustled in the night wind, and he was reminded of the crash of water against the shore. In his mind, there was little difference between the deepest reaches of ocean and forest. Neither were fit places for human habitation. The cry came again, closer this time. It rolled down into the camp, shaking the very huts to their foundations.

Very soon now, he thought. As if to prove him right, there came a great creaking and splintering from the trees on the eastern side of the camp, as of something very large moving very quickly through them. Another roar. Men were shouting in alarm and loggers scrambled for cover. Vordenburg pushed through them, drawing his sabre as he did so, his eyes on the easternmost huts.

When the explosion came, he was ready. He sprinted into the billowing smoke, parting it with a slash of his sabre. He heard Karole shouting after him, but he paid the man no mind. Loggers stumbled past him, bleeding—burnt. They'd obviously been caught in the explosion. Vordenburg ignored them. There would be time for apologies later. The grenades might well prove ineffective against their quarry, but at the very least they might stun the creature long enough to dispatch it.

The smoke began to thin, drawn away by the breeze. Vordenburg slowed. He heard a guttural grunt and a large shape reared up suddenly, bracing itself against one of the huts. He had an impression of a shaggy bulk, and a smell like stagnant water resting in a hollowed log, and then it flung itself towards him with a howl that made his teeth ache. He ducked aside, narrowly avoiding the sweep of a broad fist.

The C96 bucked in his hand.

His quarry shrieked and went for him again, long arms looping out as if to enfold him in a crushing embrace. He stamped forward with a fencer's grace and slashed at the thing's chest and head with his sabre. The stink of it made his eyes water, and its cry—whether of pain or frustration, he couldn't say—momentarily deafened him.

It reeled back from him, and he got a glimpse of its twisted countenance in the moonlight. It resembled the face of a man, but stretched over far too much skull, with a mouthful of sharp, wolfish teeth and eyes like dark stones. Things that might have been roots were tangled in its thick pelt, and when it breathed, the air smelled of pine resin.

But fearsome as it was, it seemed too small to be the creature he had heard about. The Leshy was supposed to be a veritable titan, but this thing was only half again larger than a man. An ogre, rather than a giant. He felt a twinge of disappointment. He had been looking forward to fighting a giant.

The creature took a step back. He saw now that its dark hair was scorched, and something black and glistening stained its side and legs. The grenades had hurt it after all. It panted heavily, its lungs working like a bellows. A rifle barked, and the creature flinched and spun with a bone-shaking growl. Karole and his men emerged from between the surrounding huts, their weapons levelled. "Fire!" Karole bellowed.

Rifles spoke, and the creature howled as the fusillade struck home. It swiped wildly at the air, like a child stung by insects. Vordenburg seized the moment and darted in, sabre flashing. The creature staggered and attempted to slap him away. He retreated with his blade extended before him. "Close the trap," he called out. "Surround it. Don't let it escape!"

His words came too late. It was already bounding back towards the safety of the tree line as Karole's men moved to cut it off. One unlucky soldier got too close, and the creature snatched him up and tore him in two with barely a pause. An instant later, it was gone, vanished back into the trees.

Vordenburg cursed and started after it, but halted as Karole called out to him. "Where are you going, Vordenburg?" the other man demanded. He had his revolver in his hand, and though it wasn't aimed in Vordenburg's direction the threat was clear.

"To find it and kill it."

"You said the grenades would do that," Karole accused. He barked orders at two of his men, and they hurried to cover up the body of their fallen companion.

"I said the grenades would help." Vordenburg cleaned his sword on the sleeve of his coat and sheathed it. "And they did. It is injured. We'd best kill it, before it recovers."

Karole hesitated, and then holstered his weapon. "How do we do that?"

"The same way we would any beast. We run it to ground."

"You mean... follow it? Into the forest?"

Vordenburg nodded. "The sooner the better."

Karole was obviously reluctant, but quickly set about gathering food, water and packs for the dozen men he'd volunteered to accompany them. Vordenburg had prepared his own bag earlier, suspecting that it would be needed, and waited impatiently near the tree line. When Karole and his men were ready, Vordenburg led them into the forest.

Initially, the trail was easy to follow. Broken trees and churned earth marked the direction of the creature's flight. It was only as they lost sight of the lights of the camp that the trail became somewhat opaque. Vordenburg had begun to fear that the beast had slipped away when he spied something glistening on the trunk of a nearby pine. He touched the sticky mess smeared on the bark, and sniffed his fingers. "Fresh blood. It came through here."

"Smells like tree sap and rancid meat," Karole said, wrinkling his nose.

Vordenburg snorted. "Did you expect it to smell of mint and honey? Come. This way. Tell your men to keep their eyes open. If it is as badly injured as I think, it will be all the more dangerous."

Karole stared at him. "More dangerous? How can it be more dangerous?"

Vordenburg ignored him and kept moving. He heard Karole shout something to his men. Though it was foolish to make so much noise, Vordenburg didn't chide him. If nothing else, it might draw the beast out of hiding.

The carpet of pine needles crackled as they followed the blood trail into the labyrinthine depths of the forest. The shadows grew long, like curtains hanging between the trees. The moon was bright enough for him to see. He concentrated on the path ahead of him, senses straining to catch the smallest hint of his quarry. Abnatural or not, it was still a thing of the forest—an animal. When animals were injured, they ran for home. Monsters did the same. Still, he felt a growing sense of unease about the whole thing. It had almost been too easy to put the beast to flight. It was a wonder that Karole hadn't managed it without him.

"This is a mistake," Karole murmured, when they at last stopped to rest. He sat down on a tree stump and mopped at his face with his handkerchief. "We should not be here, in these woods. We should draw it out again. Perhaps the grenades will work next time."

"Scared of the Leshy, then?" Vordenburg asked. But he didn't think it was fear he saw in Karole's eyes, or at least not fear alone. There was frustration there as well; perhaps even some resentment. He had glimpsed it more than once since they'd met, but put it down to Karole's annoyance at his presence.

"The Leshy doesn't exist," Karole said, vehemently. "Forest spirits are children's tales. This is merely some... throwback. Some antediluvian holdover, driven out of hiding by our presence."

"I have seen stranger things," Vordenburg said. "I was in the Alps once, and I..." He trailed off, listening to the whisper of the wind through the pines.

"And you what?" Karole asked.

Vordenburg held up his hand for silence. He had the sense of being watched, though he wasn't sure whether it was by the Leshy or something else. The thought bothered him and he rose from the log he'd been sitting on, suddenly eager to be elsewhere. "We should keep moving," he said. "Get your men up."

"Now who is scared?" Karole asked snidely.

"Only a fool is without fear," Vordenburg said, looking down at him. "You are right, though. We should not be here. These forests belong to the Leshy. Man is an invader. Hard to blame the beast for treating us as such."

"You sound as if you have sympathy for it."

"Some, perhaps," Vordenburg admitted.

"But you still intend to kill it," Karole said. It wasn't a question.

Vordenburg nodded. "It is what I do. Now—up. All of you. The night runs on, and the beast has a head start." He gestured briskly, and Karole and the others rose doggedly to their feet. Karole's men were tough; but the deeper the group went into the forest, the more nervous they became. They acted like men returning to the scene of a crime.

Pondering this, Vordenburg led them on through the corridors of pine following a trail of blood, broken branches and torn ground, until at last, as the moon reached its apex, they came to a clearing. It appeared suddenly, like a new-made wound in the hide of the mountain.

Moonlight filled the clearing. Heavy stones rose from the rough earth, and in the dim light Vordenburg could just make out the crude carvings that decorated them, made by the hands of men centuries dead. Vordenburg went to the nearest of the standing stones and frowned. He felt an unidentifiable chill as he contemplated the carvings. "A temple, perhaps," he said aloud. "Or the remnants of one. A sacred place to some forgotten god."

"Fairy tales," Karole said, automatically. He did not seem surprised by the presence of the stones, and that made Vordenburg suspicious. Something told him the other man had been here before or had, at the very least, known of its existence. "The Soviet state does not recognize the existence of so-called deities. The only thing man should worship is the state."

Even as the words left Karole's mouth, one of his men screamed. Vordenburg turned—and ducked, as a broken body flew over his head to crash against one of the stones. The twitching corpse left a red smear on the face of the stone as it slid to the ground. Karole barked an order and, for a second time, the night erupted in gunfire. The clearing shook as the unseen creature roared, in pain or perhaps challenge.

A trap, Vordenburg realised, firing his C96 into the dark between the trees. The beast had led them into a trap. It had laid a trail, faked weakness and drawn them away from the camp. "Clever bastard," he muttered, not without a little admiration.

Another man screamed, and then a third. A body smashed into a tree and pinwheeled to the ground. The Leshy was among them before they could react, moving swiftly despite its wounds. The beast rose up over a man and brought its fists down on the unfortunate's skull with a sickening crunch. A sixth was jerked into the air and torn in two like a wishbone. The half dozen survivors were screaming, cursing, but their weapons were having little effect.

"Fall back into the clearing!" Vordenburg shouted. He wasn't certain that was the right choice, but it was better than being picked off one by one. Karole and his remaining men hurried to obey. Vordenburg was the last to retreat, his eyes on the trees. The creature had stopped at the edge of the clearing; he could just make it out, crouched among the pines. Why hadn't it followed them into the clearing? Was there some power in the stones that it feared? Or perhaps there was another reason. It had led them here after all—but why?

He took a step back and something clinked beneath his heel. Something that gleamed in the moonlight. He paused, stooped and retrieved it. A spent casing from a bullet. There were more of them scattered about. Old ones. Weeks, if not months old, given the dirt that clogged them. He felt no surprise, only annoyance. He closed his hand about the cartridge as the Leshy roared again. There came the sound of splintering wood and then a tree arced over the tops of the stones and crashed down into the clearing.

Instinctively, he knew it was trying to keep them from leaving. Trying to trap them here. Was it hoping to pick them off... or was it waiting for something? Reinforcements, maybe. The thought wasn't a pleasant one. He felt as if he'd suddenly walked into the middle of conversation. What else hadn't he been told?

Another tree tumbled through the air, striking a stone and exploding into a blizzard of splinters. A man cried out and reeled away, clutching his face. Karole and the rest of his men returned fire, to no effect. Vordenburg wondered how many times this same scene had played out since his hosts had decided to start logging this part of the Urals again. He decided to ask. He pushed away from the stone and prowled towards Karole, pistol in hand.

"Where is it? Do you see it?" Karole asked frantically.

Vordenburg ignored the question and tossed his discovery to Karole. The other man caught it, and made a show of examining it in evident confusion. "What is this?"

"You knew this place was here, didn't you?" Vordenburg asked. "Maybe you found it by accident. Maybe it's why you decided to begin logging in this region. But you knew about it, and you knew about what was protecting it. Tell me, how many men did you send after it the first time?"

Karole frowned. "What do you mean?"

"I wonder, did you send them after it had attacked you—or before? You told me yourself that you'd heard the stories. You must have suspected that there was something in these woods. Perhaps finding this place confirmed it. So, you decided to kill the Leshy. Or capture it. A gift for your superiors, perhaps. Or maybe they ordered you to do it."

Karole's face might as well have been a mask of wax. "I do not know what you are talking about. We have more important matters to deal with." He glanced towards the trees, clearly anticipating another attack. And with good reason.

"It set a trap for us. It knew. It expected you."

Karole stared at him. "What does it matter now? This is why we brought you here! Do something!"

Vordenburg levelled his C96 at the other man. "It matters because I say it matters. Why didn't you tell me?"

"Are you mad? You will not shoot me!" Karole spoke loudly, and several of his men swung their weapons in Vordenburg's direction.

Vordenburg ignored them and kept his attentions on their commander. "Answer the question."

Karole grimaced. After a moment, he said, "We killed it."

Vordenburg frowned. "Explain." He risked a glance at the trees, and caught a glimpse of something hairy passing through a shaft of moonlight. The Leshy was circling them. Waiting for its chance. Or maybe just waiting.

"We tracked it here after the first few attacks," Karole said, through gritted teeth. "That's when we learned about this place. We killed it. Lost a dozen men in the doing of it, but we did it. We killed it and sent its head to Moscow in a box full of pine boughs. But it came back. Somehow it came back."

"Or maybe you didn't do as good a job as you thought," Vordenburg said. Again, he found himself wondering why it didn't simply attack. He glanced at the standing stones, noting the similarity between the crude shapes depicted on them and the Leshy itself. In some parts of Russia, the Leshy was thought of as a god, of sorts. A nature spirit. Was that the answer? Was this place sacred to it, or to those who'd once worshipped it? Is that why it had fled here the first time, and why it had led them here this time?

"Perhaps there is more than one," Karole countered. "I don't know, but it was decided that a—a *professional* was required to solve the problem where we had failed." He practically spat the word. "Only you don't seem to be doing that good a job."

"Only because I did not know the truth of what I was facing." Vordenburg lowered his weapon. This changed things somewhat. If terrestrial weapons did not affect the beast, then other methods were needed. "If you had told me, I would have come properly equipped. As it is, I am forced to make do with what I carry. Hopefully it will be enough."

"What are you talking about?" Karole demanded.

Vordenburg patted the katana sheathed at his side. "You asked earlier why I need two swords. Simple, one is merely steel—but the other is blessed. A holy weapon. You may not believe in such things, but I do." He holstered the C96 and drew the katana without flourish. "Now, draw him in and we will see if this professional can succeed where you failed."

"Draw it in?" Karole hesitated. "How do you expect us to do that?"

Vordenburg lifted the katana until the tip was just under Karole's nose. "Run."

Karole took a step back, a confused look on his face. But it only lasted a moment. "It wants us here," he said, slowly. Vordenburg nodded and sheathed his sword. Whatever else, Karole was no fool. Even so, it took him several moments to get his reluctant men moving out of the dubious safety of the stones, and only after he resorted to threatening one of them with his pistol.

At Karole's urging, they crept forward, as if making a break for the tree line. As Vordenburg had expected, the Leshy moved immediately to cut them off. It emerged from the trees and bellowed, brandishing a broken branch as it did so.

Vordenburg circled around, keeping the stones between himself and the Leshy. Karole and his men scattered as the beast charged towards them. It was trying to drive them back into the stones. As he readied himself, he saw the creature snatch up a man and fling him bodily into the clearing.

The Leshy killed another in the time it took him to get into position. The beast was battering the dead man's body with the branch when Vordenburg sprang into the open and charged. The Leshy turned, startled, and hurled the branch. Vordenburg ducked beneath the improvised missile and grabbed the hilt of the katana. The weapon seemed to leap into his palm, eager to be put to use. It had been forged by a sorcerer, with the intent to slay a supernatural beast, or so his grandfather had maintained. Whatever its origin, the blade could cut through almost anything, and bore the blessings of the gods of two lands.

The Leshy came for him, and Vordenburg leapt to meet it, sweeping his blade out in a tight arc. It cut through the mossy hide of the Leshy, and spattered the surrounding stones with blood. The Leshy threw back its head and gave a mournful wail, exposing its chest in the process.

Driven by a hunter's instinct, Vordenburg seized the opening and lunged. The katana slid smoothly through the Leshy's chest. The Leshy stumbled forward and fell, bearing Vordenburg to the ground beneath it. The impact crushed the air from his lungs and he felt his ribs crack beneath its weight. He groaned and tried to shove the Leshy off of him, but it wouldn't budge. "Damn it," he panted.

He heard Karole laugh and saw the other man walking towards him. "You did it. And with only a sword. Impressive."

Vordenburg grimaced. "Help me out from under it," he growled.

Karole raised his revolver. "I think not. It is dead, again—and you will join it. Fitting, I think. Both of you, relics of an outdated system." He cocked the revolver. "Rest assured, comrade, that you will be remembered as a hero of the Soviet Union."

Vordenburg tried to free his arm from under the Leshy's bulk, but it was too heavy. He ceased his struggles, however, as the trees around the clearing began to bend and sway as if caught in a strong wind. Karole hesitated, looking around. "What is this? Some trick?"

"Not mine," Vordenburg said, his eyes never leaving the other man. He strained and felt the butt of his revolver, still in its holster beneath his arm. Karole glanced at him, and then out at the trees. They were creaking now, as if some great weight was bearing them under.

A moment later, one of Karole's remaining men screamed as something snatched him out of sight. Karole whirled. "What was that?"

"I think I know what the beast was waiting for," Vordenburg said, and laughed, despite the pain in his chest.

His fingers ached as he stretched them to their utmost. He almost had the gun out. A few more moments were all he needed.

More men screamed, as dark shapes bounded into view and carried them away into the trees. Their cries rose to piteous heights before falling abruptly, permanently silent. Soon, only Karole remained. "No," he muttered, shaking his head. "No, I killed it."

"Yes, and in doing so, you defiled this place," Vordenburg said. "You defied the lord of the deep woods. And now he has come for recompense."

A great roar, like a mountain falling in on itself, filled the clearing. Trees cracked and fell, slamming into the ground. The wind howled through the stones. Something as dark as the deepest woods, and as vast and incomprehensible as the Urals themselves, heaved itself up to loom over the clearing.

Leshy. The true Leshy, Vordenburg knew. Come to avenge the death of its child. The old stories said that the Leshy had children, though they had not described them. But wasn't a child just a smaller version of its parent?

Karole stared up at the shaggy titan, eyes wide behind his spectacles, his mouth open, no sound coming out. The Nagant hung forgotten in his hand. Far above, the Leshy's eyes blazed like distant fires in the night forest. Another booming roar beat down on them, and, as if in reply, cries and shrieks rose from the trees. Karole turned one way and then the next. "What does it want?" he hissed, his voice gone shrill with panic. "What do we do?"

"Only one thing for it," Vordenburg said, as his hand closed around his pistol at last. He drew it out from under the creature's bulk as quickly as he could. "We have to give him what he came for." Karole turned, a puzzled look on his face. Vordenburg fired.

As the shot echoed through the clearing, all other sound ceased. Karole, his skull perforated by Vordenburg's shot, pitched forward onto his face and lay still. Vordenburg waited, heart hammering in his chest. The wind dipped, and the trees stilled.

The Leshy was gone. Appeased, perhaps, or at least satisfied, Vordenburg wasn't sure and didn't care. He was just grateful that his guess had been right. The Leshy had desired a blood-price for its fallen child—a price that it now apparently considered paid.

It took some time, but he managed to drag himself out from under the creature's body. Aside from a few cracked ribs, he seemed to be in one piece. Limping slightly, he retrieved his sword and other pistol. He considered removing the creature's head and taking it back as proof he'd done the job, but hesitated.

Though he could not see them, he could feel the eyes of the forest on him. The father might be gone, but his children remained. He thought unlikely they would ignore the desecration of another brother's body here, in their place of power. "Fine," he murmured, and sketched a bow to the surrounding trees.

Let the forest keep its dead, and let Karole's masters keep their money. He had his life, and that was enough. Something crunched beneath his boot. He looked down and saw Karole's spectacles. He smiled.

After all, it was more than could be said for some.

HUNTING DOWN THE UNHOLY

PETRA RAPAIĆ

BENEATH THE HOMOLJE MOUNTAINS, in the village of Čeremošnja, close to the cave of the same name, firewood for Priveg is being collected throughout the whole day. In the evening, a huge fire is to be lit for the souls of the dead to warm themselves. The Marga is to be danced around the fire, so the strong lads can outmatch one another, celebrating a good and fertile year.

Baba Stana has, in her lifetime, seen plenty of rituals and each one had gone impeccably, since the beginning to this day. Even the ritual at which, in the time of her grandmother's grandmother, some tourist from Ithaca stopped by to speak to the dead. Everybody knows about the Homolje Mountains and the caves which lead to the bowel of the earth, to the souls of the departed.

The Homolje are not just the gates to the underworld, where the souls emerge once a year. There are all sorts of things here, including an imprisoned dragon. It's no wonder, considering, that the losing streams run dry every once in a while and young maidens go missing. Incantations and witchcraft sometimes help, sometimes don't, depending on the cause. And the cause is, according to baba Stana, always the same—the dragon. The day they captured him, water began to dry up, gold stopped flowing as abundantly as it's supposed to, and those remaining two river gold panners lost their desire to squabble over gold-bearing rivers and took each other as brothers.

The world was dying, and it could've been a lot worse if not for those from Čeremošnja to keep watch, but what on—they had no idea. They held onto the ancient rites because they were supposed to, by the grace of God.

God's grace did not grant much this evening, or if it did, not to them. For the first time in baba Stana's memory, the ritual was going wrong. They had no issues gathering the firewood, but the fire didn't take immediately. The dead had come out of the cave's dark entrance, driven by habit and, with no fire to attract them, scattered about. Whom they would visit and drive mad before some priest delivered them back to the underworld, God knows.

As if out of spite, because it had been raining the whole day, the wood released more smoke than fire, blinding the lads as their dance for the dead wound around the flames. Instead of upstaging each other and competing in strength and agility, they teared up and staggered, a little bit blinded. At one point, the leader stumbled and got pretty singed in the blaze.

Baba Stana watched them from among the gathered folk and grumbled. She knew no good would come out of this. Still, they would somehow weather a bad year, she thought. Most of them had children and relatives in Germany, money would be sent, they'd get through the winter.

However, when the time came for the fire to be put out and the burning pieces of coal to be distributed among the households, well, that's where it all went sideways. Magic was supposed to be wrapped around the coals, a web was supposed to be raised around the village when everyone took their piece home, thus protecting themselves against the dragon. It was in baba Stana's genes to be able to sense both the magic and the protection.

This year, for the first time, she felt nothing. She held an already cooled-down lump of coal in her palms, should have given it to the woman in front of her, and she could not do it.

"It's not working," she whispered. "The magic is no more."

And just like that, a curse befell Čeremošnja.

THE WEREWOLF

It is said that, if you've never walked through Homolje in the night, you've no idea what darkness is. Ognjen drives through the Homolje night and feels at home. In his eyes, the nature is so beautiful he's almost crying. He wonders how it had never occurred to him to visit this part of Serbia before and makes a promise to himself that he would come here at least once a year from now on.

He'd like some music, but his companions don't seem to be in the mood for the compilations that get him going. Gavra is somewhat indifferent, while Ravi looks as if she'd gouge his eyes out if he as much as opened his mouth.

"I'm listening," she'd said. "Now hush and leave me be."

He did exactly as she told him.

They've known each other long enough that he doesn't take her words personally. He feels that this mission is of a special importance.

They'd stopped once on their way and walked down to the water. It was gurgling, but fairly noiselessly. Ravi had started crying and said that a great crime had been committed here. Surprised, Ognjen had explained to her that the river is quiet because this was where Empress Milica had been given the news of her husband's passing. He'd volunteered to investigate the region they were going into, unlike Ravi, who 'listened' on the spot, and Gavro, who couldn't care less.

"Such a typical human thing, thinking everything revolves around them," Ravi had mumbled before ordering them to move on. She hasn't said a word about what she thinks happened at that section of the river. She called shotgun and continued staring through the window. Gavro kept taking up more space at the backseat and there was no way to find out what his thoughts on the mission were, if he had any. When his eyes weren't closed, a pair of sunglasses kept watch over them, day and night. Ever since they'd started their trip, he hasn't said a word.

The proximity of the forest and the mountain sets Ognjen at ease. The sheer vastness of it entices him to shift and run til the end of his life, but he contents himself with staring over the jeep's steering wheel, heedless of the turned-off headlights. His vision is better in complete darkness. Ravi had told him to floor it and forget the cops—there aren't any at night in Homolje, and even if there were, she'd know how to get rid of the curious. Good, since their boot is packed with suspicious gear.

They pass through the village during that darkest hour before the dawn. In the well-maintained wooden houses, the folks are still asleep. The occasional rooster is the only sound, accompanied by the inevitable barking. Ravi frowns with no wish to 'listen' to the settlement and tells him to drive on. They stop in a field outside the village, get out of the car and turn east.

Legend has it that the first dragon was born in the sunrise, when the bloody disk touched the edges of the two worlds. Ognjen has never wondered whether it was true, but he understands why some think it is. The shades of the dark, so wonderful and warm to his eye, retreat in front of the fiery avalanche of color. What little of the moon had been in the sky until now disappears.

THE PRIEST

"We can't reach the cave by car," Mitar explains to the guests, a little resentfully. The way Stana had described them, he was expecting a bunch of wildlife experts or dull-witted witches, anything other than three mercenaries. At any rate, he'd expected Stana to stay in the village, too, and take part in the events she'd concocted, but no—the lady had packed her bags posthaste and gone to stay with her daughter in Beograd, entrusting him, the cleric, to bring the newcomers up to speed. Had the old priest Đorđije, when he passed the parochy down to him, not dragged him aside and, under the seal of confession, explained to Mitar that all the legends were true—the dragon, the fairies, the dead, and anything else he could think of—Mitar would have stuck the goddamned baba and her muddlings where the sun don't shine. This way, he knew that the baba kept the people under protection in one sense, and he in another.

"You go on foot, with a guide. The terrain is mostly unapproachable and caution is in order," he explained on.

Laughter from the square-shouldered blond lad interrupted him. "Reverend, if you know the way, lead on. The terrain's configuration is the least of our worries."

"I'm still waiting for the payment to come through," the girl with long silver hair reminded them. She was sitting cross-legged on the car's hood, with a laptop in her lap, impatiently typing.

"Yeah, yeah." The lad grinned. "There's time until the evening." He seemed to be itching to get on with it, regardless of whether they get paid or not.

The third lad, dishevelled and ginger, was leaning against the vehicle and staring at the mountain. He hadn't come closer to say hi, he hadn't taken his glasses off. "I could fly there," he spoke for the first time since father Mitar had joined them.

"Not without us, you won't," the girl growled.

"There are no landings for a helicopter there, either way." Mitar ignored the lad's smirk and the blond's confused look. The business needed seeing through. "Why don't you explain to me what your qualifications are against these... fairies and karakondžulas... and what have you."

"The karakondžulas, despite your beliefs, are no more than the product of a dirty consciousness. Also, don't mess with the fairies, and they won't mess with you."

"Don't they steal children into their ranks?" Mitar didn't let himself be sidetracked.

"No, what for? Fairies are nature's children, they need no offspring from some tech-crazy person."

"We haven't been called here because of a fairy issue," the blond lad said.

"You start with the small things." Mitar waved his hand. "Stana tells me you can take care of the dragon, the aždaja, whatever it is that is in there. His head in the field can break the curse, make the land bear fruit again." He glanced at the mountain, restless.

"You don't know what you had imprisoned there?" The lad with the glasses finally turned to him.

"I've just told you."

"A dragon or an aždaja. Can't have it both ways."

"Is there a difference?"

"A big one." The redhead spreads his lips in a smile. "You see, reverend, the aždajas don't have wings. They live in the water and trouble the humans. They materialize from a snake which has devoured another snake. A dragon, on the other hand, does have wings, breathes fire, loves high spots and lives in caves. Just like the ones, I've heard, you have around here. And then there are the alas, too—flying snakes with huge heads, voracious and dangerous."

"Aren't they all dangerous?"

"Not to everyone." The redhead shrugs and abruptly loses his interest in going on with the conversation.

"I hope you have an ala." The blond grins. "We charge double for one."

"Listen, I have no idea whether you are mercenaries or dragonblood heroes." Mitar sneers. He pulls a cell phone from the pocket of his cassock and types out a message. "The payment is coming in no time, don't you worry. There's just a single catch—you need to withdraw the money in person, or it goes back. Insurance in case of, God forbid, you get killed."

"You think God has something to do with dragons?" the blond asks.

Mitar smiles. "They're referred to a full sixteen times in the Bible. Also, a thing you forgot to mention, from all the flying reptiles, the dragons are the only ones capable of procreation."

"We didn't forget," the girl says wistfully.

"What of werewolves? Are any werewolves referred to there?" the blond asks hungrily.

"There are no werewolves in Homolje," Mitar asserts.

The ginger laughs. The blond frowns. The girl types on her laptop. Some fifteen minutes are spent in an unpleasant silence, avoiding each other's gaze, while their eyes glide toward the mountain.

Mitar jumps when there's a loud *ping!* from the laptop. The girl shuts it closed with a triumphant smile on her beautiful face. "It came through."

The blond opens the boot of the car and indecisively stares at what looks like a heap of garbage to father Mitar: stakes, small bottles of water, walnut shells, some sort of dried herbs, spindles, feathers, and twigs.

"You don't have a minethrower?" All hope's gone from Mitar's voice, which is nothing compared to the feeling that envelops him when he hears the redhead:

"Come on, Ogi. You don't need anything from there."

"Sure?" Ogi's look at the other lad is indecipherable, and the redhead nods.

"You fight fire with fire," he says.

THE DRAGON

Dragons don't have it easy. They come into existence from forty-year-old snakes, though, to this day, no human has managed to discover from which ones, and the dragons, after their transformation, blissfully forget. It is said the butterfly would live longer if it forgot it used to be a caterpillar. Also, Gavrilo thinks, how can a snake tell it has turned forty? Is it a spontaneous process, something written in the genes, or is the snake's intellect similar enough to the human one that it can count and remember? And why does it need to be sixty years more until it gets its second chance at transformation, and what is it that makes it become so bitter and malicious in the meantime that it transforms into an ala, stronger, more powerful, and capable to transmute into whatever it wishes to be?

Gavrilo has no idea, since he's never met his father, and whenever he asks about him, his mother suddenly shuts her mouth and changes the subject. There is a lot that he doesn't know about his own kind, and after tonight, he'd probably never get the chance to find out. As they're making their way through the underbrush, he's entertaining the thought of simply going into the cave during the day, finding the reptile and having a man to man—alright, dragon to dragon—chat with him. There are a couple of flaws in the plan. Firstly, the priest cannot say for sure, but he thinks the dragon has been incarcerated for about a hundred years, if not more. He'll be furious and hungry for revenge.

Normally, nobody feels like talking in such a state. Secondly, his mother is pretty certain that purebred dragons can't stand halfbreeds like him. The legends may glorify them as much as they want, and call them the dragonblood heroes, but the fact is, side by side with real dragons, they seem no more than poodles next to wolves. Wolves next to werewolves. Whatever.

He shakes his head, stops thinking. They fought an aždaja once, the biggest trick was to draw it out into the open. Hopefully, it won't be a problem with this dragon. Could a dragon turn into an ala if he got furious enough? Maybe they'll manage to double their fee after all.

There are only so many ancient and truly malicious creatures left in the land. What are they going to do when they eradicate them all? Freelance at crossroads by regulating traffic for the unholy? Sell anti-drekavac repellents? He has a hunch that, should they survive the following dawn, boredom would be a welcome feeling.

"Here it is," the priest says as they break through to the cavern's gaping entrance.

Ognjen immediately starts pacing around, measuring and mumbling to himself. Ravi takes a deep breath and closes her eyes, doing that 'listening' of hers. Gavrilo, with his hands in his pockets, stares at the sky. Sunlight barely makes it to the ground past the trees' tall canopies. It's gonna be a pain to spread the wings here. Other than that, he's strangely at ease and calm.

"He's angry. Very," Ravi says.

"Wouldn't you be?" Gavrilo quietly replies.

She approaches him and watches him with worry. "You'll be careful? Please."

"Gimme a break, mom, I'm a hundred and fourteen."

"This one is not like the others."

What others, Gavrilo thinks. "What is he like, then?"

Ravi offers no reply. The priest is standing nearby, cleaning dirt off his cassock and feigning not to hear them. Gavrilo understands him completely, sometimes it's better to live in blissful ignorance.

Ognjen has finished his calculations. "Gavro, brother, there's enough space for you. It would be ideal if the dragon came outside, especially during the day. We would get the advantage of both the familiar terrain and the light. I hope his vision has been seriously damaged by so many years of darkness. The worst that could happen is for him to drag you into a fight inside. If it comes to it, run."

"Are you teaching me how to fight, Ogi?" Gavrilo smiles widely. "Don't make me beat your ass right now."

"Calm down, kids, I taught you better than this," Ravi says, even though it's obvious they're teasing each other. "Father, thank you for the company, but it's best for you to go back during daylight."

"If God would have it," father Mitar says.

"And the luck of heroes bear it," Ognjen says.

Gavrilo keeps quiet. Everybody relies on what they like the most.

THE FAIRY

"How do you lure a dragon?" Ognjen asks.

"Ice cream," Gavrilo is quick to answer. "And pretty girls."

"What flavor of ice cream?" Ognjen asks.

"Strawberry."

"And if I have plazma biscuits or chocolate?"

"You got any?"

"No."

"Nothing then."

"And the girls?"

"Pretty ones. Clever, of course. Can't be afraid of heights."

"'Cause your head is in the clouds."

"Sometimes." Gavrilo's lips twitch in a smile. "Best if it's a fairy."

"Where do I find you a fairy, my dragonblood hero?" Ognjen laughs.

They keep quiet, watch as the time passes and the sun changes the shadow's position among the canopies. They're lying in the grass, head to head, like the hands in a clock when they're showing three forty. Gavrilo has folded his palms under the back of his head, while Ognjen's are resting on his muscular stomach. Ravi had wandered off somewhere. Ognjen waits for her to come back before asking the next question.

"How do you capture a dragon?"

Ravi stands opposite her sons, in the position of twelve; the top of her shadow touches their heads.

"With a lot of difficulty," she says.

"What about all those tales of skins? You know, the ones where the dragon transforms and leaves his skin in a hidden spot, and some crazy baba takes it and burns it."

"Is that the one where the dragon, in the shape of a lad, hisses like an angry viper, tells the girl she'll never see him again, turns into a dragon and leaves?" Gavrilo mocks.

"Pure fantasy," Ravi snorts. "A dragon is no snake to shed his skin each year. Horny housewives used to tell those fairytales for fun while they spun."

"No one told them that's not the way it goes?" Ognjen asks.

"Why would they?" Gavrilo laughs. "While the old babas stumble around in the dark, looking for a skin twenty meters long, the dragon sleeps with the girls in peace."

"What do you reckon', how did they capture this one?"

Ravi takes a heavy breath and sits next to them. Suddenly she seems tired and worried. "This dragon is old. He may have dropped a scale somewhere and the babas used it for witchcraft. He may have drunk from a spring he wasn't supposed to, and a fairy took offense. Most probably, he accidentally went in and slept where he shouldn't have, and the souls of the dead captured him, looking for the warmth of the living. Had the humans not been stubborn in maintaining the ritual to keep the dead in one place, the dragon would've freed himself ages ago."

"Feels like we should let him be. No one's fault that he made the mistake to sleep in the hallways toward the underworld."

"And the peasants?" Ognjen asks.

"What about them?"

"The village has already been cursed. What if he turns on them?"

"Why would he?"

"Gavro is right; no human being can imprison a dragon on their own, there needs to be something more, aside from a wish and an incantation: a name, scales, blood, a fairy's help. But Ogi is right, too, we have no idea what the dragon's reaction to humans will be at this time. If not for their fires and rituals, if they hadn't unknowingly positioned themselves as the guardians of the dungeon he's in..."

"There was nothing unknowing about this." Ognjen growls slightly when he's angry. "What's with those lumps of coal the local fortune teller mentioned? Said they protect the village from the dragon?"

Ravi shrugs. "Human magic. I have no idea. The village isn't cursed because the dragon willed it, but because they've betrayed him. Nature gave him the power to do good, and this is what the humans did. Pure law of nature."

"Though... how can he tell when there's no moon in the sky?" Gavro asks.

"He never stopped counting," Ravi's answer echoes ominously.

FAMILY

On a moonless night, a lad enters a cave, where darkness swallows him in an instant. He doesn't want to give the dragon the advantage of a running start. He's taken off his sunglasses earlier and given them to his brother. He can't see that well in the dark, but his eyes are red like fire.

Outside, not that close, his brother and his mother are waiting for him. The brother's eyes have a gold glimmer, his muscles tremble with the urge to jump in after him, though he knows he won't get the chance. The mother's eyes are black now, with no pupils. A fairy's eyes look like that when she's worried or angry.

Prepared for the worst, they think that the dragon who's never stopped counting would be close to the exit as soon as it starts getting dark, and quite far away before midnight strikes, so they're not surprised when, just a few minutes later, eerie cries emerge from the innards of the dark.

In front of the cave, there's suddenly an explosion of awkward movement, two dragon bodies intertwined, making the air swirl as the trees are getting bent to the ground by the harsh swinging of powerful wings. To the ordinary human eye, they would appear like raging demons, a torn-off piece of the night, condensed by fury and the urge to kill. The ordinary human brain would draw wrong conclusions and proceed to grow completely bonkers. The reasons not to go anywhere during the night in Homolje are plenty, and the hunters for the unholy are adding another one this evening. Fact is, only children fear the dark, while the adults fear what lives in it.

The dragon, finally free of the dark in the cavern's labyrinth, filled with souls of confused human beings, was determined to rejoice in the calm and quiet of the night and the height of the sky. The presence of an unexpected adversary, no more and no less than another dragon, drove him too mad to think. The old dragon wanted nothing other than freedom, and he couldn't care less what or whom he would run over to finally experience it. Still, in the madness of the one who's had their plans thwarted, he remembered he wasn't supposed to breathe fire, not because he would burn down the trees, which he couldn't care less about at this moment, but because he would render himself blind and offer the opponent a perfect view.

In a burst of despair, he flew upward, ignoring the branches which were tearing up his wings and his adversary who was plunging claws into his back. They split up for a moment, under the thin glow of the stars, while the trees underneath danced in the insane rhythm of fluttering, torn wings. Dead set on using his newfound freedom for as long as he could, the old dragon dashed as far away from the mountain as he was able to. Unfortunately, he chose the route which would take him to the village, which reinforced his opponent's goal of intercepting his path.

Another scrummage and the ripping of claws across the stomach. A wounded beast's bellow and a fall into the void.

Ognjen and Ravi found them writhing in the stream, snarling at each other, too weakened to continue the fight and too obstinate to admit defeat. Ognjen shifted mid-run and landed as a big, bristling wolf at his brother's side, ready to fight.

Under usual circumstances, no opponent could match the old dragon's strength. Tonight, though, there was a young dragon in front of him, one who had, unlike him, eaten regularly, kept working out outdoors, and it seemed as if he could sense fairy blood in his adversary. Truly, nature had given him a double blessing. Triple, if the werewolf was helping him.

"What times have come," the dragon growled, hoarse from keeping silent for ages, "when kin strikes against kin, on behalf of the treacherous mankind?" The brook seemed to be giving him an additional strength, and he planned on chatting them up until he recovered it in full.

The wings on both of them hung in strings, useless, but there were still a few strong limbs to be chopped up.

"And when I told you to get rid of them, you didn't want to, you stubborn mule," the fairy hissed from the streambank.

The dragon snapped his head around so quickly it made his jaw creak unpleasantly. "Ravi? Ravijojla, is that really you? Why are you dressed like that?" he asked in shock.

"None of your business," she retorted, despite the fact that tenderly green tears were flowing from her eyes. "All of you, turn back into human form, right away. You hear me?"

They heard her, oh, how they heard. On the other side of an uncomfortable rustling and distortion of space, a wiry man stood in the stream, waist-deep, overgrown in red hair, with a pair of red eyes unable to peel their gaze off the fairy.

Gavrilo feebly staggered toward the streambank while Ognjen helped him.

"No, stay in there," Ravijojla commanded. "The water has healing properties."

"Sure." Gavrilo dragged himself to the shallows nonetheless and dunked in, submerging all the way to his nose. Ognjen stood above him, his keen eye discovering similarities between the older and the younger dragon.

They'd done a proper number on each other in their skirmish, resolved on digging out each other's intestines. The water was quickly healing the wounds.

"Brother," the werewolf whistled.

"Don't have the strength right now," Gavrilo groaned.

The older dragon started through the water to get closer to the fairy, disregarding his injuries, and Ravi stepped into the river, keeping him in place.

"Why are you so stubborn?" she murmured as his strong arms wrapped around her.

"I've missed you," he whispered in return as she hugged him.

"Mother?" Ognjen dared to intrude.

"Mother?" the dragon repeated soundlessly, separating from the fairy just to look her in the eyes. "I understand that the dragonblood is mine, but where did the werewolf come from? You didn't...?"

"I've adopted him," the fairy said threateningly as her eyes went darker. "He's been with us ever since he was a pup. Got something to say about that?"

"Absolutely nothing," the dragon said quickly, ducking his face once more into the falls of her silver hair. "Absolutely nothing."

OUT OF LINDEN AND OAK THEY MADE YOU

SREBRENKA PEREGRIN

"IS THE CHILD FROM Here?" I ask Dean, trying to make the H capital in my voice.

My skin is in goosebumps from the double chill: both the air and the thought that our world may not be the only one which we can tread in the mountains. I move closer to get a peek through his looking rod. He does not let me, but hurries to get to her.

"Gods, she is a fragile thing, isn't she?" Dean breathes, his eyes full of compassionate tears. He snuffles them away and spits out a clot.

I am disgusted with his manners but must agree with the words—the girl's hair is like black fleece, her eyes the color of olive leaves. She is a child of the Adriatic coast. She is shivering in dirty, ragged remains of her clothes, for which I cannot say whether they were a dress, or trousers. Dean is already taking off his own coat, to shelter her from the late December wind that carries the promise of snow.

He touches her hand before I can have a look through the rod. By the time I catch up, the rod is on the ground, the girl draped in the coat, and nestled in his arms. It is too late: If she is from the Otherplace, she will appear corporeal here as well. I cannot argue with Dean, however. He did the same with Branko and me, the day he found us.

By the time we had climbed Velebit high enough to come across Dean, I had stopped counting the days on the road.

Branko was already answering to the name I had given him. He would not tell me what they had used to call him. Perhaps his name had died with his parents.

I found him clutching them both on a street in Nadin, shot with the rest. I do not remember how I tore his hands away—at twelve, he is almost as big and strong as I am. I could not make him board the bus that was supposed to take us to safety. He screamed and thrashed, and I gave up. If I had not, the bomb that had turned the bus into crumbles would have been the end of us both.

That was when I started calling him Branko. There is something protecting the child.

We climbed no more buses, or cars, or boats. We walked. We walked all the long miles from Nadin to Velebit, and somehow, no one stopped us. Then we climbed up the rocks, and through the brush, on paths and off them. The only thing keeping us warm was the Burberry coat I had brought from Munich. Our feet were blistered and our hands raw.

And then we were on the other side, away from the sea and the sound of guns in the distance, for a while.

If someone had asked me, I could not have told how. It was as if I had been walking in a dream. I only woke up from it when Dean took us to his hut, made me some concoction of his, and put me to sleep for two days.

It was on the fifth day that he showed me the looking rod. I had seen it before, of course, for our host went nowhere without it. We traipsed with him in the forests stretching in all directions from his threshold, looking for scraps of food and firewood. But I had not realized that the rod was anything more than a walking stick for the old rebel-turned-mountain-hermit.

"It's how I see... Otherplace," he said. *Drugodje* was the word he used. I had never heard it. He waved the looking rod around, lowering his eyebrows when I did not appear to understand.

"*Drugodje*, you know? Gods! The place between the... the places."

"I don't know, Dean," I told him honestly.

He planted the looking rod in front of us, still holding it with one hand, and waved the other one at me. "Look; look at both places. Through the stone."

The looking rod was Dean's height—a gnarly branch with a hollow circle made of stone tied to the top. At first, I saw nothing. We had been picking mushrooms, for Saturday was his Mushroom-Day, and had stopped to get a breather. Our hands were streaked with earth, pungent, and sticky. We were in the middle of nowhere, forests stretching about us like a rough, stark blanket. Just below us, however, there were some rocks I could focus on.

When I looked at them, they were solid chunks of stone, washed gray with rain and soft with moss on the northern side.

When I looked at them through the looking rod, there was a path between them, where there should not have been room enough for a path. Moreover, the path was green, twinkling in the shadows of the late afternoon, as if made of phosphorescent dust. The rocks were greenish as well, but very light, almost as if the pure white stone were awash with green shine.

"Where does the path lead?" I asked Dean.

He shook his head. "*professional*. We don't go there."

It was then I learned he always consulted his looking rod before stepping on any path, or touching any thing in the forest, living or not. It was how he knew which mushrooms to pick. Usually, it was how he determined whether to help a wounded animal, or wring its neck and cook it, or leave it well alone.

Perhaps he needs no such aid when it comes to people. Perhaps there are no people in the Otherplace.

"What do the things from... *There* do... if you take them?" I puff as we trudge back to his hut. My Burberry coat is tied a little too tightly, in a vain attempt to make myself warm. Dean is carrying the girl, who appears to be sleeping in his arms, and I the mushroom basket and his rod.

Dean shrugs and walks on. He may not know or may not want to tell me.

"Are you sure she is no threat?" I ask. I do not like how fast I have caught on to his superstitions. They would have laughed at me, back in Münchner Bank on Frauenplatz, to have heard their Head of Loans so quickly succumb to old wives' tales from her homeland.

He still does not answer. I would not let this pass, if I were my old self, back in Munich. But I am not. I came to get my parents out of Nadin, but I was a day late. Now I am a refugee in Velebit, hauling around dead people's child that I have named, and living with a crazy old man who has spent the last twenty years avoiding the *capitalist swine*. I have not had the heart to tell him I used to be one of them.

It does not seem relevant. None of us are who we used to be. War chews us, and if it spits us out, we are a shred of our former selves.

"Come on, you would not put us in danger, would you?" I ask, on the verge of screaming myself.

We are almost at the hut. Dean stops, turns, and spits out something again. "No."

"I have a child to look after!" I tell him, refusing to move.

I have no idea who Branko used to be before he was clutching his dead parents in the street. Whether he liked school or detested it—liked the radio or the TV, or both—had a brother, a sister, both or neither. What does it matter? Now he is a large boy, rancid from not washing often enough, who either sleeps with his hand in mine, or wakes up screaming.

The only reason he was not picking mushrooms today was because Milana came round from her tent further in the forest. Before I came to Velebit, I never imagined so many people living here. To be precise, Milana did not use to live in the mountains. She was an avid hiker and naturalist, and only decided to stay when the war with Serbia began. In this past month that we have been here, I could not once get her to say anything more about herself. Perhaps that is why Branko likes her so much.

They both come out of the hut when they hear me complaining to Dean.

I have never seen anybody's face crumple that fast, not even when I told people they were to be laid off, as Milana's crumples when she takes the three of us in.

"Na— Nnn—" is all she manages before rushing to Dean and trying to pry the child from him. Her hands are sinewy but translucent with hunger and cold.

"No, no," he tells her. His head sways, his arms hold the girl. "No, Milana."

Double her age and weight, he shakes her off, and rushes into the hut. My brows meet when Branko follows him, instead of coming to my embrace, or to Milana's aid. She is kneeling on the ground, convulsive from a dry crying fit. I am the one left to take care of her. It is strange; I have never touched her. Now I squat next to her and slowly put a hand on her shoulder. She violently shakes it off and her stomach heaves.

I have no patience with hysterics. If I could have gotten through to Nadin, and walked away from it, never wrinkling my nose at the stench of the dead, and the dust—so much dust—choking me, she could calm down a bit. I tell her so, but she pretends not to hear. I take a deep breath, grab her by the upper arms, and lift her. She struggles, though weakly. I half-push, half-carry her inside the hut, where she collapses on the nearest chair.

Everything is strange inside.

The persistent reek of mold, mushrooms, and sour smoke has been replaced by a freshness that reminds me of early summer. Fire on the hearth burns brighter than usual.

And Branko—he appears to be *whispering* to the girl. It is not in a cheerful way. They are both more serious than children ought to be. Her lips move slightly, and perhaps it is not him who whispers.

Only Dean stoops over the fire in his own way, crow-dark and suspicious. He pours one of his herbals into a cup, and gives it to Branko, who passes it to the girl. Another cup is brought by Dean's hands to Milana. She purses her lips. I have never seen her eat or drink, though she collects meat and mushrooms from Dean now and then, and brings nuts in exchange.

Dean leaves the cup aside and waves her off with a hand.

When his back is turned, she takes a sip. It's bitter on the tongue, hot in the throat, calming in the stomach. I have had enough cups to know. Her eyes keep darting towards him, but he never faces us until she has drunk most of it. He observes Branko and the girl. So do I, as I untie my coat and put it carefully over the other chair.

When Milana has had enough of the tea, she follows Dean's gaze, and coughs.

"I'm sorry," she says. "I know it's not her, and yet—"

Dean looks at her, then me, and nods. "I get it."

"I don't," I say.

There is a hunger in Milana's eyes that makes them into a burning liquid. She gapes at the girl as if she still wants to go to her, put arms around her, whisper to her instead of Branko. Another exchanged look. Milana just lifts her knees to her chin and hugs them. She is so thin she is almost the same build as the girl.

Dean huffs. "Alright, I'll tell, then."

This he does, in his clipped speech, and checking with Milana that he got things right. She had a daughter before the war, a small thing, just like the girl we found. They liked hiking together, but Milana did not take the warnings about the war seriously enough. Some time in May or June they went into the mountains, and came upon a group of armed men. No more than four or five. She did not know if they were from the Serbian or Croatian side. It did not matter.

When they chewed them, and spit them out, they left them for dead.

Milana could not face the girl's father after that. The two remained in the mountain, going further and further away. From the war, the guns, the people, themselves. Her daughter went so far away she vanished one day.

"What do you mean?" I ask and look to Milana for an answer.

She shrugs. "Perhaps a wolf got her, or a bear. That's what I think. Dean says she found one of the paths to..." Otherplace; she does not need to say it. She looks at him, accusingly this time. "I keep waiting. Hoping."

That is the only solace, perhaps, in seeing our loved ones dead. We know they are not returning. Perhaps in dreams, to ask us to take them away, so we can feel guilty for not managing it when they were alive. We may want to save them, but we do not for a second believe we can.

"No people come from *Drugodje*," Dean cuts her off.

I inadvertently look at the girl. She is not a girl any longer.

Branko does not look surprised enough that he is talking to a block of wood.

The wood is dark, with curly bark. Its leaves are olive colored. To me, in the flickering light of the fireplace, it appears moist. It glistens and oozes, so when Branko touches it, his hands get slimy. Only then does he make a face, partly fascinated and partly disgusted.

There is no time for the woodling's reaction, though. Dean rushes headlong and shoves it right into the fireplace. It shrieks, twists, and shrivels, and he takes the rake he keeps in a corner to push it deeper into the flames. Milana screams in the background, once, in high and hoarse tones.

My only thought is of Branko. I am next to him in an instant and I try to wipe his hands in a blanket.

"Gods! Not my—!" Dean yells, looking over his shoulder, while he keeps pushing the struggling woodling further into the fire.

Milana interrupts with a "No!" and jumps at him, trying to take the rake away. Dean holds her off with one hand, while fighting the woodling with the other. I turn away from the scuffle to check if Branko is alright, putting my hands on his face.

"What is that?" I ask, not because I expect an answer from him, but because I cannot think.

Branko licks the slime remaining on his little finger, thoughtfully. His eyes find mine and, for the first time since I've known him, he speaks. I am surprised at how childish his voice still is. It clashes with his plump frame that only got tougher, not leaner, since we have been in the mountains.

"She's a *Nemra*," he tells me. The Never-Dead.

My fingers freeze on his cheek. His lips are crumbling and appear moist at the same time. I stare while his skin gets darker. Just as I manage to withdraw my hands, his face becomes woodlike. He still sits in front of me, but the change is quick. He utters an "Oh!" as he sees his arms turning into branches, and a "What!" escapes my own lips.

I jump away from him. Dean has pushed Milana away so violently that she is lying on the floor, perhaps unconscious. The woodling is still in the fire but does not burn. My cry makes Dean turn around. He does not hesitate like I do. He throws himself at what used to be Branko, who is confused enough not to resist as Dean throws him into the fire as well.

Instead of burning brighter, the fire begins to die down. The two are too much for it, bulky, slimy, thrashing around. *Alive and fresh.* They are not kindling. Dean's attempts to keep them in the hearth are a lost cause.

"Help!" he shouts at me.

I grab the first thing, his looking rod, and try to keep them inside with the pointy end. As I have a look through the stone circle, I see no greenish light, or anything that would give a hint that they are from Otherplace. *What, what, what?* keeps playing in my thoughts as I poke at the two clumps, half-human, half-wood. The fire is nearly extinguished. There is so much smoke my throat begins to burn and my eyes water. Dust is everywhere, and I hate it—but it is not dust; it is ashes.

From the ashes, two woodlings emerge, shaking themselves off. One used to be a girl, the other a boy. Now they are both wood, lichen, and that pungent, dripping muck.

The larger woodling plucks the rake away from Dean. The smaller one grabs the looking rod. I try to keep it to myself, but the woodling is too strong. The rod leaves my hands and the creature, this time cheerful, laughs. Dean pushes the bigger woodling away, trying to get to his looking rod. But the smaller one is lithe and avoids him easily.

It crouches next to Milana, grabs her by the forearm, and wails, "Save me from him, please, please!" Milana is now fully awake and determined.

I am so surprised by her wrapping her arms around the woodling that it takes me a moment to notice it has turned into a girl again. Her black hair is disheveled and covered in ashes. Dean has noticed sooner and has stepped back. I hope to see my Branko around, but he is still a piece of wood, holding the rake in what must pass for hands.

He rushes to Milana and the girl and threatens Dean with the rake in case he tries to approach them.

Milana's eyes flash from the floor. Desire and despair have whetted them.

"You will not get her, do you hear me?" she tells Dean.

She is embracing the girl with a thirst not easily quenched. "Not if I have to pluck out your eyes!"

She seems ready to do so, though I doubt she is strong enough.

"Why are you defending it?" I ask.

"She's my baby, my girl, she's come back to me," Milana says, and holds the girl tight. I notice there is some slime on the woman's cheek.

"She is not..." I think better than to argue with her and pull at Dean's sleeve. "Let's go! Let's go!"

"But the—"

"No time for that!"

We scramble out of the hut, into the gathering dusk. I have no idea where to run to. I hope Dean does. Just as he trods down a path, and I follow, I hear a voice behind my back. It is childish and hurt, and says, "Mum?"

It is not a name anyone has ever used for me, but my gut knows it is me he is calling.

I stop dead in my tracks and, despite my better judgment, turn around. Branko stands just outside the hut. He does not hold the rake any longer. He is not a piece of wood, either, though there is a certain dampness to his skin. His eyes are two pools in the gathering dark, and I cannot imagine he is anything else than my big, quiet, traumatized boy.

Although I want to run to him, I stand still and command myself to stop shaking. In the background, Dean's advance through the woods has stopped. Old leaves do not betray his steps.

"Yes?" I say.

Branko stretches his arm and offers my Burberry coat. I want it badly—I will freeze in the mountains without it. This late in the year, perhaps with it as well. And yet, I do not dare approach. *What if he has left the ooze on the inside?* a scared voice chirps in my head. I stop it. This can be checked, carefully. Perhaps there is some humanity still left in the boy, and the gesture is genuine.

"If I come for it, will you hurt me?" I ask and feel stupid. Somewhere behind me, a pair of feet start their way back. Dean is braver than I am. If I had managed to get away, I would not have returned for anyone. But I might be wrong on that.

"Hurt you?" Branko echoes. "No."

"She means—will you make her into... *that*," Dean says, now next to me.

Branko's face is a maze of different thoughts. He settles on one. "Don't you want to be *Nemri?*"

"No!" I say.

"But why?" he asks as Dean approaches slowly to take the coat from him. He lets go of it but keeps his attention on me. "It's good."

"How? How can it be good... not being yourself any longer?"

Branko follows Dean and comes closer. We stand under the leafless boughs, clear cold skies, and the shadow of misunderstanding one another. His head cocked, he tells me how it is good. I listen, pulling the coat on, hoping to cast some light into the shadow.

It is good because he doesn't hurt any more. His memories have faded. The longer ago, the less he remembers. He still knows I am his mum. *I am not*—but we accept the roles others offer, especially those offered with love. I say nothing, therefore, and he goes on.

It is such a relief from what was. He does not need the past. What good is it? It is hurt and humans. It is not what lies ahead. This place of humans is not a good sort of place. It needs changing or escaping from it. But people can do neither. They are stuck in the past, the pain, the possessiveness.

We are not, I want to say and cannot. We are.

Being a woodling is better. It is clean, comforting, and kind. "She said she will never let anyone hurt me again. Woods are strong and healthy. We are growing." There is a promise of a green tomorrow in his words that is felt even in the midst of winter.

"He's got a point." I think my thoughts are betraying me out loud, but it is only Dean murmuring. "A strange one, but still. Is there a catch?"

Branko shrugs, a copy of Dean's shrugs that he has seen in plenty. Dean shifts his own shoulders as if they are pricking.

"Ask her," Branko says. "She can show you better than I can explain."

I start shaking my head; no. I do not trust that creature. She just needs to touch me with a slimy finger, and I will turn into her. No: I will turn into a piece of wood. Who knows what I will be—let alone if there is a person left behind the bark to actually *be*. No, and no again.

The shadow is trying to pull me into itself.

"Call her outside," Dean says. "We're not coming any closer."

At least he has not fallen prey to the green words. *Not fully, or not yet?*

Branko trudges back to the hut and is gone for a while. When he returns, both the girl and Milana are with him. Milana is aglow, as calm and content as I have ever seen her. She smiles, holding the curly haired girl's hand. When she notices Dean and me keeping distance, she lets go, and nods as if she understands.

The girl—*the Never-Dead*, I correct myself—raises her other hand. She looks at the two of us through the hollow stone circle that is not tied to the rod anymore. As if satisfied, she pulls it onto her thin arm, where it rests like a bracelet, placidly by her side.

"What do *you* see through my stone?" Dean asks, ruffled.

It is his turn not to be answered. The Never-Dead watches him and moves her lips a little, as if speaking herself or imitating him, but says nothing. She turns to Milana and nudges her with an olive glance.

Milana steps forward and says, not meeting Dean's eyes, "The same as you. Paths that are to be."

"Leading to *Drugodje*," Dean says.

Milana's face turns away like she has to remember how to say what she means. "Other? It is the same place," she says in a musing voice. "The only difference is that there are no humans there."

"Gods, I knew it! It's foul, and..."

The *Nemra's* hand with the stone bracelet goes up. Dean falls silent. She takes the stone circle off again and comes closer to us. She raises it and shows us the world through it. Slowly, I understand. All the greenery, and the glow, is there because the world has changed. It is a world of trees, not people. A world of peace and quiet, where woodlings may roam, or plant themselves in place.

The girl turns the circle around—I did not know it makes a difference, but it does, at least in her hands.

It is a similar world that we now see, only ancient. It is like looking at someone's memories, though I am not sure if she could have witnessed it. I am not sure if I am witnessing it, or if someone is playing with my senses.

The world I am shown was soaked with power. It was not the power people have, sharp and cold, but warm and vast. It was a world that gods walked upon.

There were three. Their names were them, so I know, although I have not been told, who they were. The one with lightning for his gaze and sky for his robes was Perun, and I see him working on something. So intent he was on the work he did notice me. His arms, which were the handles of great axes, remodeled the hands and hair of a human into the crown of a woodling. As he did this, he perished into the leaves, only the sigh of the wind remaining of his might.

The dark one, under whose feet water churned as he stepped, and whose hair was darkness swollen in the underground, was Veles. He took to working with the torso and the legs of the human and gave the woodling its trunk and roots that move. In the next moment, he was gone, collapsing into soil so that only his bones remained in each stone buried.

But the woodling was only completed when the third one arrived. Her hair was wheat, her arms were all the mothers' embraces through centuries, and her breath was life itself. When Mokosh kissed the woodling, it received life unending, and she was gone into it.

The woodling is strong with Perun, moist with Veles, and alive with Mokosh.

It is the will of the gods of old. It is what they left of themselves in this world before they vanished and were forgotten. It is a hope of a better place, the one where woodlings are wild and free. Perhaps it will be a better place than the one it is now, where people made of trees wreak havoc.

Made of trees? I think I have thought it, but I must have said it out loud, because Branko answers me. "Out of the linden tree they made a woman, and out of the oak a man."

It sounds vaguely familiar, as if I learned it a long time ago, or knew it in my bones.

"And then they tried the other way around," Dean arrives at a conclusion, "to make trees out of people?"

"Yes."

I do not know who said it. Perhaps it was even me, agreeing that it makes sense. I have walked into the shadow and seen it was not made of misunderstanding at all. It was an offering of peace. Perhaps it was me, agreeing to the proposal.

I finally say, "Just let me do one thing."

As I go towards the hut, I notice Dean holding hands with Milana. I wonder if he has always loved her, and can touch her now that she, too, has forgotten about the past and the hurt. I do not know what he needs to forget, apart from the capitalist swine.

I know what I need, and yet, I do not want to. Not fully, or not without leaving something for others to remember. I enter the hut and take a deep breath; mold, mushrooms, smoke.

While the four wait outside for me to take Branko by the hand, and walk into the green world of tomorrow, I take a pencil and a piece of paper. I sit on the chair where Milana crumpled for the final time. I touch the pencil to my lips, its wood so familiar now, then lower it onto the paper. I write, *"Is the child from Here?"*

And I know the answer now—from Here and from Tomorrow.

THE GENTLEMAN HAT

IVANA GEČEK

2022

THE NURSE IS LOOKING at me suspiciously from behind her small, fogged-up glasses. I'm convinced her lips are making a sour, thin line behind her blue medical mask. There's a name tag on her neat uniform that says *Kristina*. I hear her tongue clicking disapprovingly: the sound of it fills the quiet corridor, mixing with the soft drizzle of the rain outside.

"Only family is allowed to visit him," she says.

Inconvenient, but not unexpected. I'm flashing her my brightest smile even though I'm wearing a mask, hoping to somehow charm her. Smiling with one's eyes has gotten somewhat crucial these past two years. "He was my favorite teacher in high school. I wouldn't insist otherwise, but I'm only in town for a couple of days and would like to see him for a few minutes. I want to thank him for everything and tell him I went to a good college. I think he'd appreciate that." I smoothly slide a box of chocolates from my bag on the counter and tap lightly on the envelope that's attached to the top of it. "I wanted to give him something sweet, but I think you may deserve it more. I can only imagine how hard it is working in a nursing home, especially these past few years."

"Well... yes, it really isn't easy," replies nurse Kristina, looking around hastily before snatching the envelope and shoving it in the pocket of her scrubs. *Jackpot.* For the first time in my life I'm thankful that corruption's such a common and well-spread thing in this country.

The nurse's nonexistent cordiality suddenly springs through the roof: after checking my ID and vaccination card, she leads me to the old man's room, explaining his condition to me with a sing-song voice. "He doesn't hear at all, but his sight is very good," she tells me as we stroll through the long, white corridor. The smell of air fresheners and antiseptics fills my nostrils and makes me slightly light-headed; I concentrate on my breathing while listening to the nurses instructions. As we reach his room, she pushes a piece of paper and a pen in my hands. "He's good at lip reading, but it's best to be prepared, dear," she says with a wink, before happily hopping away in her heavy clogs. I see I really made her day with my generous financial compensation; I almost feel bad that I'm about to ruin it all for her.

I enter the room and close the door behind me. Thankfully, the old man doesn't have a roommate; I guess that's one of the perks of a private nursing home. My supposed professor is laying in bed, looking small and fragile. He reminds me of a dried up, wrinkly raisin. The glasses he's wearing lay crooked on his nose. Looking at me questionably, he puts away his crossword puzzle and reaches for his mask. He hooks it behind his ears and slowly waves at me, urging me to come closer. His eyes are glued to my hat.

I sit on the chair next to his bed and reach for the photograph from my bag; best to get it over with quickly. The heavy scent of the old paper fills the room and mixes with the old man's slight smell. I tap the photograph and then hand it to him. His blotchy hands are shaking as he squints at the picture. Taking my mask off, I look into his eyes. I'm definitely at the right place. They're wide and scared, anxiously shifting between the photograph and my face, desperate to find some sign that this is all just a misunderstanding. An image of a scared deer pops into my head.

He reaches for the help button, making a weak, guttural sound, but I'm much faster. He barely lifts his limp hand halfway before I pull out the knife.

It's all over and done in under two minutes. It looks like my moves were effective, but still, it was harder than I expected; he put on a good fight for a man who had one foot in the grave. My arms ache and my chest heaves as if I'd just finished a bloody cardio training session. Surprisingly, no one came rushing to the door, even though the old man somehow managed to knock over the fake flower-filled vase from IKEA and a glass of water from his night table. The raisin was much stringier than I thought he would be, but all's well that ends well: I didn't even need the pen and paper that Kristina had given me. I think he got the message.

The clock on the wall tells me I still have a few minutes left. I fix my crooked hat and try to clean my hands and face with some paper towels, but nothing's really coming off. The room reeks of the metallic smell of blood and the piss the professor let out in panic. *Bladder control is no joke*, I think to myself as I put my mask back on.

There's a photograph on the old man's nightstand which had miraculously managed to stay intact. I take it in my hands and watch the happy, nuclear family for a few minutes: smiling parents, a cute baby daughter licking ice cream while staring at the camera, flashing it a big smile. The only thing that's missing is a big, loyal dog sitting by their feet, preferably a golden retriever. Looking at the happy family rhapsody contained in the small black and white photograph, I keep waiting for the remorse to kick in, but instead, a sense of fuzzy, warm emptiness spreads through my body. I stretch it, feeling it from my head to toe.

After a couple of minutes comes nurse Kristina, knocking politely on the door before entering. I put the photograph back in place and listen to her loud shriek and panicked run as she bolts back out of the room, screaming for help. A sudden wave of exhaustion flashes through me; not knowing exactly what my next move is, I sit back in the chair and close my eyes. A sense of completion fills my head and makes me dizzy. With a blissfully blank mind, I fall asleep.

The tranquility stayed with me even when I was pushed into a police car, cuffs etching harshly into my skin. Somewhere along the line, it stopped raining; I feel the soft rays of sunshine stroking my face gently through the glass window. I don't know how long this feeling will last, but I'm hoping it's going to remain inside of me forever, filling my lungs with the serenity I know I don't deserve.

I close my eyes again, smiling. *Finders, keepers.*

2021

"I'm telling you, he ran through the door in the blink of an eye! Barely lasted a month. A horror and sci-fi writer from Germany that came here during the pandemic to write in isolation. Said that the ambience was inspiring him. The old house, the dark forest with a lake, sleepy hollows, that kind of shit. After a month of his inspiration, he starts rambling about some sounds coming from the forest. From the lake, to be specific. Starts calling me in the dead of night, crying and whimpering like a scared little dog. Hilfe, hilfe! A real man, am I right? If you ask me, he was hittin' the bottle a little too hard. Hell, most artists do. That much I do know! Anyways, he went nuts and tried to convince me to come here and hear it for myself. I said nein, nein, he goes ja, ja! His damn noggin went auf Wiedersehen! Maybe the isolation got him... Some people can't handle being alone. But who knows, maybe he was a nutcase from the beginning. With the kind of shit that he was writing, I

wouldn't be surprised. Vampires, werewolves, demons...
What a troubled mind, am I right? You couldn't pay me
high enough to peek into his messed-up head!"

Damir finally finished his rant and started rolling himself
a new cigarette, a used-up medical mask hanging loosely
under his chin. Talking and smoking at the same time, he
more resembled a steam locomotive than a fifty year old man.

My dad told me a groundskeeper would greet me on my late
grandfather's property: I caught him leaning on his car hood,
smoking a cigarette, Megaton radio blasting through open windows.

Not taking no for an answer, Damir insisted on helping
me with my bags and showing me around the property. The
state of it wasn't horrible, but it was obvious that no one
had really lived here since my grandparents moved away in
the early sixties. Still, I was impressed with the estate: a big
two-storey house, green meadows filled with wildflowers,
and an oak forest hiding a small lake inside of it. Taking in
the beauty of it, I wondered why my grandfather wanted to
keep the property vacated for so long. My father never took
his words seriously, though: a week after his death, he called
up Damir to ask around for potential tenants.

Damir hung out much longer than I'd liked; his smug
smile and grabby hands that were constantly grazing my
hips and back were making me feel uneasy. After giving me
a detailed tour of the house and showing me the forest path
leading to the lake, he finally headed back to his car. "Call
me if you need anything, darling. I'm going to come back in
a while to see how you've settled," he said cheerfully while
opening his car door.

That won't be necessary, I thought to myself. "That's
very kind of you," I replied instead. "Would you like to stay
for a cup of coffee?" The words were out of my mouth
before I could even think them through. Damned be the
pathological politeness that my mom instilled in me.

He thankfully declined my offer, saying he couldn't miss any more of his work. With the agility of a young man, he hopped into his car, winked at me, blasted the radio and drove off, disappearing quickly down the hill. Sighing tiredly to myself, I tried not to inhale the dust his car made while drifting away dramatically. *What an overkill.*

Later that day, I sat on the bench by the lake, taking in the view. The deep, emerald green water was speckled with golden reflections of the setting sun. Being a city girl my entire life, I felt a bit doubtful about coming here, but I found the rich shades of green a welcomed change from the gray streets of Zagreb. A soft breeze tickled the hair on the nape of my neck, bringing a whiff of earthy freshness with it. The trees that circled the lake formed a thick cocoon of leaves and wood around it; instead of feeling isolated or uneasy, I felt strangely at peace, like I'm being hidden from the rest of the world and its expectations.

Closing my eyes, I inhaled deeply a few times, wanting to get the oak-scented air into my lungs as deeply as I could. My lips curved into a small smile while I thought about how unnecessarily I worried about adapting to a quieter lifestyle. Glancing back at the water, I felt the sudden urge to caress my palm along its surface or dip my toes in it, but ultimately decided against it, not wanting to disturb the potential inhabitants that may reside in it. The sun was hanging low, grazing the hills and casting a golden hue all over the woods. A sense of insignificance flashed through me, but it was soon replaced with a tight clench in my chest.

After a while, this morning's excitement started fading away. The reality of the last two years, ever present but forcefully pushed to the back of my mind, threatened to burst out: the pandemic, getting fired, and the haunting feeling of isolation all came flooding through. The tears fell silently from my eyes as a dull pressure gathered in my forehead.

Massaging my temples and praying that it's not a beginning of a migraine, I felt the need for some company but didn't dare call my friends for a whining session so soon. While the weight of our late twenties was pressing on us all, ranging from unhappy relationships, loneliness, and parental expectations to moral dilemmas, it was especially burdensome for them. Dealing with the usual problems and balancing soulless, criminally underpaid jobs, money issues, sick parents, and overall low morale was taking a toll on them.

And then there's me: someone who came from a wealthy family and wanted to be independent, but always relied on their parents as human cash machines. When my office downsized last year and I got fired, it would have been tragic only if it had actually affected me; the reality is I hated my job and didn't really need the money. I'd studied social work out of some silly, romantic notion that I could make a change, but it only made it painfully obvious how much out of place I am, my hands helplessly tied by nonsensical laws and unnecessary paperwork. My biggest humanitarian achievement was forcing my family to donate to a different charity every year, which they only agreed to because they thought it would make them look good.

"Maybe we should do something with kiddie cancer next," my father had said the last time we made a donation. "Do you have something like that?"

"Yeah, that's a good idea!" my sister had chimed in. "The boob cancer one you suggested is a bit depressing, don't you think?" she'd added, looking at her breasts.

Ever since I was little, I've felt out of place in my family, often dreaming that I was actually adopted; as I grew older, the fantasy only got more elaborate with each day.

I could trash talk my family in my head all day, but the sad truth is, I'm no better than them. As soon as things got difficult, I accepted their suggestion to come here and play makeover with my grandfather's estate to turn it into a fancy money-making Airbnb instead of making a name for myself, as many other people were forced to do. My rock bottom looks awfully like a jackpot, and as unbelievable as that sounds, no one hates it more than me.

I cried for a long time by the lake, watching the sun go down, disappear behind the dark green hills. The night slowly veiled my surroundings with a rich darkness that's only possible in uninhabited spaces. It started to get chilly, the crisp, autumn air pinching my cheeks. I zipped up my light jacket fully while looking at the lake in front of me, the fog gathering around it and hovering over the smooth surface. The surrounding hills merged into one big mass, dark and mystifying. I could see why the writer had liked this place. A gothic rhapsody hidden deep in the center of Zagorje.

After my moment of self-pity by the lake, I woke up feeling determined to make myself useful. The next week flew by, filled up by unpacking and exploring my new surroundings. Soon, the dusty, old house stuffed with heavy carpets and needlepoint paintings started to feel a bit more cheerful; I scattered my personal belongings all over the house and filled my bedroom on the second floor with a bunch of books and comics I'd dragged with me. I even put my rainbow magnet I got at last year's Pride on the fridge, although I didn't really see the point of advertising my preferences out here. The only Tinder matches I might get would probably be the Blair Witch and the Creature from the Black Lagoon.

To make my hands busy and my head empty, I decided to clean the whole house myself, without hiring cleaners to help me. *Who's the spoiled brat now?* I thought, happily assembling cleaning supplies. I started with the basement, looking for some familial skeletons in the closet, but after spending the whole morning inhaling dust, I felt disappointed: I didn't find anything remarkable. I was hoping for some old incriminating letters, undisclosed love confessions hidden among the pages of a book, mysterious diaries filled with juicy family secrets, but to no avail. No old photographs of my grandfather in women's clothes or my grandmother partaking in a feral orgy. Is it really possible that I'm the only degenerate in this family? *How boring.*

My biggest catch was a family of mice hiding in the wooden closet, which I was forced to rehome; as a former social worker, my heart was breaking as I gathered them in a box and placed them in the garden.

Later that day, while sitting by the lake and flicking through the few photographs I'd found in the basement, a strange incoherence filled my head. Looking at the portraits of my grandparents and what I assumed to be their friends, I found not a drop of fondness in my usually compassionate heart. Outside of some shared physical attributes, I might have as well been looking at a couple of strangers who had lead lives completely detached from mine. No memories of them were stored in my mind, only plain, objective facts: my grandmother died from a stroke before I was even born and my grandfather was an eccentric hermit, secluding himself from his friends and family in the plains of Slavonija. I would usually only see him about two or three times a year, around the holidays, but as I grew older, those visits had gotten sparser and sparser. On those rare occasions that I saw him, I was put off by his peculiar behavior, which often bordered on religious madness and fanaticism. He would always carry a rosary around, twiddling it in his hands like some kind of a holy fidget toy, making his guests dunk their hands in a Tupperware container of holy water before entering the house. Although I found all of that to be incredibly strange, I didn't really question it at that age.

"He's just a part of a different generation," my father would say. "Things were different back then."

I wasn't sure if that was true, but my tween brain was satisfied with that explanation, not really wanting to dive deeper into my grandfather's mind, sensing something sinister behind it. Then again, maybe I was imagining the darkness and hollowness that hid in his eyes; watching a bunch of scary movies in one's formative years will do that.

My reminiscence was brought to an end by a loud splash of water coming from the lake, making me jolt in surprise. A few birds flew from the branches, chirping. The usual smoothness of the lake was now being filled with concentric circles that slowly spread along its surface, merging softly at the edges.

I'll have to find some tamer fish, I pondered, recovering from the horror movie-worthy jumpscare. *Fucking hell.*

My new routine was doing wonders for my mental health. It must be all that fresh air and the hills that were surrounding me. Johanna Spyri was definitely up to something when she wrote Heidi. I made ten inspirational moodboards on Pinterest and watched a dozen of house renovation vlogs on YouTube. Looking up gardening vlogs with a cup of coffee in my hands became my new daily morning ritual, and I wasn't even ashamed about it. I was sure that I could transform this estate into a fabulous vacation destination in no time. With some renovations and subtle landscaping, I could imagine Kate Bush doing her interpretative dances in the meadows, calling out for Heathcliff.

After successfully clearing out the basement, I started on the attic, the two looking uncannily alike: a few piles of old clothes and some furniture hidden under gray, dusty sheets. I did, however, stumble upon a black box stored beneath a glass showcase while vacuuming. An image from *Hellraiser* popped into my head, making me apprehensive for a second, but curiosity got the best of me: I peeked into the box, hoping to finally find something interesting and slightly incriminating.

What I found was a vintage men's hat. Unlike the rest of the clothes and garments I'd found in the house, I actually liked it; it fitted my head perfectly, blending nicely with my somewhat boyish aesthetic. I wore it the rest of the day, loving the look of it as I glanced at myself everytime I passed a mirror. *Thriftiness at its finest.*

Feeling especially inspired that day, I started an impromptu digging session in the garden, but quickly realized that planting actual plants was not as easy as the gardening vlogs showed me. I found myself exhausted, leaving the backyard at twilight, excavated like a labor of moles went through it. *It must be because I'm almost thirty*, I concluded, dragging myself up the stairs. Some say that thirties are the new twenties, but then again, some say that queen Elizabeth is a lizard. *Trust no one.*

I threw myself on the bed, contemplating if I have enough willpower to take a shower. Outside, the wind rustled the shriveled leaves, making a soft murmur that was better than a white noise machine. Already half asleep, I reached for my phone, but my hand didn't move, remaining still at my side.

I tried again, mildly annoyed, not thinking much of it in my tired state, but it still didn't budge. As confusion inside me slowly started to grow into unease, a loud crash came from downstairs.

Under different circumstances I would've jumped, startled by the sound, but my whole body was still, unable to move. Panic started to rise in my chest as I heard a weird, shuffling noise from the ground floor, gradually getting louder and louder. Slowly but steadily, I heard something dragging over the stairs. The noise didn't sound like an animal, but didn't sound human either. Beads of sweat rolled down my neck, soaking the pillow under my motionless head.

A string of hysteric curses slipped from my tongue as I shifted my eyes at the bedroom door I'd carelessly left open just a few minutes ago. I tried to somehow calm my heaving chest, but failed miserably.

"Who is it?" I shouted with a hoarse voice, receiving no answer. Whatever was making its way up continued creeping closer, making my scalp burn with terror.

"I called the police, they're on the way!" I screamed, trying to keep the desperation out of my voice. I still couldn't move, my body stiff and hard like a wooden figurine. With dread, I thought about what I'd do if my lips stopped moving next. Not wanting to waste my voice for a moment longer, I prepared to shout another threat, but then the shuffling noise suddenly stopped, leaving an eerie silence in its wake. A speck of relief ran through me as I took this beat of quiet to convince myself that this is all a bad dream with a particularly nasty case of sleep paralysis, but after a few seconds, the silence was abruptly broken by a piercing shriek.

It jabbed my ears sharply, making them pulse with nauseating pain. It felt like a thousand little needles poking my eardrums, making my eyesight blurry and fuzzy for a few seconds.

An intense, fishy odor started coming through the door frame, quickly spreading through the room. The stench was horrible: I gagged as it filled my nostrils, reminding me of rotten fish and dirty water. That's when I saw the thing's head peeping at the top of the stairs, pulling itself up with its hands.

I watched in silent horror as the creature slowly made its way towards me. It looked like a decomposed corpse, face ashy and unnaturally pale underneath streaks of wet, bronze hair, while its bloated chest and arms were covered with patches of dark, rust-orange pelt. A small gasp escaped my lips as I discovered the thing was dragging a long, scaly tail behind it, the scales glistening in the dim light of my bedside lamp.

Under different circumstances, I would be thrilled to see such a thing, but now, the only thing I could think of was *I'm about to die by the hands of a zombie siren*. She crawled sluggishly, dragging herself on her hands, leaving a trail of gray, jelly mucus behind her.

I closed my eyes when she finally came next to me. I could feel the weight of her hands dipping the bed, her foul breath heavy on my face. My ears pulsated dully, but the pain subsided slowly, leaving a mild vibrating sensation behind. A sharp fingernail traced the skin on my neck in an almost caressing manner; I waited for the pain, but it never came. Instead, she licked my throat a few times, slowly, tasting the blood I didn't even notice leaking from my ears. Her long and pointy tongue was cold against my exposed skin, sending a trail of goosebumps along my whole body. Just as I thought I couldn't take her slick, icy touch anymore, she headed back out of the room, as slowly as she'd come.

Suddenly able to move again, I bolted to the door, almost falling over the mucus the thing had left behind. I closed them, locked them, barricaded them with a chair and then fell to my knees and retched a few times, all in under half a minute. Somehow I dragged myself back on the bed, shaking with fear and adrenaline like a leaf. I cautiously touched my ears, but they didn't hurt at all anymore. The only evidence of the pain was the little bit of blood behind my right ear she didn't get.

I sat on the wet sheets until morning, eyes glued to the barricaded door. When I finally mustered up the courage to leave my bedroom and descend to the ground floor, I found everything pristine: nothing was out of order, except for the old hat resting on the kitchen table. I swore I'd left it in the foyer, hanging safely from a brass hook.

"So? Have you started seeing weird shit yet? Did you become Jack Torrance, screaming bloody murder?"

I laughed nervously at my friend Ana, clenching the phone tighter in my hand, but her words stuck with me long after we hung up a few minutes later.

Something that always irked me while watching horror movies was the often illogical behavior of the characters. Why in the world wouldn't the tortured protagonist just tell someone: *Hey, I started seeing some really weird stuff, I may need some help*, and just skip the whole shebang? *If I started seeing some crazy shit like that, I would definitely tell someone*, I always thought as I stuffed my face with popcorn. While I don't really believe in the concept of karma, I may have brought this one on myself.

How do you even say something like: *A few days ago a smelly siren licked my bloody throat clean*, and not sound like an attention seeker who's screaming for help? The only option I had when Ana asked me if I was roleplaying *The Shining* by myself was to deny it and casually change the subject, clutching the survival backpack I'd packed and always carried on my back to soothe my nerves.

To get to the bottom of this, I even considered sending an e-mail to the writer who had lived here before me. *Dear Mr. German Writer*, I would start, *Guten Tag! I'm writing to you as the current tenant of the house that you supposedly went mad in and ran out of screaming and crying like a scared, helpless child. I was wondering, in case it isn't much of an inconvenience, if you could explain to me what the actual fuck is going on in this place? Did you also get nightmarish and very lifelike hallucinations while staying here? Did you also notice something like a busted up siren from hell crawling around the house like a broken Rumbot while screaming like a lovechild of a hyena and a screamo band vocalist? Thank you in advance for your answer! I really hope I didn't trigger some kind of a*

psychotic episode with this message. Mit freundlichen Grüssen,
The Girl Who Thinks She's Losing Her Fucking Mind.

I really hoped that I wouldn't have to face the same
dilemma that Chris MacNeill encountered in *The Exorcist.*
Where on Earth would I even find such a smart, eloquent,
considerate and handsome priest like father Karras? I'm not
sure that I'm ready to throw my rigid atheism through the
window to allow some money-hungry local priest to cleanse
my house of evil spirits with a few Hail Marys and a splash
of stale holy water. I'm doubtful I could remember any of
the prayers or how to cross myself correctly, which is very
important because, unlike my devout grandfather, I'm
convinced that religion's just 99% a placebo effect.

Although I was on high alert, the days were uneventful,
merging together in a mass of unease and trepidation, until one
night the doorbell rang. Gripping the biggest kitchen knife, I
peeked through the window; Damir was standing outside of
the gate, trying to light a cigarette in the pouring rain.

"You know, you shouldn't really do all of the digging and
shoveling yourself," said Damir while scratching his head,
looking at my unfinished landscaping in the back garden
with strained eyes and raised eyebrows. He took a long sip
of wine and continued. "It's just not a woman's job. Don't
get me wrong, I'm not saying you're not capable, right? I
know these days women like to do everything that men do,
but why bother with this? You could have just called me. I
know my way around a shovel! Hell, you should see the
garden at my house. You'll have to come by sometime!"

I smiled politely and made a non-committal *mhm.*
Damir's been here for more than two hours and there's no
signs that he'd be leaving anytime soon. He's pulled a bottle
of wine from his jacket, inviting himself in under the guise

of checking up on the house. I found out many things I didn't need to know about him: divorced (*unhappily*), right-winged (*unquestionably*), unvaccinated (*proudly*). Luckily, he didn't question me too much; I was starting to get worried as I saw him glancing at my rainbow magnet with a poorly covered scorn, eyebrows furrowed. I could already see the headline: *Rich Girl Gets Hate-Crimed by a Local Man and Gets Buried in the Surrounding Woods.*

"Anyways, this is going to make a fine renting place. What do you kids call it these days? Airbnb?" he said, reaching for the thankfully almost empty bottle of wine. "It's a shame your grandpa moved away so quickly. He could've just drained the lake if it was such a bother to him. He certainly had the money for it, am I right?"

The hairs on my neck stood up as shivers ran through my body. I never thought that the word *lake* would trigger me, but it's 2022 and here we are.

"Why did it bother him?" I asked, trying to stay nonchalant.

"He didn't tell you? I guess it's for the best. It's not really a nice bedtime story for the grandkids. But it isn't really my place to tell it, you know?" Damir reached for his tobacco.

Nonetheless, he told me the whole story almost immediately, confirming my theory that men are often worse at gossiping than women.

"There was a string of drownings in that lake, back around the early sixties. Five young men drowned, all of them your grandpa's friends. Rumor has it they were all drinking a bit too much. I don't judge, okay? I sure do occasionally like to have a few myself. But drinking and then going for a swim? It's like they were asking for it, if I can beg your pardon."

He paused for a moment, licking and rolling his cigarette. Outside, the rain got heavier, thumping loudly against the windows.

"Anyways, your grandpa moved away very quickly after the accidents. As he should've, am I right? Seeing his friends all die such a stupid death. The only one who stayed close, and well, alive, was Jakov Horvat. He's still around, pushing ninety in a fancy nursing home in Varaždin. He moved to Zagreb, became a professor. Got himself a nice little family. And then, suddenly, before he turned forty, went deaf as a doorknob. Who the hell goes completely deaf out of nowhere? Some say that he did it to himself. I don't really believe that, though he always was a bit wacky. Well, who wouldn't be, after all of your friends snuff it? Anyways, he has a pretty cozy life now. His daughter lives in Australia and makes loads of money, doing some fancy mumbo-jumbo with computers."

He rambled on about the professor's daughter as I got up to make some coffee, giving myself an excuse to process all the information I'd just heard. My mind went blank, Damir's words reduced to a background noise. Trying to gather my thoughts, I didn't even notice him come behind my back and lay a heavy hand on my shoulder.

"Look, don't be scared, sugar. It was a long time ago. I won't let anything bad happen to you, okay? You worry too much, all alone up here."

I felt his hand graze my hips. Shivers ran all the way up to my neck as I instinctively went to push his hand off, but froze instead, feeling like his hand paralyzed me the same way the creature did the other night.

"You can't completely cut out a man's hand, you know?" he whispered in my ear.

Before I could react, a familiar shriek punctured my ears, making me fall to the floor and cover my ears firmly.

Damir jumped away from me, looking around frantically, his eyes teary and wide. "Do you hear that?" he asked me desperately. A broken sob escaped his throat. "It's beautiful."

He ran out of the house before I could respond, leaving me shriveled up on the floor, ears throbbing with pain. Once the shrieking stopped, against my better judgment, I went out to look for him, armed with a phone in one hand and a knife in the other. There was only one place he could be. I really was raised to be too polite. *God damn it.*

It was quiet as I got to the lake; it stopped raining somewhere along the way. Damir lay near the benches, almost merging with the pitch-black ground. I checked his pulse: it was a bit slow, but he was still breathing. His shirt was damp and torn, covered with a familiar slime, while his neck was already bruising, a few strands of copper hair still clung around it.

I reached for my phone to dial an ambulance when I heard my name whispered softly. My body shivered, enfolded by the cold, autumn air as I slowly took off my clothes and entered the water. She was waiting for me at the bottom of the lake, bathed in dim moonlight, her arms open. I nestled deep into her gentle, warm embrace as she whispered her story tenderly in my ear.

1962

Zora looked at her dusty boots and sighed. Ever since Marta got married, getting to her was a hell of a journey: a ninety-minute bus ride from Varaždin and then a half hour long hike up the steepest hill. Her dress, much like her boots, was a dusty mess, with sweat stains peeking under her armpits and tainting the fine fabric which she had paid a fortune for. When she finally arrived at Marta's house it was already twilight and the dinner party was in full swing. Chugging a generous sip of *višnjevača* that someone handed her, she wondered if it would be considered rude if she just guzzled the whole thing and poured herself another glass to make this whole thing more bearable.

"Nice hat, Zora. Is it your brother's?" said one of Marta's friends as she sat down next to her. *No, darling, it's actually your dad's,* Zora wanted to say, but somehow managed to keep her tongue still.

Zora was used to people making snarky remarks about her appearance. She made herself an easy target and actually enjoyed it most of the time: the feeling of heads turning as she walked by made her stomach burn with excitement.

It had all, honestly, started with boredom: there was nothing else to do in their small town other than daydreaming and making a little buffoonery here and there. Zora incorporated a bit of havoc in her everyday life, provoking her mother and her teachers with inappropriate language and sticking out her tongue at the priest during Sunday service. As she got older, her usual provocations didn't cut it anymore. She started hanging around local bars and roadhouses, looking for some cheap thrills to pass the time. She didn't mind the rancid booze or the lousy men; one day she would look back on it with laughter while traveling Italy, France or even the whole world. Working alongside her mother as a seamstress was only temporary. If she could just keep saving money and avoid getting married for a little while longer, she'd find a way to get out of this shoddy town.

In the meantime, she could at least look the part: one day, after seeing *Breathless* at the cinema, she came home from the hair salon looking like Jean Seberg. That was the last straw for her mother, who was relatively used to her daughter's shenanigans and usually refrained herself from sharing her opinion; she grabbed the long, brown ponytail which had formerly been attached to Zora's head and started whipping her with it in a fit of rage. Later, when the initial shock faded, she replaced the anger with a childlike sadness.

"Who on earth will marry you now?" mother muttered to herself almost lamentably. *Boys don't care how shitty you look if you play by their book*, Zora wanted to say, but kept her mouth shut, arms and back still burning from the whipping. The next day, however, her mother cheered up a bit: she'd managed to sell the hair on the market for two months' worth of wages.

The hat was Zora's latest visual addition, quickly becoming her statement piece: ever since she bought it in Zagreb while looking for some new fabric, she rarely took it off. It was love at first sight, making her feel giddier than any man she'd ever gone home with.

The hat caused some serious racket, and it wasn't even the fact that the hat was meant to be worn by men. Poor people like her were used, even encouraged to wear clothes that were intended for the opposite gender, often inherited or passed on by various family members, neighbors or friends. The fact that shocked everyone was, apparently, the sheer madness of spending a copious amount of money to buy such a fine, luxury item. If Zora had just bought a bunch of cheap, functional clothes, people would've maybe begrudged her excessive spending habits and moved on, but buying a practically decorative, expensive hat just for the joy of owning one was considered to be the peak of eccentricity. Now she was known in town as *the wanton girl with the expensive gentleman hat*, which was a title Zora wouldn't admit she actually enjoyed.

Zora drained down two more glasses of *višnjevača* and considered washing them down with some rakija, when she saw her best friend walking into the room with a small, moving bundle in her hands. All the girls gathered around her: the whole room was instantly filled with gleeful commotion, making Zora want to roll her eyes.

"He's so cute!" they cooed, pinching his slobbery red cheeks and poking his snotty, button like nose. The girls shifted the baby among each other's arms like they were playing a game of hot potato. The air in the room suddenly became too heavy, so when someone had to take food and drinks to the guys who had secluded themselves by the lake, Zora couldn't volunteer fast enough, feeling like the walls of the room were closing in on her.

The cold late autumn air was pinching her cheeks as she trailed the forest path to the lake. Although she tried to walk confidently, her legs were wobbly from all the alcohol she'd drank on an empty stomach. As though her mood wasn't foul enough, she managed to almost fall a few times, stepping into piles of mud left by this morning's rain; she was certain her shoes and dress were going to be completely ruined by the end of the night. *Just splendid.*

She found the guys gathered on the benches by the lake, drinking in a circle. Someone whistled as she came closer, making her eyes roll. *How original,* she thought.

"Nice hat, Zora!" said Tomislav, who was Marta's husband. "Do you also have a matching pantsuit that goes with it?"

They tolerated each other in Marta's presence, but enjoyed a bit of a squabble when they were alone.

Before she could come up with a witty comeback, though, Petar, his best man, chimed in. "Can I borrow it?" he asked, standing up from the bench, scanning her from head to toe. With his broad shoulders and bulky chest, he towered over Zora's petite form easily, but she never let herself get impressed or intimidated by it. She knew that his bark was worse than his bite.

"I would let you," she replied, "but I don't think you're man enough to pull it off."

She was definitely not in the mood to play this game with him tonight. The guys laughed and cheered as she left the basket and stormed back into the forest. Even Jakov, always the quiet and serious one, allowed himself a little chuckle at the expense of his friend.

Her gloating, unfortunately, didn't last long: soon she felt a firm grip on her forearm, squeezing her tightly and making her stop. Having known Petar for some time, it was naive to think he would back off so easily.

"Why are you playing such a fucking prude all of a sudden?" he whispered in her ear, words slurring together. "Making me look like a fool in front of the guys, when we all know how much you like spreading your legs for anyone."

Seeing red, she turned around and spat on him. A gob of her saliva landed all over his face, leaving a tense silence between them.

It was all blurry for her after that: it was impossible to determine who started the shoving or landed the first slap. She doesn't remember tumbling down and feeling a sharp, searing pain in the back of her head. She doesn't remember Petar shaking her limp body violently, cursing and calling out her name. She doesn't remember the guys gathering around her body, alarmed by Petar's wailing. She doesn't remember Jakov checking her pulse and quietly suggesting they call the town's doctor, only to be shut down by the others. She doesn't remember Tomislav running to the house and returning with some rope. She doesn't remember them working in unison, tying her limp limbs to heavy rocks. She doesn't remember Jakov violently retching behind them, his glasses lying even more crooked than usually on his nose. She doesn't remember being dragged to the edge of the lake and being pushed in, slowly sinking into the darkness. But somehow, when she opened her eyes again, she just knew all of that nevertheless.

She became conscious that she was a rusalka, a creature her grandmother used to tell her bedtime stories about. And somehow, she came to accept it very quickly, watching her breath shape into iridescent bubbles.

That was her life now, her new state of existence. *Come hell or high water.*

The biggest change, as imagined, were the legs, or better said, the lack of them. Her scaly tail annoyed her at first: she felt clumsy and awkward, rolling around in the mud like a newborn baby, but soon she moved with an elegance she didn't know her new body possessed. Soft hair covered her skin, leaving her arms and belly with a fur-like texture; she loved watching the copper strands of it float softly, caressed by the green water. Her hair grew rapidly, almost reaching the end of her tail, turning gold orange. The locks were soft and wavy, but could turn hoarse if needed: they were prehensile, she discovered, and could inflict serious damage if she wanted them to.

None of it really scared her or made her uncomfortable. After all, she was a woman, used to constant pain and bodily changes from a young age, but the irony of what she'd become didn't pass her by. All her life she fought against something, a fiery pit burning in her stomach. She didn't want to be defined or caged by other people, especially men, and now she was here, a *rusalka* in this smelly little pond in the middle of the hills. When the thought of it became unbearable, she would swim to the surface of the lake and scream and cry for what felt like hours, wondering if Marta could hear, all the way in Slavonija where she'd run away with her husband after Zora's disappearance, feigning ignorance and playing the role of a happy housewife.

Petar came back to the lake a few months after the accident, stumbling around, apparently in a state of drunken grief. She almost took pity on him, seeing him cry and cradle his head like a little child, but then remembered the sigh of relief he'd let out when her body finally sunk all the way down, the rocks pulling heavily at her limbs. She didn't savor the horrified look on his face when she peeked with her head to the surface. This wasn't a killing of pleasure: it was a killing of pure need mixed with hot, searing rage. Her hair grabbed his legs and started pulling him into the water, wanting him to have the same experience as she did.

They all came back, one by one, except Tomislav and Jakov. One ran across the country and the other, not having the same luxury, hid behind the nearest hills. That didn't stop her from inflicting psychological terror on them both. She cackled as she sent them feverish nightmares and grueling visions, amused by their attempts to stop her: Tomislav praying desperately to a God he didn't believe in and Jakov going as far as stabbing himself in the ears with knitting needles.

After she killed the others, making it all look like a series of unfortunate drownings, the thrill of it started wearing off. Her bloodthirst left her; with nothing to do, she mostly lay in the mud, head empty and heart heavy. She was a bit ashamed of her behavior when that writer came to stay in the house. He was a nice man; it definitely wasn't necessary to taunt him like that. But who could blame her? She always loved a bit of tomfoolery, and the clueless German was the perfect target for some psychological teasing. It was the most fun she's had in decades. *Couldn't they have killed me somewhere more fun?* she often thought to herself. *Why couldn't they have killed me at the Plitvice Lakes? Oh, the things I could do there...*

Somewhere along the line, she started forgetting things. Her human life became distant and blurry, resembling an abstract watercolor painting, turning her memories into a dull thud heard from a distance. She couldn't remember the taste of her favorite fruit or the way her mother laughed. Slowly, she sank further and further into a state of apathy, lying in the mud for years, caught in a limbo of reminiscence mixed with melancholy.

And then one day came the girl: Marta's granddaughter, crying her eyes out by the lake, waking her up from her trance. Zora didn't even have to meddle with her head as much. The girl was pliable in her arms, already broken by her own self-loathing. Zora didn't feel too bad sending her away to do her dirty business and to wave an old photo of Marta and her in front of Jakov's face, reminding him of his unpaid dues. At least she gave the girl the purpose she so desperately craved.

The day Jakov died, Zora didn't swim up to the surface. She didn't even notice her body changing back, making her the same hotheaded, daring girl from all those decades ago. Looking at the top of the lake, she swore she could see her favorite hat floating above. Smiling, she closed her eyes, rays of sunshine dancing on her eyelids.

It was quiet by the lake. A few birds flew into the blue sky, and the wanton girl with the gentlemen hat with them, finally free.

MORANA'S SONG

PETRA VALKOVIĆ

THE FIRST LEAF FELL on the hard ground, quietly unnoticed. The weather was changing, days growing shorter, and the wind was blowing colder with each passing hour of darkness, howling through streets and alleyways as the cry of a thousand dead souls. People were hurrying home and were scarcely seen outdoors after the sunset. Not so long ago, they were bursting with life. Now they were worriedly trying to close the flapping wooden shutters of their windows. *Every change is a shock, no matter how small it is*, she thought as she walked down poorly lit passages. She wondered if anyone still sang the old song that was hovering in her mind like a cloud heavy with rain. Her song.

Hide, Morana is here
Lo, the winter is near
Her long nails will catch you
And quickly cut you through
Run, the nightmares come
Run and beat the drum
Children, be still and beware
Or she'll chew your bones and spit them bare.

This dreadful song played in Morana's head for ages, come wintertime. People used to scare children with that haunting tune. Nowadays, it was remembered by a few; old village women, storytellers and keepers of the old lore. Withered old crones, as she herself was called. Yet she was no crone, let alone withered. But she was old. Old as the world itself.

Morana was there when the ice giant Leđan led the rebellion against the gods. She'd sided with him. It was in her nature to do so. Her reputation was horrible. After all, she was the goddess of winter, death and bad dreams. No one really liked her. Together, Leđan and she had frozen the entire Earth but were eventually defeated. Leđan had been turned to stone and Morana had gone underground and stayed there for many centuries, emerging when necessary as she still had duties to attend to. Humans were not immortal and cold weather had to come to bring spring in the end. Such was the circle of life and the cycle of the year. Their whole existence, of gods and humans, was one big wheel. And round and round it went. Endlessly. Tirelessly. Boringly. But it was needed. She was needed.

However, she'd decided to get away from squabbling gods and all the drama that causes bad weather in this human realm, which she now resided in. She was minding her own business and laying low.

Morana shook away her memories, only to frown when she found the song in her head, still. She walked through the empty town, tucking her chin into the collar of her black leather jacket with hands in her pockets. Although her signature color was white, she liked black, it complemented her long raven hair and made her smooth, pale skin shine. She was tall and slender, a figure to behold, her long legs dressed in tight black jeans with flat black boots on her feet. Men were easily enthralled by her cold ethereal beauty. They always were. Morana could seduce anyone, but her heart was continuously broken each year, for none could equally love her back. It had been some time ago that she'd changed the story and started breaking *their* hearts. She feared rejection, so *she* rejected instead. She liked this arrangement more. It gave her some kind of a status quo feeling. At least from her part.

But the white color always reminded her of her primal personality, something pure as snow itself, natural and innocent. She always had to wear something white, ever since she was born. At first, it was a dress she proudly donned. One disappointment after another and white was reduced to trivial things such as socks or some trinkets hidden under layers of black. This evening she'd chosen the simplest white bracelet with a single, thin leather strap. It felt like wearing one last thread of her old self twisted around her wrist.

Her feet turned left at the next crossing, following the narrow street and down the slippery stone staircase covered with a thin layer of moss. She knew every nook and cranny of this town, and this particular secluded corner was the entrance to her underground hideout. A club of sorts, her kingdom of tunnels, shady businesses and all kinds of creatures. Some were seeking shelter, some were scheming and plotting, and some just wanted a good drink while catching up on some gossip. It was always busy at nighttime, a hive of voices and sounds.

As she walked through the corridor, something small came running toward her. Amid his frenzy, she recognized Malik, the red-capped, foot-sized dwarflike creature. His inexhaustible energy drove her crazy sometimes, but he was good at running errands that nobody liked.

"Mistress Morana, mistress Morana!" he shouted excitedly, hopping from one foot to another, mumbling to himself.

"Calm down, Malik! I don't understand a word you're saying!" Morana crouched down and caught him by his little shoulders. "What is it? Focus! Is there something important you have to tell me?"

He grimaced, trying to remember. *Svarog, give me strength not to slap him!* she thought, rolling her eyes. Malik bit his thumbnail and raised his eyebrows. "Yes, yes, mistress! You have a guest. Lord Stribog is here!"

"Stribog? What does he want, did he say?"

"No, mistress. You know me, I don't meddle in the affairs of gods."

Morana bit her tongue, half smiling. "Malik?"

The little one grinned, baring his teeth. "But he seems troubled. And he came alone."

"Thank you. That will be all," she said, worries swirling in her head as she watched him sprint to the large warehouse.

The goddess of winter rubbed the tattoo on the small area between her thumb and index finger. An old Slavic symbol for a snowflake, an X with similar signs at the ends of each diagonal, it was the mark she was known by. She pressed it often when she was stressed or nervous. Meeting with the god of wind was seldom a reason for celebration, although they had been allies for a long time.

The club was its usual busy self, all tables occupied, waiters carrying the drinks and the music playing in the background, loud enough to cover the small talk and business negotiations.

Morana found Stribog by the fireplace with a shadowy corner at his right, quietly sipping his favorite brand of ale from a giant mug. His appearance was one of an old man with a long white beard, his face wrinkled with time and the strong winds he wielded. He wore a long dark blue coat with a high collar and his emblem embroidered on the golden hem of his sleeves.

Stribog sensed the cold coming up to him. He looked up and smiled, his stormy eyes reflecting the flickering fire and showing a streak of worry.

"Well met, Morana of Winter," he said with a nod.

"The pleasure is mine, Wind-lord. What brings you to my humble abode?" she replied and bowed politely. She always held him in high regard as one of the elder gods and one of the few who had defended her after the unsuccessful rebellion, even sought her out after her self-imposed exile.

"A very serious matter. If we're done exchanging pleasantries, I'd like to explain."

Morana looked around suspiciously. "Not here. Let's find someplace quiet. You never know who might be listening."

"I quite like it here by the fire," murmured the old man. He raised his hand, gently stroked the air and made an invisible dome, impenetrable to sounds. "Now we can talk in peace. No one can hear us."

She tried not to gasp at the sight and sat in an armchair opposite him. "I'm listening."

"Someone is stealing from the gods. Their most treasured possessions. Pieces of their strength." His brow furrowed with a hint of sadness and shame. "My horn. Without it, I cannot summon my grandchildren, the lesser winds, and send them across the land. I cannot control the weather, cannot send them to bring clouds of rain, spring and winter when needed, or to scatter plant seeds. I am almost powerless, as I am the only one. I cannot do my duties alone, for I cannot be in all places at the same time."

Morana didn't dare to look him in the eyes. Once a proud warrior-god, he suddenly seemed so lost and humiliated. "When did it happen?"

"Probably last night, while I was sleeping. First I thought I had misplaced it somewhere, but then Tatomir came with news of these outrageous thefts happening all around Svitogor."

"Tatomir! That scoundrel! Are you sure it was not his doing? He's prone to thieving himself. And he is treacherous."

"So are we, Morana. You seem to forget that. In fact, the three of us would be the most likely suspects for this particular event. They call us unruly, mischievous, uncontrollable, unpredictable," he said, spreading his arms wide. "We are useful outcasts. So, no, it was not Tatomir's fault. He's missing his golden sickle. And he is devastated."

She laughed scornfully. "He's devastated? That'll be the first!"

"Do not judge him for his temper, for it is equal to yours," Stribog said calmly. "You would be crushed if you lost something so precious. Do you still have all your valuables?"

Morana patted herself to see if anything was missing. "Yes, everything seems to—" Her face went paler than it has ever been when she saw her bare left wrist. "My bracelet! My white bracelet is missing! But how?! I've had it on my hand the whole day!" She winced in despair, her fingers gripping and tearing the fabric of her armchair. "Do you know what this means? My powers will diminish and I will grow older and older each day. What if all the ages come crushing at me all at once?! I'll be the shrivelled old hag everyone keeps calling me, bitter and resentful. And we all know how it went the last time I was like that."

The Wind god shrugged. "As I recall, you and Ledan brought the Ice Age upon humankind. There was barely any life left in the world."

Morana sprung to her feet, flapping her arms in the air, causing a swirl of snow above their heads. "You see? This is bad. This is very, very bad."

Customers who were near and who saw this little snow globe event froze in their seats, fearing to move before it was all clear, but the staff merely lifted their heads and continued with their business, being used to the turbulent nature of their boss.

Stribog waited for Morana to calm down, but it was not going to happen soon, so he interrupted her. "That is why we need Tatomir."

She suddenly stopped, with an exasperated look on her face. "You already called him, didn't you?"

"I let him into our circle. He's been here the whole time."

"Of course you did. Wait, what?" She looked as though she had been slapped in the face. "He's here?"

The man in question came out of the shadowed corner with a grin on his face. "Hello, Mora. Lovely as ever." He bowed courteously.

Tatomir was a young and handsome man, but old as the world itself. Just like Morana. His light brown hair was cut short but still managed to look dishevelled from air traveling. He was always clean-shaven, and it was worrisome to see him grow a beard. The mischievous Moon god, the messenger of the gods, was clad in modern, but ragged gray and black traveling clothes and wore combat boots. He still had his saber used to kill the spawn of darkness with him, the one which he was known for.

"Tatomir." Morana nodded, folding her hands across her chest. "So, you heard everything?"

"Yes, he did. I'm an old man. I didn't want to explain everything twice," replied Stribog in Tatomir's stead.

Tatomir laughed out loud. "You're just a few minutes older than I am. And you're not fooling anyone with that grandfather look." Then he winked at Morana. "Don't worry, I'll still like you when you turn into an old hag. I always had a soft spot for lost causes."

"Being one helps a bit, doesn't it?" she threw him a taste of his own medicine.

The Moon god smirked. "Such poisonous bitterness! Were you like this even when you had your white thing or is it more recent? Like, today recent."

Morana snapped, but Stribog got up and stood between them. "Enough! You bicker like children! Pull yourself together before something worse hits us."

"Like Gerovit, you mean? He's gone completely mental when one of his seven swords got stolen. He's wreaking havoc as we speak. And may I remind you he is a god of war?"

Tatomir raised an eyebrow, looking at the goddess over Stribog's shoulder. "Mora, my wolves are outside. They need to be fed properly or they'll start eating fairies. If you please."

"Of course," she said through her teeth. "Can we all now sit and talk about this pickle we've found ourselves in?"

"I thought you would never ask!" Stribog sighed, returning to his armchair with a loud thump.

Morana grabbed his mug and took a large sip of ale. She was done with politeness. She was beyond upset. Drowning in her chair, she looked at Tatomir, who was pacing back and forth. "Now, what of my bracelet?"

The Moon god stopped for a moment and turned to her. "Did you perhaps hear your song? 'Cause I did and I knew something was off. I haven't heard it in ages. Next thing, my sickle was gone."

"Yes, but I thought I'd imagined it. That it was in my head."

He scratched the back of his neck. "No, this person knows you, knows all of us, our weaknesses. Knows you hate that song, and they played it over and over again to distract you. That's how they stole the bracelet from you."

Morana leaned forward with her elbows on her knees. "How do we get our things back?"

Stribog's stern face grimaced. "First, we have to find out who is behind this. Tatomir assures me that no gods are involved. Nor any of our creatures. He flew all across the land, collecting bits and pieces of information, and concluded it must be a human. One well-versed in folklore."

"You did all that? I'm impressed," Morana said, looking at the Moon god with a new light in her eyes.

"Yes, Mora. I have a heart, you know. Maybe I'm a trickster, but I'm not selfish. Well, not completely selfish. I care. Even for you, although we once fought on different sides." His silvery eyes were sorrowful, as he had never been able to escape the prejudice everyone had about him.

Morana still hadn't quite forgiven him for filching her pearl of death, which he'd later returned, but her demeanour toward him softened a bit. He surely wasn't the same god he once was. None of them were.

"Good to know." She cleared her throat. "Stribog, could Bura help? Have you managed to contact her? She's around these days. I can feel her cold blasts bite every now and then. She's good at catching rumours."

"I will see to it." The Wind god nodded, wiping spilt ale off his beard when he took the mug back from her.

"And I will dispatch my Mora Squad to infiltrate people's dreams and poke things out. Things hidden in the subconscious. A few nightmares won't hurt anyone," she said with a wry grin.

Tatomir finally sat and stretched his legs in front of him. "Aaaand, I'll just wait here. I'm a bit tired."

"You're never tired. You're the messenger of the gods, constantly moving." Morana looked at him skeptically.

He sighed, raising his hands in the air. "Well, now this messenger needs a respite. If you don't mind."

"Not at all. Be my guest. Just don't do anything stupid. I'd hate to freeze you, here in front of everyone," she replied, relieved she'll avoid spending her precious time in his boastful company, for a short time, at least. He was a handful and she rather enjoyed the silence.

Stribog broke the dome and the two of them left the club, leaving the Moon god with a dejected look on his face.

It was still evening, though late, when the duo returned. They found Tatomir surrounded by creatures at the bar. He was buying them drinks and telling his tall tales as they laughed and shouted. Morana rolled her eyes and Stribog grabbed the Moon god by the shoulders and pulled him away from the flirting fairies. "Move aside, you idiot! I hope you haven't been blabbering about our business!"

"Relax, old man. I'm not that stupid!" Tatomir raised his voice in anger and yanked himself from the Wind god's grip.

Morana smirked and followed them to their previous meeting place. Stribog once again made a cancelling noise dome and sat down.

Tatomir leaned against the wall by the fireplace, lifting his chin, with an impish smile, at the old god's messy hair and beard. "Bura must've been pretty talkative."

"Indeed she was. Svarog, that woman can talk!" The Wind god shook his head and straightened himself up. "She told me some interesting things. A man's name came up. He calls himself Borna the Dark and he is a warlock."

"A warlock?" Tatomir suddenly got serious. "I didn't know they still existed."

"Why wouldn't they?" Morana asked. "Practitioners of all sorts of witchcraft never ceased to pass on their knowledge, good or bad. This one got involved in dark magic."

"Hence the 'Dark', I presume." Tatomir tsked, then narrowed his eyebrows. "Anything else?"

"My moras told me he's got a thirst for power. Wants to become one of us, the gods. The most powerful one, as it seems. Since he stole our most valuable things."

Stribog leaned in. "Bura said that he got a scroll with some ancient spells. Once he collects all major possessions and performs a ritual, that is it. All of us will be subjected to his will. You know we have our roles, the day's and the year's cycle to maintain. He won't respect that. It will—"

"All turn to one giant mess!" Tatomir said, looking at the fire in frustration. "And where are all the other gods? Sitting blissfully in Svitogor, leaving things to us. Look at us. Not a single god trusts us."

"They must think we're up to something." Morana pursed her lips and rested her chin on her fist. The Moon and the Wind god nodded in confirmation.

"It is time to prove them wrong. To clean our slates. Nobody will call us volatile again," Stribog said decisively.

"Slow down, grandpa! We haven't even started yet. You found the name, now we have to find the place." Tatomir swallowed his laughter.

"That's easy. All deals are struck at midnight under an oak tree. We just have to find the right one," Morana said casually, crossing her legs. All eyes were suddenly on her. "You didn't know that?"

"Nobody ever tried to strike deals with us," the Wind god answered, his face saddened.

"Can't say I'm surprised." Morana sighed. "Let's get going. I want to be off the gods' black list once and for all. If this will get them off my back, I don't see a better time than now. Borna would want to do this as soon as possible, trust me. He has all he needs, now. That's what I'd do."

Tatomir looked at her in awe. "Mora, I must say I like when your temper's up. There's nothing more attractive than the look of murder on your face."

She gave him a killer glance. "Can you just stay quiet for once?"

Tatomir coughed it out. "Fine. Let's go on a field trip and find ourselves an oak tree to hug."

All three of them stepped outside an hour before midnight. The trickster god whispered something to his wolves and they spread out running as fast as their legs could carry them.

"What did you say to them?" asked Morana suspiciously.

"To find that bastard and rip his legs off," he answered,

half grinning, half-serious. "Just joking, I know we need him alive. They will help."

Stribog shook his head. "How will they find him? We don't even know what he looks like."

"For all your long beard, I thought you'd be smarter. They are wolves, they already know our scents and they'll track his, the different one. And we all have traces of it on us since that warlock left it behind when he stole our things."

"I hate to admit it, but he's right." Morana shrugged. "We'll have to split up to cover more ground. Whoever finds him first will summon the others using our tattooed signs. Agreed?" The Moon god and the Wind god nodded in agreement. "And don't get any funny ideas. We're all in this together. Balance must be respected."

"Wise words," said Stribog.

"Well, when you mess up the world, you get a lifelong lesson." She cast down her eyes, slightly embarrassed. "I don't want to see it repeated."

A few miles away from the town, there was an old—an ancient forest, one might say. At its crossroads, below a great oak tree, sat a man well in his thirties, waiting for midnight. Midnight was the time for witches, bargains and rituals.

A warlock would know all about it. Borna first got into witchcraft ten years ago, exploring the dark web on behalf of the government. His hacking skills granted him access to all sorts of forbidden or deeply hidden content. He found out that the cults of the ancient gods' worshippers still existed, he found books of spells and summonings, and even artefacts, sold on the black market.

That's how he got his hands on Czernobog's scroll of power. It cost him an arm and a leg, but he had no trouble obtaining money. He had stolen rich people's identities before.

This time it got him the secret of immortal life and unimaginable power. He would've been a fool not to take that chance.

His life was invisible, anyway. Nobody paid him much notice, just another face in a mob, and not even a handsome one. Borna was a skinny, pasty man with a receding hairline in an early midlife crisis, and this would get him the long-coveted attention. He would be venerated as a supreme being. People would crawl before him and build him temples. Images of grandeur had become an obsession and he knew he wouldn't find peace until their fulfillment. Thus he found a way to steal the most prized possessions of the old gods. Combining them would get him to the top of the pyramid.

Borna the Dark, a warlock of ten years, looked at his wristwatch and saw it was half-past eleven. Once again he checked he had everything needed for the ritual. Czernobog's scroll was well hidden in the inner pocket of Borna's long coat. The wooden tripod with no nails stood before him, with branches underneath it and a brass cauldron on it. First, Borna poured a jar of Vodan's water into the cauldron, then threw the rest of the stolen artefacts into it. He poured fairy blood over them and lit the fire beneath the cauldron. He calculated there would be just enough time for the tripod to burn and the water to boil. At midnight he would recite the incantation and spill his own blood into the mix to seal the deal.

Somewhere in the distance, Winter cried in anguish, Moon lost control of the tide, Wind ceased to blow and wolves howled in unison. Hard times befell the old gods. A new one was about to be born.

Morana watched in horror at her shrivelled hands. She was growing older by the minute and her raven hair had already become white as snow. Upon her head, there was a crown of thin leafless branches and her clothes had turned to black rags wrapped around her like dark shadows. Her shrieks scared the birds and beasts out of the forest.

Kneeling on the ground, she felt the pulsing of her tattoo. Someone was summoning her. She pressed the sign and found herself behind Tatomir, who was standing in a puddle, shaking off seawater from his wild hair. He turned and looked at the old woman suspiciously.

"Excuse me, have you seen—"

"It's me, you fool!" she snapped and he took a step back in surprise.

"Morana? Gods, you really weren't kidding about the hag look!" Tatomir held a hand on his heart. "You scared me half to death!"

"Keep pushing me and it won't be just half." Her voice sounded as crotchety as she felt. "What happened to you?"

The Moon god sighed droopily. "I tried to stop the rising tide. The wave was so massive, I couldn't stop it. I tried calling you to help me freeze it, but then it dropped me here and flooded the entire town on the other side of the forest."

"Where is Stribog? Did you summon him as well?" She barely managed to get up, holding one fist on her knee and the other on her hip. "I wasn't aware half the time I was transforming."

"He should be here somewhere. We were there together. He tried to blow the wave away, but it created an even bigger mess when he suddenly lost it."

"Lost what?"

"His ability to control the airflow at long distance. Did you notice how quiet it is? Not a whiff of fresh air."

There was a loud rustling coming from the trees. Stribog fell hard on the ground, materializing in front of them, grumbling through his teeth, his mane and beard full of leaves and small branches.

"This was not an easy landing," said the Wind god, getting up to his feet. He looked at the two. "I see you also had better days."

"That's an understatement." Tatomir sniffed, crouching. "At least my wolves are doing well. I hear them running, they're onto something."

"I hope they run fast, the chaos in my mind grows stronger with each passing minute. I don't know how much I can hold it till it unfolds." The Winter goddess grimaced through her words as if they were razors.

Stribog looked at her with a slight caution. He had seen that look before. A long time ago, when the world was younger. He felt it as a sting to his heart for he knew this time they won't be able to stop her. They were useless.

The three of them waited for the wolf pack to return, slowly regaining their composure. When the first wolf's head came out of the dark, the Moon god smiled. The rest of the pack followed in unison. He spoke to them, scratching their backs. They howled in return and vanished into the darkness once more. "They found the bastard's trail! Let's go! Come on, you two!"

"I'm not as fast as you. Can't fly, remember?" Morana said, agitated.

"Then hold onto me. I'll carry you," Tatomir offered. "And don't tell me I've never done anything for you."

He extended a hand and she took it, embracing him around his waist. "Thank you," she said sheepishly and he smiled. Stribog was already ahead. They flew fast, following the wolves, and the Winter goddess held tighter, almost burying her long nails in Tatomir's skin.

"Well, Mora, if you were any younger..." He grinned through the air and she would have slapped him so hard if she hadn't been afraid of falling.

Stribog suddenly stopped in mid-air and signed to them to do the same. He put a finger to his lips and nodded at the firelight under the oak tree. They descended and laid low behind the shrubbery. What they now needed was a plan to break the warlock's ritual.

"It's almost time," Tatomir said quietly, looking at the stars.

"How do you know?" Morana inhaled deeply.

"Don't insult me, Mora. I know my stars."

"Fine! What do your stars say?"

"That we have fifteen minutes to snap that maniac out of his god game."

"What do you suggest we do?" asked Stribog, his voice barely making a sound.

The Winter goddess looked at him compassionately, for she also felt herself faltering. "Whatever we do, we have to move fast or we're done."

"I'll distract him." Tatomir stroked his beard. "You two try your best not to get us killed."

Borna rolled out the scroll and started reading aloud. Fire sparks danced in his dark eyes as he recited the long-forgotten words. An ancient force shook the cauldron and smoke went up in the air.

Immersed in his own world, he didn't notice a blurry figure emerging from the treeline, light-footed and sly.

"Greetings, warlock!" shouted the Moon god, approaching him and waking him up from his transcendental trance.

The human's gaze suddenly sharpened, focusing on the intruding stranger. "Who are you?" he asked in a commanding voice.

"The nerve on him..." muttered Tatomir to himself, then offered a wolflike grin as a warning. "I am the one you stole from, human!"

"I think I'm more than that now," Borna said, forming a cold, sinister smile that would make anyone shudder.

"And I think you are full of yourself, Borna the Keyboard Master." Tatomir smirked. "Seems like everybody's calling themselves witches and warlocks these days. I bet you can't even summon a goat, let alone the power of the gods."

The man scowled, but continued to read the scroll.

Tatomir interrupted his chant with random things, a series of words that came up in his head at the time just to get him out of track. "Borna. Borna The Warlock. BTW. That's what I'll call you. Because, *by the way*, you're not a god. And you'll never be. You simply don't look the part. We had a meeting, you know. Svantevid saw a glimpse of you and decided he won't be introducing you into the ways of us immortals. Said he won't shed a single sunbeam to lighten up your basement look. Our dear Vesna nearly fainted when she heard you're runnin' up for your seat in Svitogor. She's had her fill of marriage proposals and no doubt you'll be coming with one of your own. Let me tell you something, BTW. Did you put chamomile in that mix? I know some say it's tricky, because it's all grannies' favorite tea flower, but it really could be a banger once you mix it with faerie blood. You should try selling it to the local drinking establishments. I swear on my sickle, which you stole—how rude—it will be the greatest thing invented since rakija. See? I'm giving you ideas here and you're acting as if I'm not here. Why, if I were someone else, I'd be offended. As I was saying..."

Borna flushed red with anger but did not break up the spell. His time was running out.

Stribog and Morana were sneaking up from each of his sides as carefully as they could. With the last of his strength, the Wind god threw himself at the cauldron, spilling the contents. The artefacts fell to the ground. Each of them was drawn to their masters with such strong force it was impossible to resist. All except for Morana's. Her bracelet was no longer white, but smeared with faerie blood. She felt no pull, no greedy frenzy that overtook her fellow gods.

The goddess gathered all of her winter, her death and her nightmares into one ear-piercing cry. Nothing similar was ever heard on this Earth or will be again.

Tatomir and Stribog fell into the mud, powerless, their eyes white, with no recognition in them.

Borna still stood above them reciting, seemingly unaffected by the Winter-cry. He cut his hand and, holding it above the fallen gods, performed the last part of the ritual.

Before his blood even began to drip, Morana caught his hand and froze it mid-air, her sapphire eyes cracking his like glass with a surge of ice power. She savoured his every scream before she sent a swirl of hellish nightmares into his mind.

Insanity took over his arrogance. He should've known better than to mess with such a dangerous deity. Borna the Warlock started running away like a madman chased by the ghosts in his head, for he had hurt many.

Morana spread her hands and froze the entire grove just to see him stumble. He slipped and felt his frozen hand break under him. His hoarse screeches resembled a crow's. Morana laughed as she left him eyeless, handless and mindless.

She was still old. Old, but more powerful than ever. She had lost the bonds that had held her other self on a leash for a very long time. There was no longer anything pure about her, just a brutal and raw force of nature, wild and imminent. The goddess turned her back to all that had brought this upon her.

All the gods that had been robbed found themselves underneath the great oak, around the cauldron, pushing each other to get to their personal artefacts. The mighty Perun, Veles, Gerovit, Lada, Vesna, and even Svantevid, behaved like spoiled children searching for their toys, with no dignity whatsoever. They almost trampled over Stribog and Tatomir, who were still stuck in the mud, trying to find their bearings.

Stribog's anger rose as he took his horn and blew one strong blow. All the winds gathered at his command and threw the gods on their backsides. "Enough!" he bellowed, rising in full power. "Look at yourselves!"

Tatomir smiled proudly beside him.

The gods stood up straight as birch trees that surrounded them.

Perun dispelled clumps of frost from his clothes, his eyes scanning everyone present. "We seem to be missing someone," the Thunder god said. "Where is Morana?"

Tatomir stepped in front of the gods. "We all got our things back. Hers was destroyed beyond repair."

"That means she's out of control. Unhinged." Vesna put her palm over her mouth in shock.

"Please, Vesna, don't even bother pretending you care. As you consider yourself 'too pure' for hate, I'll say you never *liked* her. None of you did." The Moon god waved her off.

The goddess of Spring gasped. "I take offence at your notion."

"Of course you do. Sulking befits the child you are," said Stribog angrily.

Gerovit unsheathed one of his swords. "Morana must be stopped."

Tatomir laughed scornfully. "You mean 'killed' or 'horribly maimed'. Really, Gerovit? That's rich, coming from you. Oh, as a matter of fact, why aren't we punishing you as well? You have brought far more damage than Morana with your rampaging. If you have, by chance, missed it, she's saved us all from a crazed warlock who wanted to govern over all of the Earth with us as his primary subjects. Call me foolish, but I don't think that ticks the right box for punishment. We should be thanking her."

"Then, by all means, go talk some sense into her." Veles laughed. "If you get killed in the process, you will be sorely missed."

Tatomir smirked. "Stribog, Morana and I. You underestimate us. We're not under your control and that scares you. If I succeed, you'll treat us as equals. No more sidelines for us. I think it's only fair. Deal?"

Svantevid stepped up, holding out his hand. "Deal."

"I always knew you were the smart one in the family," Tatomir said with a roguish smile. "Stribog, are you coming with me?"

"Yes. Who else is going to keep that crazy head of yours on its neck?" he answered and once again called upon his wind grandchildren to come with him.

They left the gods on the frozen crossroads with the overturned, muddy cauldon.

Morana felt someone's presence closing in on her. She turned around and caught sight of Moon and Wind, her former allies. Now they had come for her, presumably by the order of those self-righteous bastards that always wanted her restrained.

She sent a snowstorm in their direction, only to find it stuck in the middle of the forest, between them. Stribog blocked her blows by sending winds to crush the storm. Poor Tatomir stood in the centre of it, battling the strong storm fronts with his forearms crossed in front of his face, protecting his head.

"Mora!" he called in the strongest voice he could muster.

"Mora, please stop! Please! They mean to kill you! Don't give them a reason!"

Her striking blue eyes filled with fury. "Funny how they see a threat where I see opportunities! I am free, trickster! Free at last!"

"You're not free, Mora! You're just angry! And rightly so! But you can prove them all wrong by being better than their petty assumptions!"

"I don't have to prove anything to anyone! Not anymore! I am me!" she howled with a blizzard.

"Please, please stop! I don't want to see you hurt!" Tatomir yelled, wiping icicles from his face with the sleeve of his jacket.

"Why do you care?"

"I told you, I have a soft spot for lost causes!" Her storm wavered a bit and he smiled, his heart growing. "You are worthy, Mora! We are all worthy, you, me, and Stribog! We deserve our due respect! I made a deal for us! Please, don't leave us hanging! Make them swallow their insults. They already think you're beyond help! They expect you to kill me!"

Morana was blasting blizzard after blizzard, the last stand of her madness against the sparks of reason coming to her mind. A tiny voice was kindling inside her, saying she wasn't alone. Not anymore. She refused to listen to it until it grew and she could bear it no longer. Winter was not alone. Someone cared enough to risk their own life to save hers. She slightly pulled the storm to herself, her hands shaking. "Tell Stribog to scatter the winds and my attack will cease! And don't get any ideas!"

Tatomir signalled the other god to stop the whirlwind and Stribog obeyed. The goddess lowered her hands and fell to her knees. She was breathing heavily under her wrinkled skin. Morana wasn't physically tired, but her mind was exhausted by all the inner struggles she'd had with herself in these short moments of her insanity. The forest was as quiet as a grave.

Wind and Moon hurried up to her. Tatomir caught her and held her as she cried. Cried for the first time in her long life. Stribog made a dome around them so the other gods couldn't hear her breaking.

"It's all right, you're all right." Tatomir rocked her in his arms and removed her crown of branches. "You don't need this anymore. Your crown will be one of icy crystals and it will shine like no other."

"You're a fool, trickster." She smiled with tears on her cheeks. "But I like you now."

"That means you'll finally forgive me for that death pearl I stole from you aeons ago?"

Morana curled up and laughed the faintest of laughs. "Yes, I think we are even now. Thank you." She looked up. "And you, Stribog. I'm sorry I almost wiped you out."

The old god nodded silently in return.

Tatomir cleared his throat, cutting in. "Don't flatter yourself. I was in the midst of your clashing powers and I'm still standing. Not wiped out."

"But your face is still blue from the cold. At least we made a good impression," added Stribog, brushing his beard with his fingers.

"We'll call it a draw, then, and be done with it," said Moon, helping Morana to her feet. "Now, my old lady, let's clear our names and take our rightful place among the other gods."

"Just don't expect me to live with them in that shiny castle."

"Shiny castles don't appeal to me. Give me a clear night sky any day. I'm happy among the stars."

"And I am happy traveling the air," said Wind. "It suffices to say we're not made for great halls and parading heroes. But I will take their supply of mead. One last mischief. Are you in?"

Tatomir grinned. "You really need to ask? Perun will be pissed, of course I'm in."

Morana burst into laughter and couldn't stop herself from being happy for once. Nor did she wish to.

"Look at you all glowing!" said the Moon god, smiling. "Svarog really outdid himself with this gesture. I must say, I wasn't expecting this."

"Shut up!" Morana hit his hand, laughing.

She looked at her long white dress with her snowflake emblem at the end of the sleeves and at the waist. It was designed for her specially, to wear in winter and to keep it safe during summer. The goddess was once again reminded of how she used to be, how she was created. Something pure as fresh snow, something necessary as the final cycle of the year and of life itself. All things must come to an end, and Morana is always there waiting, not taking anyone before the Fates decide.

She was still the mistress of nightmares, but distributed her power to her Mora Squad as per the agreement she'd signed before the other gods in her own blood.

Now she stood on a snow cloud with Tatomir at her left side and Stribog at her right. They watched the cities and villages beneath them. Small lights lit up as a wave when the night cloaked the Earth in darkness. Winter was ready.

"Shall we, my lady?" said Stribog with one arm open.

She nodded and kneeled, digging her fingers in the airy softness of the snow cloud. Snowflakes began to fall and Stribog sent them flying. Not long after, it spread a thin coat over the hills and valleys, rooftops and treetops. Layer after layer, and a bed of snow was created all over the land.

"Are those...?" Tatomir struggled to see, then paused in awe.

"The imelike." Morana smiled as she saw these smallest of winter fairies, but the most joyous ones, ones that brought help and happiness to people in need. They peered out from the trees and bushes and hopped lightly in the snow. She felt things changing because of the imelike. They used to be afraid of her before and were seldom seen in the open. Tonight was different, with a different feel in the air. Winter was born anew.

"Well, I'll be off then. Got some sky business to attend to." Tatomir bowed with a hand against his chest. This time he wasn't teasing. He'd made his peace with Morana and respected her for who she was. Now even more than before. He sprung in the air and smiled. "And, Mora... please don't wear off that white dress too soon. This mood suits you. It's been long since I've seen you this happy."

"I promise I'll try!" she shouted, laughing through the swirl of air. "And you keep away from your trickery!"

"It is like asking me not to breathe, dear goddess!" He laughed in return. "But, I promise, you will be spared." Tatomir flew high in the night sky and turned himself into a full moon. Wolves howled all across the valley.

The Wind god tucked his horn in his belt. "It is my time to leave, too. Summon me when you need me, before Vesna appears. You know I favor you, but I also have to bring spring to people. I'll leave one of my grandchildren to spend winter with you."

"Thank you, lord Stribog, for not writing me off. And I thank you for your help," Morana said with a bow, her long raven hair floating in the air.

Morana was left alone on a cloud of her own making. A song began to rise in her head. A song she knew well. But this time she wasn't afraid of herself. This time she was going to try harder and better to stay this way as long as she could.

Hide, Morana is here
Lo, the winter is near
Her long nails will catch you
And quickly cut you through
Run, the nightmares come
Run and beat the drum
Children, be still and beware
Or she'll chew your bones and spit them bare.

DEATH WILL SEE

LAURA J. VELIGOR

THE LAST DAY OF Winter finally arrived, and as customary in the small town of Evening, all the townspeople busily prepared for the celebration of the coming Spring.

Unique for their reverence of the changing seasons, each solstice and equinox were thoughtfully celebrated by the people of this ordinarily sleepy, forest-side town. In fact, so quiet and quaint was Evening, one would scarcely believe such a community capable of the howling madness they engaged in if not for witnessing it firsthand. And for those granted the privilege of observing these sacred events, their confounded awe matched only the bewitching impulse they felt to join in the wild revelry that came just before and just after periods of habitual calm and normalcy.

Four times a year, the townspeople prepared sweets, spiced drinks, and lavish foods in the days leading up to the celebrations, each home smelling distinctly of the offerings left behind by the departing season's generosity. The music band gathered and rehearsed for the long-standing tradition of caroling: Summer, Autumn, Winter, and Spring each honored with their own collections of songs, poems, and fairytales, performed to the joyful melody of violins, accordion, and clarinet. The town square became decorated with bouquets of herbs and wildflowers, garlands of braided grass, and colorful ribbons strung with carefully selected river shells, gently chiming against each other with every sway of the wind, creating a symphony of delicate little bells.

Regardless of the celebrated season, the holiday air always smelled of fresh and woody smoke as bunches of twine-bound juniper twigs were lit and carried like miniature torches, signaling to the spirits—said to watch these rituals from unseen places—that the people here bravely and readily welcomed the turning of the wheel.

The Spring celebration in particular, an especially honored occasion, meant the return to life. Extra gestures of gratitude carefully entwined their seasonal practices—ranging from placing smooth, hand-painted stones on the flowerbeds and lighting candles in honor of those lost during the cold season, to the creation and purposeful destruction of an effigy called *Winter.*

No one could say where the tradition came from, but each year called upon a different household to create the doll used in the rite. At a minimum, a figure would typically be built from straw and shaped with cloth and twine to vaguely resemble the form of a person. Most families got a bit more creative in their design by either dressing it in cold-weather clothing or creating a costume for it, befitting the personification of Winter. In rarer, albeit thrilling instances, the assigned family would engage in near-witchcraft in the conception of their doll. Past years saw one with mysterious symbols and unrecognizable words scrawled across its entire body, and another curiously bestrewn with salt, candle wax, and ash, as if a spell had been cast upon it. Yet another had supposedly been sewn beneath the light of the full moon and stuffed with protective herbs: mugwort against injury and sickness, sage to heal grief, vervain to deter evil spirits, jasmine for enhanced intuition, and rosemary for purification.

An annual procession then came together to carry the doll to the large stone bridge just on the edge of town that overlooked the rushing Noć River. Along the way, they dipped it into any water source they passed—a puddle, the beverage of an onlooker, a birdbath, a heap of leftover snow—all to ensure the Winter season was completely washed away from every corner of their community, thus bringing about the delights of Spring.

In a solemn hymn, they pleaded with Death herself to take Winter and leave them in peace the rest of the year:

Let us carry Winter from our hearts and raise her over our heads—
Death will see from afar how ardent and earnest we are
and take the coldness with her.
Let us carry Winter down the road, beyond the sleeping flowerbeds—
Death will see from afar how humble and worthy we are
and take the darkness with her.
Let us carry Winter to the river and toss her over the edge—
Death will see from afar how wild and merry we are
and never take us with her.

Then, without remorse, the crowd would do as they sang and toss the effigy over the railing into the deep water below. Being superstitious people, they remained extremely careful to never turn their heads, let alone cast a curious eye back toward the bridge on their return to town, for it was said that if anyone did look back at the scene of the released effigy, Death would take them the following year.

To distract from the possibility of this ominous prophecy, after the rite, the band enthusiastically hoisted their bows and quickly transformed the shared spirit from devout ritual to that of relieved jubilation. In an excited parade, the townspeople chased the music back to the square, where a bountiful feast and ecstatic singing and dancing carried on well into the night.

While this annual practice remained widely accepted and even enjoyed by most of the residents of Evening, there existed a sensitive few who looked on at the display with an uncomfortable sense of guilt, and this was especially true for a child named River.

River always struggled with the notion of tossing a person-like figure off the bridge and began to cry the moment the effigy disappeared over the railing. Looking on, she imagined the pain of hitting the water and the misery of realizing no one followed its journey. And although her mother and grandmother had explained the significance of the tradition many times, it still remained a horrifying experience for her.

A few years ago, in an effort to foster her daughter's warm-hearted nature, River's mother built a lean-to shelter in the forest for each doll to recover from its ordeal. Not a builder by trade, she often joked that she could have been a carpenter in another life, for they were surprised to discover how well-built it actually ended up being. The structure sat against a giant boulder containing a natural ridge running parallel to the ground, which created a sort of narrow shelf. The roomy space fit a couple chairs and allowed for a few people to stand comfortably within. Time and again, and without much need for repair, it withstood raging storms as well as the high, downslope winds known to the area. It even endured the curiosity and, sometimes, refuge of wild animals. And for many years to come, it would continue to hold in its hidden corner of the forest, about half a mile from the bridge, just a few strides from the banks of the Noć.

Each holiday, before the Spring celebration commenced, River and her mother visited the secret spot to ensure it had held up in their absence and to tend to any damages it had sustained from the snow. They decorated it with a sign that said, "Welcome, Winter!" and little presents of dried fruits and chocolates, pressed flowers, coins, and yarn bracelets. Over time, the space had also accumulated an antique oil lantern, a small selection of books, a chipped teapot, a garden gnome, and a tattered doormat placed outside the daisy embroidered linen that curtained the entrance—stolen and repurposed from grandmother's attic.

River loved envisioning the doll climbing out of the water and gratefully fleeing to the cozy shelter. She pictured it eagerly indulging itself with tea, candy, and books, eventually becoming so exasperated with the gnome's bad table manners, that it packed up any necessary provisions and set out on its next grand adventure. In this way, the existence of the hideaway turned something that was once a source of great sadness into a happy secret shared between mother and daughter.

River excitedly looked forward to the moment during the procession when her mother would lean down and whisper, "Enjoy your stay," as if the doll about to be forced over the railing was going to check-in for a relaxing weekend at their charming inn on the edge of the woods.

This year, the task of building the effigy belonged to the Sosna family. They constructed an impressive six-foot-tall creature, enrobed entirely in hand-cut paper snowflakes, which seemed to peer out through giant, glittering star-shaped buttons in place of its eyes. Carefully, they'd transported the creation to the old gazebo in the center of the square to await its ill-fated journey to the bridge. And here, in a brief moment of being unattended due to the last rush of chaotic preparations occurring all around it, the effigy received a visit from the Cyprys family: River, a young person of twelve; Mar, River's mother and the town midwife; and Mar's mother, Zofia—endearingly known to River as Babcia—a quiet and superstitious woman who had lived in Evening all her life.

"The eyes are... something," Mar began with a hint of sarcasm. She stood before it, head tilted and hand resting on her hip as if unimpressed with how the effigy slumped against the aged wood of the banister.

River smiled at her mother's comment. "At least it's pretty. Not like last year."

"No, not like last year," Mar agreed.

All three stood quiet for a moment remembering the horror of last year's effigy; it had resembled a monster more than anything else, shockingly adorned with real human hair on the top of its head.

River, uncomfortable with the memory, broke the silence for them. "I wonder how many there are?"

She reached out and ran her hand along the robe made exclusively of cerulean snowflakes. The paper had rough edges, as if multiple sheets were stacked together to save time, and then hastily trimmed with very dull scissors.

Just then, the nearby clock tower chimed its massive bronze bell in announcement of the hour, just as it did every hour of every day. Today, however, and in celebration of Spring, it indicated to all that the time to meet Death on the bridge—and surrender Winter to her—had come.

The sudden and loud noise made River startle, causing a fine cut across her left index finger as it jolted away from the stiff paper. Without pause, Zofia grabbed her granddaughter's hand to assess the damage.

"I'm alright, *Babcia*," River assured her grandmother.

Zofia continued to inspect the cut, and in noticing some blood, cast a worried glance at the tiny drop of crimson left behind on Winter's robe. Quickly, she used the end of her intricately patterned shawl, draped gracefully over her head and around her shoulders, to wipe it away. To no avail; a saturated stain remained. The doll's eyes sparkled knowingly as the crowd holding lit juniper bundles gathered close, ready for the procession to begin. And as the effigy was lifted gracefully into the air on the shoulders of two volunteers, so followed the Cyprys three who walked attentively behind.

River linked her arm securely through Zofia's as they traversed the patches of ice that often formed on the road this time of year, when the warming air allowed the sun to melt the snow, yet the lingering cold continually re-froze it. Soft voices arose from the crowd to unite in heartfelt melody as the procession traced the path to the bridge. And upon reaching the river, they raised the doll up as high as they could to promptly heave it over the railing, applauding as it fell. The edges of its robe fanned out like fluttering, angelic wings before meeting the dark water in a resounding splash. For only a moment, it bobbed amidst ghostly blue snowflakes bursting in all directions, then caught the current and floated serenely away.

"*Enjoy your stay*," Mar whispered to River conspiratorially, with warm amusement in her voice.

Both began to laugh. This inside joke between them had continued to grow in effect with each passing year, for it gratefully separated them further and further from the times when this moment had resulted in tears.

River echoed the sentiment back, which came out in a half-whisper for her giggling. "Enjoy your stay!"

A few people turned around at the noise. Mar just smiled and nodded at them, pointedly ignoring the disapproving stare of her own mother observing their silliness.

The entire gathering then turned their attention away from the Noć and set off toward the celebration of Spring.

Mar wrapped an arm around River's shoulders and turned her with the crowd. "Come on, then. Off you go."

The little family followed slightly behind due to Zofia's labored walking on the uneven, uphill dirt road. Violin music filled the air, and from the juniper torches billowed a calming haze that had enveloped the trailing Cyprys' in its scented cloud.

Transported by the scenic and dreamy atmosphere, River became lost in her thoughts. The cut on her finger burned, and although her grandmother gently batted at her each time, River continued to thumb it nervously. Unable to dissuade curiosity, she lifted her hand to investigate the irritated injury, and in doing so, failed to notice the gnarled tree root protruding from the path.

In what seemed like an instant, River's boot caught the twisted wood curling up out of the earth. She landed first on her knee before it painfully buckled, and then on her stomach where the wind was knocked abruptly from her lungs in protest of the impact. She opened her eyes to see that her nose lay just a few centimeters away from the ground.

"Oh!" Mar instinctively bent down to River's level and took her daughter's elbow to help her up. "Are you alright?"

"Yeah, I'm ok," River replied, embarrassed.

"Here, let me help you."

With her mother's support she made to stand, but her balance yielded to the sharp pain in her knee causing her to fall a second time—this time, landing on her hip. Frustrated and focused on the aching injury, River rolled into a sitting position, facing her mother and grandmother, who also had the misfortune of sharing the direction of the bridge they'd just departed. Unintentionally, River's gaze traveled beyond the two women and landed on a cloaked form in the distance.

"River, what is it?" Mar frantically assessed her daughter in an attempt to understand the look of pure terror in her expression, scanning from the top of her favorite red beret to the bottom of her brown leather boots.

River hardly breathed. The looming figure appeared tall with its firm posture and unmoving presence. It stood shrouded completely in darkest black, its face obscured by a voluminous veil gently flowing in the breeze off the water. Even across the distance that separated them, River could make out an exaggerated headdress of what looked like things off the forest floor—sticks, feathers, and dead leaves—placed faithfully like a crown. And whether or not it was, the being seemed aware of her regard. For the moment River's mind silently supplied its name, it gave a single and painfully slow bow, then languidly turned away from her to look out over the Noć.

River had seen Death. And if the chilling superstition shared across generations rang true, she would be taken the following year.

Nearly one year had passed since the events of Spring; events largely unnoticed but quickly shared by a distressed mother to a friend, and from that confidant to another, and soon known by all in Evening.

As each day grew slightly longer, and each afternoon slightly warmer, so grew the tense ball in the pit of River's stomach and the pang of hopelessness in her heart. Many in the town seemed to share in her weariness—or at the very least, sensed how she felt, for they dared not mention anything regarding Spring in River's presence. Even more alarmingly, they whispered to each other when they saw her in town, ceased their conversation completely if she got too close, and only seemed to muster a half-smirk that implied pity whenever she passed by. Although endless reassurances had been offered that the myth of seeing Death on the bridge existed simply as an ornament of an embellished tradition, the upcoming celebrations dawned only two short weeks away, and River was terrified.

She mindlessly traced a circular motion along a small dip in the wood of her grandmother's kitchen bench. The spot—now revealing pale oak and velvet softness for the little thumb that had nervously cleared the canary yellow paint away over the course of many years—spoke volumes to her grandmother who watched on with worry. To Zofia, the discrete gesture signaled unease, and even though the fears of a child were easily consoled with the comforting magic only a well-used kitchen could produce, River's current predicament hardly suited a child. For behind the unintentional disclosure was something Zofia could barely endure herself, let alone alleviate for her granddaughter with offerings of plum cake and rose jam.

Zofia sat next to River and took her hand away from the bench, placing it in her lap. River looked up at her grandmother. Wisps of wiry, gray hair feathered out from beneath her customary shawl as her *Babcia* gazed down with genuine concern over the hooked end of her nose. River was relieved not to see pity in her expression—although she immediately felt a twinge of guilt.

"I'm fine," she lied unconvincingly, not wanting to cause too much worry.

Without words, Zofia adjusted them both so that her arms wrapped snugly around her granddaughter in a hug. A tear escaped down River's cheek as she burrowed into the reassuring embrace being offered, taking in deep breaths of the sweet orange and warm amber that was her grandmother's familiar perfume.

She felt the life she had lived up to this point disappearing before her eyes—whether due to a dark prophecy being fulfilled or simply the result of fearing one, she did not know. And whatever this meant for her own fate, she didn't feel ready.

Not long after, Mar arrived home lugging a wooden box. She let it fall gracelessly to Zofia's terracotta kitchen floor, causing a little cloud of hay dust to whoosh out of a crack in the opening as it landed. River and her grandmother simply looked to Mar for an explanation.

"Guess who's been nominated to make the effigy this year."

Wayward pieces of hay stuck out from Mar's long, dark braid and across the wool of her black coat. Zofia shook her head and stood to busy herself in the kitchen.

"Is that really a good idea? You know, with everything that's going on?" River asked as she approached the box to inspect its contents.

Opening it, she could see that it was unsurprisingly filled with tufts of straw as well as a large spool of thick brown twine and a couple narrow wooden boards.

"I told you, we're not going to let anything happen to you," Mar promised as she patted her daughter's head and passed by to deposit her coat and bag in the hallway closet. "It's going to be fine. Don't worry."

River reached up to fix where her hair—dark like her mother's, although much shorter—had been tousled. Whenever she brought up concerns about what happened last Spring, she was always met with some version of this same response. And while the words initially provided some comfort, they became somehow less convincing the more they were repeated. Now, upon hearing them, River just felt more alone in her fear.

Zofia discreetly nudged a plate of cinnamon rugelach across the counter toward her granddaughter.

"Shall we get to work?" Mar suggested enthusiastically, re-entering the kitchen.

"We're going to build it now?" River asked.

"Why not? It will give us something to do."

"I just—I don't know if I'm feeling up to it," her daughter protested.

"Come on, it will help get your mind off things. And, it will be fun!"

River always dreamed of building the Winter effigy.

Each year, upon seeing what the selected household created, she couldn't help but take note of both the things she would do differently given the chance, and which elements might inspire her own design. So, while the prospect of taking on a more significant role in this year's celebration made her anxious, it also filled her with excitement.

"Ok, let's do it," she conceded.

"Excellent!" cheered Mar. "I'll get to work on the base while you start looking for something to dress it in."

River swiftly grabbed a pastry and raced out of the room, promptly doubling back with a question. Peeking her face around the doorway, she called, "How big will it be?"

Upon hearing the question, Zofia paused mid-step on her way to retrieve the kettle whistling on the stove. Mar looked at her mother, who stood motionless with her back to the room, then gave a curt reply.

"About your size, River."

"Great! Can I use my clothes?"

"Yes, that's a good idea."

Smiling, River bounded away again in search of items to dress and adorn the Winter doll with, unaware of the tense energy she'd left behind in her wake.

That night, after they cleared the mess away and each Cyprys lay restlessly in their respective bed, soft moonlight tore through the curtain seams to illuminate the inanimate creature leaning unnaturally against the canary yellow bench in the kitchen. At four-and-a-half-feet tall and constructed of two wooden boards nailed together like a "T", the creature was shaped by twisted bunches of hay held together by a rough jute chord. Its head—too large in proportion to the rest of its body—was decked with a crown of fir branches plucked from a tree just outside and pinecone earrings where one could imagine its ears to be. It wore a sleeveless dress of oatmeal linen that River never liked due to the plain color and for the fact that she hated wearing dresses, and a swooping necklace of braided, sage green yarn strung with wooden macrame beads. Slipped under the twine of both wrists at the end of each, stiffly hanging arm was a little corsage of lush fir to match its crown.

Throughout the rest of the week, the doll sat on the bench, ignored by all in the home. Mar worked later nights than usual. As a dedicated midwife, it was not uncommon for her time and attention to be needed at odd hours. She conducted exams, provided counsel and remedies, supported those uncomfortable or unwell, and assisted and protected the journey of new people entering the world. However, as a dedicated midwife, it was uncommon for Mar to keep such odd hours without the accompaniment of her delivery bag. River found it carefully stashed behind a pile of folded blankets on the top shelf of the hallway closet. When asked, Mar explained she'd been visiting the herbalist to aid in the preparation of a special tea blend for her patients. Residing not far from the Cyprys' on the edge of town, in a home mostly transformed into a workshop and greenhouse, the herbalist crafted various tonics and tinctures, salves, perfumes, oils, and herb and spice blends. A mysterious albeit necessary presence in the small community, the expert healer secretly reveled in the whispered accusations that her extensive knowledge was somehow unnatural, and that her work was the result of a spell rather than practiced skill. This reputation was not helped by the way she adamantly kept to herself, aside from her friendship with Mar.

At the end of the week, upon completing her assigned reading for school, River journeyed to where she knew her mother to be, hoping to appease her craving for peppermint drops. As she entered, the bell on the front door chimed, unheard—for no one greeted her as she waited expectantly at the counter, holding the little bag of sweets. River hesitantly progressed further into the dimly-lit shop, noting a glowing room just beyond a table of scented candles where the herbalist and Mar must have been brewing. She ventured closer, pausing just outside the door when she heard raised voices amidst indistinct chatter.

"This is crazy!" said a particularly loud voice.

"I agree," rushed another, "this feels wrong."

"I know what I'm doing," Mar's voice responded vehemently.

"But, last time—"

"No," bellowed Mar. "This is what we have to do."

Suddenly, River heard movement across the hardwood floor. Not wanting to be caught, she bolted for the front entrance and ran home to save herself the awkwardness of explaining why she had been spying, the stolen bag of candy still in hand.

Back at home, Zofia toiled away in the kitchen. Even for someone who ordinarily did a lot of baking, this week seemed different. At any given moment, she added or removed another batch of something from the oven. The sink overflowed with bowls and spoons, treats in various stages of preparation covered the countertop, and packaged goodies lined the cellar pantry. Most curiously, she molded, cut, and decorated each item to resemble the Winter effigy residing in her kitchen. River didn't understand why, but certainly didn't complain. Last night, with her mother again working late, she happily indulged on three delicious ginger biscuits, stamped in the shape of little dolls, complete with colorful sugar crowns and icing dresses.

As the days passed and she spent more time alone, something about the Winter effigy began to bother River. Even more disturbingly, she had nightmares about it. At first, they weren't so bad: she'd enter a world that partially reflected real life, but also included elements that were somehow offbeat—exaggerated, impossible, or otherwise just bizarre. Then, the doll would appear. Even in this other world, River felt uneasy toward it. Her slumbering mind continuously tried to write the creature away, but it remained, just as it did in reality.

Things took a turn one night when she experienced a horrifying nightmare that the doll came to life. The scene began as usual, however, when River made to walk past the bench, the effigy's faceless head swiveled up in her direction. River backed away as it slowly stood and followed in stiff, clumsy strides. She could hear the wooden post that held it upright knock against the floor with every step, and when her back hit the wall, the doll instantly jumped into the air and flew with great speed toward her.

She woke up screaming, with the feeling of sharp straw scratching at her face. In the morning, River saw marks across her cheek where the thing had reached for her. Her mother assured her it had only been a dream.

By the end of the week, the nightmares had increased in both frequency and intensity. The worst of all involved River turning into the doll. Even though she desperately tried to call out to her mother, she could not, for she had no mouth. Even though she frantically attempted to wave down her grandmother's attention, she could not, for her arms were made of straw. Even though she painfully struggled to stand, she could not, for her legs were bound with rope. In fact, she could not move at all, because she was not real.

Whether due to these constant nightmares and lack of sleep, her growing loneliness, or the recent overindulgence of sugar—River also suffered from the feeling of being watched. The sensation followed her wherever she went, starting with a small prickling on the back of her neck, and escalating to something continually darting just out of sight. Then, one night, when she found herself lingering in the kitchen later and later, pretending to read her book to avoid going to bed, she thought she actually caught a glimpse of someone staring through the window. She recognized not the features of a person, but rather the tall silhouette of one moving away from the glass. Getting up from her seat to investigate, she saw nothing through the pitch black of night. Ever curious, River quietly snuck outside, hoping to discover something innocently explained by the swaying evergreen trees surrounding the house. Instead, she found a pile of sticks, feathers, and dead leaves resting just beneath the window, probably deposited by the untamed wind that roared restlessly that day.

The next morning, River got up early to try to catch her mother before she left for work.

"Good morning," River said as she entered the kitchen.

Zofia turned her back to River and began to remove a loaf of twisted effigy bread from the oven.

"Morning," responded Mar, "You're up early."

"Well, I wanted to ask you something."

"Oh?"

"Yeah, I just—" River paused, trying to come up with a logical way to express how she'd been feeling "—I was thinking we could move the doll outside."

Mar looked at the effigy leaning against the bench, then back at River, then down at the empty mug in front of her. "Why would we do that?"

"I was just thinking that might be better because, you know, it's making that huge mess."

Again, Mar looked at the doll which had a few fallen pieces of hay resting beneath it on the floor. "I would hardly call that a mess, River."

"Ok, but, isn't it a little creepy?"

"How so?"

"I don't know, it's just always...there."

Mar laughed as she rose to put her mug in the sink. "I think your imagination might be running away with you."

River said nothing but began to second-guess herself. Maybe her mother was right.

"Plus," Mar continued, "we only have her for one more week. Why don't you distract yourself by focusing more on the decorations? Maybe she needs a hat."

"I suppose—"

"That's the spirit," Mar interrupted as she breezed by River to retrieve her coat from the hall, and then swiftly made to leave. From halfway out the door, she yelled, "I'll be home early! Let's plan to eat together tonight."

River's heart leapt. Lately, she'd been having a lot of her meals alone, and sitting down as a family was just what she needed.

That night, after completing her schoolwork, River excitedly ran downstairs to assist her grandmother with the meal. However, upon entering the kitchen, she saw Mar and Zofia already sitting at the table eating, and most horrifyingly, scooted up next to them sat the Winter effigy.

"There you are," said Mar as she got up from her seat to pull in a fourth chair from the porch. "We were calling you. You must not have heard us."

"No one called me," said River, utterly bewildered.

She watched her mother tip the chair slightly forward to dispose of the sticks, feathers, and dead leaves it had gathered from residing outside, then dragged it into the kitchen to squish it next to the doll.

"Sure we did. Well, you're here now. Have a seat, Winter."

"Winter?"

Mar laughed at her mistake. "It's been such a long day. I meant River, of course."

River hesitated but eventually made her way over and slipped into the chair, careful not to touch the creature propped next to her.

"So, how was your day?" asked Mar as she made up an additional plate, acting like nothing strange was happening.

"Why is it sitting with us?"

"I think you made a really good point this morning. She's been left alone all week. I thought we might try to give her a proper send off."

River cast a suspicious eye toward the thing and noticed its appearance had definitely changed. In place of the plain linen dress, the effigy now bore the very same pullover sweater River wore yesterday. "Are those my clothes?"

"That was your idea, remember? I was thinking that the dress is really more fitting for an effigy of Summer." Mar smiled fondly at the doll. "Now, she'll be warm."

"*Babcia* knitted that for me."

"Don't be selfish, Winter," snapped Mar.

River didn't comment on her mistake this time, and quietly studied the plate pushed across the table toward her instead.

Circumstances did not improve over the next few days. In fact, in River's opinion, they grew much worse. The doll routinely sat at the table for meals, complete with a beverage and plate placed in front of it. If River didn't arrive quickly enough, there would not be food left to include her—the plates of Mar, Zofia, and the one in front of the effigy completely filled. In these cases, River would retrieve one of her grandmother's doll-shaped confections from the cellar. Feeling uncomfortable eating the snack in front of the very creature it reflected, she instead opted to take it upstairs to eat alone in her bedroom—the scene a perverted imitation of the one occurring just a floor beneath.

Each night, the doll was wrapped in a warm, wool blanket and carefully laid out on the sofa like a child tucked in for sleep, and it eventually gained its own bedroom in the spare room next to River's. Each morning, they propped it up at the kitchen table with a mug of River's favorite honey-sweetened rose tea, Mar wishing it a good day before she left. Zofia constantly fawned over it, brushing away rebellious pieces of straw to make it look pristine. They even added new items to its outfit, including a set of lovingly knit scarlet mittens and a beautiful locket engraved with the letter "R" in place of the one made of yarn.

"What does the 'R' stand for?" River had asked her mother one morning.

"Her name."

"Isn't it Winter?"

"River," corrected Mar, as she attached an expensive pair of cherry red laced boots—the very same ones River had begged her for not long ago—to the end of its post.

"That's my name."

"I've always loved that name," Mar responded whimsically, seemingly obliviously to the meaning behind her daughter's words.

"Mother—"

"Winter, please!" yelled Mar in frustration. "I don't have time to argue. Now look, you've made me late. I have to go." She leaned down and kissed the doll's forehead, then rushed out the door.

The night before the Spring celebration, River walked to the lean-to shelter in the forest, the very same journey she'd cherished to take in the company of her mother just last year, and many years prior. Without the usual welcome sign and various other offerings, she arrived at the spot and paused just outside. A quiet rustling sounded within, and for a moment, River thought maybe her mother had kept the tradition. Slowly, she pulled back the curtain. Something inside the dark interior seemed to stare back, for she felt the hair on the back of her neck stand, and an inexplicable impulse to run. Just then, something leapt out at her. In a

whirl of obsidian fur and wild, midnight eyes, a black hare
darted from the shelter, knocking into River's legs, then
swiftly disappearing into the forest. It took more than a few
moments to steady her nerves before making her way back
to her grandmother's house.

River didn't sleep much that night. The few precious
hours she did manage continued to be haunted by
nightmares. Everything in-between sleep was ravaged by fear
as she lay awake wondering about the day ahead. Would her
family be willing to part with the doll they'd grown to love
so much? Would the celebration return life to the way it
used to be? Would Death really appear before her, again, to
take her away as all had warned?

When morning arrived, River climbed out of bed and made
her way to the closet to find that all of her clothes had gone
missing, apart from one item: the sleeveless dress of oatmeal
linen she'd never liked, its material speckled with little
pieces of leftover hay from the previous owner. The dress
hung in the corner like a lonely ghost drifting around an
empty space. She put it on, shivering, and dolefully realized
her mother had been right. It was more suited for Summer.

Arriving downstairs, she saw the effigy at the table
enjoying breakfast with her family. Only now, it wore her
cherished red beret. For some reason, even after everything,
seeing the bright hat on top of its head was too much for
River. She leaned across the table in an attempt to snatch it
away, but before she could, her mother stood up and pulled
the doll just out of reach.

"All right, it's time," Mar announced jovially. "Let the
celebration of Spring begin!"

Just then, the door swung open to reveal the people of
Evening waiting outside, the swirling smoke of their juniper

torches hanging ominously in the air. The acrid scent of burning branches filled the kitchen as a few people rushed in to collect the doll's original outfit and adornments—since replaced by River's own belongings—and to her horror, pulled River out with them as they left.

"Wait, what's going on?" she called as they dragged her outside.

The doll's yarn necklace was placed over River's head, its wooden beads hitting heavily against her chest.

"Stop, please, there's been a mistake," she pleaded, "it's me!"

The fir crown with once lush needles, now dry and hard, was cruelly pushed down over her forehead where it poked and scratched at her eyes.

"Can't you hear me?"

Her arms were roughly pulled behind her back. The thick rope that bound the true effigy now bound River's wrists together under a tight, inescapable knot. The doll watched on from the loving arms of River's mother and grandmother, who held it affectionately between them.

"Mother, please," River began to cry.

Mar's eyes stared blankly as she approached her daughter.

"I don't understand," wept River, "can't you hear me? It's me—"

The crowd interrupted her pleas with soft voices rising in the solemn Springtime song:

Let us carry Winter from our hearts and raise her over our heads...

Suddenly, they hoisted River to sit on the joined shoulders of Mar and the herbalist, as they were of similar height and already walking side-by-side. Terrified and humiliated, River struggled and squirmed to escape the hold, but the strong hands of unknown others kept her upright in the air.

"This is a mistake! Please, someone help me!" she screamed to no avail.

Let us carry Winter down the road, beyond the sleeping flowerbeds...

River frantically searched the sea of heads that surrounded her but couldn't find the one covered in a familiarly patterned shawl among them. Then, spotted just beyond the parade, was Zofia in the distance.

"*Babcia*," River called out to her grandmother, tears streaming down her heated face. "Help me!"

Zofia didn't respond and instead turned away from the crowd, picking up a basket River hadn't yet noticed, and meandered out of sight.

River was then pulled from their shoulders and awkwardly cradled, nearly upside-down, almost face-to-face with the doll that took her place. The thing had been toted along with the procession, not far behind Mar. They forcibly dunked River's head into a puddle, its ice-cold, muddy water littered with sticks, feathers, and dead leaves from the road. As they hoisted her back up, the pointy crown began to slide from her forehead, and was painfully pushed back in its place.

"Please stop," River sobbed as muddy streams of puddle water mixed with her tears.

Let us carry Winter to the river and toss her over the edge...

They approached the bridge and once again pulled River down from her mother's shoulder. Mar's strong arms firmly wrapped around her, preventing her escape.

The crowd cheered as they forced River to the other side of the railing, her bare feet tiptoeing as she struggled to stand on the narrow, icy edge. Mar's hold remained tightly wrapped around River—the only thing delaying her fall.

"Don't let me go," River begged quietly through exhausted tears.

Suddenly, something sharp pressed against her wrists and pulled at the rope that bound them.

"Enjoy your stay," Mar whispered against River's ear in a near-indecipherable tone.

"Mother—"

Then, Mar let go.

Hitting the water wasn't as painful as River always imagined it to be. The dark depths, still carrying ice from the great height the water originated from, and made even more frigid by the season very recently departed, embraced her softly, yet coldly—far colder than she ever expected. The distinction between meeting the surface and submerging fully below became a blur in her mind; the shock of cold consumed her, and an inescapable pressure strained her lungs and immobilized her body. After mere seconds underwater, River tested the bindings on her wrists and found that they easily fell apart. The bundle of rope sank past her legs and drifted slowly down to forever rest on the riverbed. Up she swam until her face broke the surface, the air much warmer in contrast to the freezing water. Instinctively, she tried to take in a huge breath, instead gasping and coughing as her lungs remained tight. Looking up at the bridge, she locked eyes with Mar who now wore the face of a mother in anguish and not that of the stranger who'd forgotten her, and then disposed of her.

Enjoy your stay, Mar had said before letting her fall. River so desperately hoped, despite the perilous circumstances she now found herself in, that she could indeed go to their secret shelter for safety, as it had been intended, and that her mother would not follow to inflict some other nightmarish scheme upon her. Before River made up her mind, the current decided and began to pull her gently away, the pointy fir crown floating steadily by her side.

From the bridge, Mar watched as River drifted off with

the Noć until just far enough away to no longer be distinguishable from what was supposed to have been thrown over the railing in her place. Painstakingly returning to the imposter by her side, Mar gazed down at the hated thing with a forced reenactment of the affection she only felt for her real daughter. "Come on, then. Off you go."

Her voice sounded hollow as she made herself wrap an arm around its sharp-cornered shoulder and turn it gawkily with the crowd. Just then, a mighty gust picked up and whipped at the group, halting them as they retreated from their spot on the bridge. The musicians ceased their festive playing as hats and scarves flew in all directions. The disoriented crowd coughed and swatted away the billow of sticks, feathers, and dead leaves swirling up with the wind and into their faces.

Without warning, in the chaos of the moment, the lightweight doll blew away from Mar's arms and collided directly with a burning juniper stick being carried nearby—as if by design. Within seconds, the doll was ablaze. Pieces of hay and twine crackled and burned in quick succession until the spot where the thing had landed flared into a bonfire, complete with a slightly scorched red beret resting just inches beyond the confines of the flames.

"It worked," Mar gasped aloud in both shock and relief.

Not wanting to waste any time, she impulsively reached down to retrieve the hat. Before taking off to where she hoped River was now safely arriving, Mar gazed into the flames where the doll, dressed and loved as her daughter, had stood only moments ago.

It would have been that quick, that unstoppable, she thought to herself, grateful for the confirmation that she'd done the right—although likely unforgivable—thing.

Branches and leaves whipped at her face as she desperately sprinted to the shelter in the forest. She could feel her lungs tightening in protest, but continued on, nevertheless.

Meanwhile, River arrived, following a clumsy escape from the rapids and an even more unsteady trek across the terrain between the bank of the Noć and the daisy-curtained entrance of the shelter. Her body felt numb, and her mind dizzy. All she could think about was getting warm inside the hideaway where she knew the tiny, yet hopefully effective flame of a lantern awaited her. What she didn't expect to see was her grandmother sitting in one of the chairs, a large basket by her side and a set of dry clothes resting in her arms.

"*Babcia?*" she called out in a hoarse whisper, unsure if what she saw was real.

Zofia sprang to her feet as quickly as her body allowed and hobbled over to her granddaughter, unraveling a wool blanket as she went. A pained sound escaped Zofia through unabashed tears as she wrapped it around River's shoulders, kissing her forehead and running warm hands up and down her arms. Before River could protest, Zofia directed her over to the chair she'd just vacated and gently encouraged her into the seat. A warm mug was placed in River's hands without delay, for which she felt begrudgingly grateful, and a basket of herb and mushroom hand pies—baked into no discernable shape—pushed in her direction across the shelf of the adjoining boulder. Her grandmother took the seat next to her.

In silence they sat while River held the mug against her chest to take in its warmth against the chill that still permeated her body. She could feel Zofia studying her and fidgeted slightly under the scrutiny. Feeling confused and more than a little awkward, she took a sip of the honey-sweetened rose tea and risked a glance over the top of the cup at the woman across from her, whose unwavering attention endured despite bulbous tears spilling down her wrinkled face. The brief eye contact prompted Zofia to reach out to River, however, before she could take her hand, the sound of heavy breathing and swift footsteps drew rapidly closer and interrupted the moment. Suddenly, Mar burst through the entrance, the charred beret still clutched tightly in her hand. Once inside and after spotting her daughter safely bundled in the corner, Mar dropped weakly to her knees, relief written plainly across her face.

"River," she let out in a strangled sob, "I'm so sorry. I had to, or else—" She looked away, ashamed. "Please forgive me."

River's mind spun trying to make sense of it all, and she didn't know what to say. It all seemed so surreal after the harrowing and unforgettable events of the past couple weeks. And yet, what she wanted more than anything in the world was to forget; to jump up and run across the distance that separated them, and to belong to her mother once more.

Just then, a sound from outside drew their attention. Whether it was the wind blowing an innocent branch against the side of the shelter or the resolute knock of an ever watchful and discerning darkness come to collect, the old woman and her daughter rose between the entranceway and River as she sat frozen in her seat, wide-eyed and afraid. Moments passed in a symphony of silent things: the held breath of Mar standing guard, the steadfast calm in Zofia's fortitude as she did the same, and the invisible presence on the other side of the curtain—unknowable and looming.

A second knock sounded, and River stood, too.

ONCE UPON A WINTER

IVAN BOTICA

KOSCHEI TRIPETOVICH LOOKED DOWN at the field that would soon be carpeted by corpses. Right now, it was glazed with soft snow which reflected the pink and purple hues of the sunset. Gusts of wind whipped at his cheeks and pushed his cloak backward, rippling. A thick forest bordered the farthest reaches of Krvavo field, which stretched out for hundreds of yards before meeting the first hills out in the distance. Snowflakes began gathering on Koschei's thick mustache. He stood there, arms crossed over leather straps and iron buckles, a saber swaying from his belt.

His sleep the previous night had been more exhausting than usual. Dreams before combat are hardly peaceful, but this one was different. It kept him walking the thin edge between sleep and wakefulness. He remembered no more than a stream of black hair spilling down the bare back of a slender woman. When she'd turned toward him, he'd jolted awake. Sweating, weak, and with the sour twang of wine in his mouth. He did not remember drinking wine the day before.

Without warning, an old woman wearing ancient furs seemed to have appeared on his side.

"This fight will be a cursed one, young Tripetovich," she said.

Without turning to her, Koschei said, "How do you suppose that?"

"Perun has spoken. I have seen it. You say you are willing to march your men for land and prosperity, but do you know the price of what you wish for?" She tapped her cane and turned to him. *Old hag*, Koschei thought. *Always the decrepit ones with the comments.*

"Lives, Priestess. Did you need oracular powers to tell you that? And what do the gods say of the weather tomorrow? Snow, perhaps?"

The oracle frowned. "One of these days you will learn how the gods regard mockery and disregard." She stepped closer to him so that he could no longer ignore her. He looked at her through the dark locks falling down his face.

"And I pray I will be here to see it," she said.

"Perun's opinions on my wars mean shit all to me, lady," he said. "Wasn't he who got us this far. Never was."

The priestess gasped, eyes shocked open. Koschei's shadow creeped over the hag against the dying sun. His mere presence was a threat to all around him, which was precisely why the people loved him.

"Do you think yourself strong enough to alter divine will, young man? To go against—"

"My lord."

The oracle squeaked. He turned square to her, looking down at her like a tired son might at his senile mother.

"Better address your superiors with their proper titles," he said. "I am tolerant with you, but you may not find that the case with others. Your predictions and prophecies are good for morale. It gives the men and women a sense of divine purpose. The fiercest soldiers are those with everything to gain and nothing to lose. I respect their beliefs because it gives them something in return. Do not think that you can impress me with the same."

"Heretic," the priestess croaked. "Heathen! You are everything the enemy thinks you are, and worse!"

"Good. It behooves me to keep up with my reputation."

The oracle squinted and craned her neck toward him, as if in provocation.

"The punishment for such insolence is categorical," she said, "My lord."

They stood in silence, each looking at the other with a scowl. The old woman's bony fingers turned white at the grip on her cane. She shivered in the cold but didn't relent. Something puzzled Koschei about her. *You have to respect the tenacity of old women,* he thought.

"Blood,"she started. "Corpses, rot, blood. And Misery. No sweetness in victory. And you, young lord... You will find no love in life. Feel no warm touch as long as you live. Death and Misery will cling to you like a shadow and you will have no peace."

"My lord," someone said from behind, "I dare not interrupt but... A messenger arrived. He wishes to speak with you."

"Thank you, lad," Koschei said and patted the skinny teenager's shoulder. "Please make sure the lady enjoys adequate rest tonight." He side-eyed the woman. "And get some yourself."

The young man nodded and offered a hand of support for the oracle. They walked back to their tents while Koschei sighed and prepared himself.

Mighty Perun, he thought, *if you object to my battles, I pray you strike me dead where I stand.* He screwed his eyes shut and waited. A minute of silence, save for the gentle whistling of the wind. He opened his eyes and chuckled, then was off marching to his tent.

The duke's tent was larger than the soldiers', but not by much. It had to project authority, but not enough to separate him from the people. Two guards flanked the entrance flap, more decorative than anything else, since any wishful intruder could sneak through any other side without too much trouble. The security of this structure was in its position. Close to the cliff on one side, beset by the Duke's most trusted men and women on the other. A hell of a task to go through for any one person. Candles illuminated the inside. A thick hide covered the floor for insulation. The duke's desk and chair were opposite the entrance, his bedding to the right of it, and a large chest to the left. Standing in the middle, a guard kept watch over a man with filthy clothes and a greasy beard. The guard nodded respectfully as Koschei entered.

After a moment's pause, Koschei spoke, "I understand you have a message for us."

Contrary to his rugged appearance, he stood dignified and spoke slowly and fluently. "I do, sir. Marshall Godinovich would like to express his deepest desire for peace with the people of Korgyra. He beckons you to reconsider promoting brothers' wars, so baneful to the work of the gods."

Koschei snorted. *Do they ever stop talking about them?* "Brothers, you say?" he asked.

"Not in blood, sir," the messenger continued, "but in history. In culture and in faith. Why, the one thing separating us is this arbitrary line over a land our ancestors had settled together centuries ago."

"Arbitrary?" Koschei mused. "Culture? Together? And where were these brothers when my people starved in the hundreds? Mothers drained of life, unable to breastfeed, fathers exhausted and shaking, incapable of swinging a hoe without collapsing. And what courtesy have you given us, brother? Lowered taxes? Given access to crops or soil that doesn't rot?"

The messenger grimaced at these words.

"No." Koschei's face turned sullen. "You parade your soldiers through our streets and scold us for not waving the flags. You hit our children for not properly saluting your officers. Tell me, messenger, which god am I to thank for that?"

The man shuffled in place. "I am certain that, if you agree to peace talks, a mutually beneficial solution can be negotiated. For duke Godinovich's mercy is—"

Koschei spat in front of the messenger's boots. Everyone in the room jerked to attention. "A shit on lord Godinovich and his mercy," he growled. "He must be desperate, resorting to such pitiful attempts."

"You'll be made an example of for this," the messenger shot back. "I almost feel sorry for having to relay this sentiment."

"No need," Duke Koschei said.

"Wha—"

Before the messenger could grasp the situation, Koschei's saber hissed out of its scabbard and flew out in an arc. Blood shot out of the messenger's throat and sprayed Koschei's face and cloak. The courier's rugged body stood frozen in place for a moment, then dropped face-first onto the duke's rug. Koschei flicked the blood off his blade and wiped it clean with a rag jammed into his belt.

"Luka, if you please," he said to the guard, "send a message back to Ivan the Merciful. And tell someone to get me a new carpet."

Luka smiled and nodded. "Aye."

The guard dragged the body out, leaving Koschei alone in his tent. The duke sank to his bedding, holding his head with both hands. His breath trembled. *Collect yourself, man. The only way out is through.*

Luka put the body on a sled, and the butcher, standing by, sharpened his cleaver. With a few hacks dealt by the butcher's meaty arms, the head toppled into the snow. They attached the sled to a pair of dogs and sent them off downhill, toward the sparkling embers in the forest, where Ivan's people made camp.

"You think they'll find their way back?" Luka asked.

The butcher shrugged, wiped his hands, and said nothing.

The air's always freshest before battle, Koschei thought.

At dawn, hundreds of Korgyran men and women formed a line before the field of Krvavo. Horsemen took positions at each flank, but their duke stood among the infantry. Shields covered their front, swords rattling against each other. The soldier's leather garments squeaked and dirt rustled under their boots. A mist formed around their heads from the heat of their breaths.

Hundreds of yards away, before the forest, a similar line faced them. The other line's spears seemed not to waver. Their unrelenting stance gave Koschei a twist in the stomach.

"You lot are the strongest people I know!" Koschei yelled, partly to forget his stomach for a minute. "Betrayed farmers, abandoned peasant folk, desperate mothers. Look at you now. Standing at the edge of glory!" his voice grew louder. "Now take what was always yours and rip out their hearts!"

The crowd shouted at once, raising their spears. The farthest ends of the line had heard little besides an enthusiastic yell from their lord, but still they joined in the war cry.

Koschei turned to Luka and grabbed the back of his neck. "Live with honor, friend."

"Die with glory, my lord," Luka said and grinned.

Chants accompanied their dash forward across Krvavo. "To war! To war! For the people!"

Cold air attacked Koschei's face as he ran. It made his eyes foggy. Didn't matter. Never did. They flew across the damp earth, traversing the slippery terrain with immense speed. The mounted right flank knew to wrap around the enemy's left, so they rode faster on, to get behind Ivan's lines and handle them from the rear.

It didn't take long before the first man came crashing in, bashed right into his shield, ax biting into its side. Koschei pushed from his rear leg, posted like a support beam, and shoved the man off his shield. The ax came tumbling after and the man scrambled to grab it for a second chance before a steel blade stung him cold between the ribs. He kicked on the ground, bleeding, Groaning. But still breathing. He grabbed Koschei by the leg and cocked his head back to blast him in the holiest of places. Unsuccessful. The duke spiked his other knee forward and caved the soldier's nose back into the head. First one down, clean.

Koschei's brothers and sisters screamed and grunted, handling their own business before another enemy noticed that his friend had failed and that the Grand Traitor lacked an opponent.

This one must have thought himself to be Svarog, by the confidence with which he held his hammer. He'd had good reason for it too, given his titan body strung with thick, wiry muscle. No shield or armor, nipples catching the rot in the cold and a hammer swung overhead by both arms. As the steel bulge went up, the soldier's hands slid toward the bottom of the handle, and his knees bent to drop his body down with the weapon. Damn, but he knew how to use it.

The impact all but splintered Koschei's shield like a meteorite and shook his bones. The force of it dropped him to his knee. In this position, he could expect to survive approximately three seconds. He took a page from the recently-dead-man's book and looked at the madman's legs to conclude where his rocks might be. He jammed his saber up and hit flesh, and the grunt that followed, almost as if in fluent common, told him he'd hit the right spot. Koschei lunged up and forward, pressing in the same direction with both arms, one of which was still stuck in the giant's fertile grounds. The hammer dropped into the snow with a thud. The body which had once held it slipped off the shield with a fixed, horrified expression. Frosty air burned Koschei's lungs and the side of his ribs hurt. Two down, not so clean.

Having found himself in a safer spot, he afforded a glance at his peers and saw Luka stabbing and slicing away like a maniac, first in line, as always. He fought like a badger, but nothing about his movements was stupid. Every sweep was calculated, every counter measured. Something about that enthusiasm always inspired Koschei. The Duke's spear maidens anchored their feet into the ground and spiked ambitious opponents with cruel efficiency. Rival forces became noticeably thinner, and his cavalry was gaining way around their left flank. He smiled.

Screams.

Warnings for cover. Koschei looked up. A swarm of arrows rose from the tree line. They ascended in a slow arc and hurled toward them. Rapid thumps and splatters of wood and flesh followed, accompanied by wails of pain. The duke raised his hand to cover himself, but a damaged round shield can only protect so much at one time. A projectile jammed itself in Koschei's thigh, making him drop his arms on instinct. Before long, another arrow found its way into his chest. It slammed in hard enough to twist his body on impact. Against his best efforts, the saber slipped from his fingers and he fell to his knees, grabbing the arrow's shaft in disbelief. Another arrow rammed his back. And another. His people shouted and cried, ran back, fell, ducked, pushed forward...

That was the last thing he saw.

Bodies, as Koschei had predicted, carpeted the field, glazed with a fresh layer of snow that had accumulated through the night. Swords, axes and spears were strewn about the battlefield, some sticking hilt-up from the ground like morbid flagpoles. The icy meadow was peppered with arrows and soaked in blood, enveloped in eerie silence. Waning moonlight sparkled on the snow.

A haze congested his mind, as if he hadn't fully woken from a dream. He pushed himself off the snow and looked down at his hands. His boots. His cloak. His saber on the ground next to him. He frowned and whipped his head around. Sacks of frozen flesh lay in place of what had once been his friends. He shook his head and grunted. The image didn't change.

As he pulled in panicked gasps, he noticed a distinct lack of winter's sting in his throat. In fact, winter had not affected one part of his body. He was not warm, but not cold either.

"What is this?" he growled, to nothing in particular.

Almost like an answer, a giggle echoed from... somewhere. The forest, maybe?

"Where are you?" he yelled. The thought of attracting bears or wolves eager to bite his throat out did not occur to him. "Show yourself, devil!" He picked his saber up from where it had lain and pointed its trembling end out into the darkness. "By every god in the sky, reveal yourself and fight me with honor!" The uncertainty in his tone shattered the illusion he was trying to portray with his words.

Moonlight was not strong enough to expose the details in the forest, but Koschei could see a faint outline. A small, human outline, partially hiding behind the trunk of a tall fir tree. He traipsed toward it, wobbly blade aimed out all the while. He tip-toed over snow and flesh, trying his best to avoid stepping on friends. When he came closer, he saw that the apparition was a girl. A child, pale, with blond hair and a bright expression. She wore a thin, white dress, which should have made her limbs freeze off on this kind of night.

"What's going on, girl," he said, "are you not cold?"

She giggled once more and ran off into the woods.

"Oi! Where're you—ah, balls..."

He sheathed his saber and ran after her. Reason reminded him how stupid it was to run into a dark forest mid-winter, but instinct told him he had no choice. When it became difficult to track the girl among the trees, he tried following her footsteps, only to find out—there were none. His neck tingled and he broke his pace. Looking behind him, he could see no tracks of his own, either. *What kind of trickery... Is the hag having a laugh at my expense?* Winding between the trees in the distance, he saw a small, pale reflection of the moonlight against the girl. With more anger than confusion this time, he bolted after her.

After a handful of odd twists and turns, they arrived at a clearing in the woods, which, by all intents and purposes, should not exist. Koschei remembered standing atop the cliff overlooking the forest. Had his eyes deceived him then? Or was his mind doing the same now? *I must be mad*, he thought. He soon ascertained insanity, because in this clearing stood a lake with a three-story mansion on a small island in its center.

It was grander and more intricately decorated than any royal dwelling he'd ever seen, large enough to house a small town's population. Its walls were most peculiar, reflecting the image of the snow and the trees surrounding it and the sparkling sky above it. The façade mirrored the natural elements of the area, but the closer he got, the clearer its own shape would emerge, the complex designs on the roof, the ornamental reliefs on the walls. He felt like the building belonged there, not unlike any plant or shrub he'd seen along the way. Like it had claimed this place since time immemorial, and everyone else was blind for not having noticed it sooner. Like an eternal palace of mirrors.

The girl ran toward it, crossing an arched wooden bridge connecting the mansion to the world. She cracked open a massive door and slipped inside. Terrified as he was, the house compelled Koschei forward. So he followed suit, testing the bridge for any illusions by tapping it with his foot first. It held sure enough.

Koschei walked over it and approached the door. Nothing lived on the small island around the palace—nothing, besides a row of white rose bushes stretching out to the sides of the entrance. He hesitated before touching the door. *The guest always brings a gift.* It was a mad situation, but standards had to be upheld. *No point in pissing off whatever lives here.*

After careful consideration and a touch of impatience, he pinched a stalk off one of the rose bushes and cut it with his knife before tucking it away in his cloak. The door, twice his height, drifted open, bathing the ice-covered island's shore in warm light. Sweet music and laughter beckoned him inside, and he couldn't resist.

Hundreds of people of all kinds danced in pairs, in a room as tall as some castles. Windows Koschei could not see from the outside stretched tall along the walls. Lights hung in crystal ornaments from the vaulted ceiling. Dark wood floors and stairs were polished to a tasteful shine and great white pillars supported the walls. The music rose and fell in a seductive cadence, a resonant sound Koschei didn't recognize. The dancers wore some extravagant black suits and dresses, with masks over their eyes. Four people stood at the far end of the room, dressed in a similar way, sawing on strange instruments which produced the swaying tunes. The girl from the forest was nowhere to be found. The music rose in volume and ferocity, swelled with vigor. The melody became threatening. Then the dancers stopped.

Countless heads snapped to face Koschei. They looked at him through black masks like a hawk might a mouse. They started toward him, gradually speeding up as they went. Koschei wanted to say something—to apologize, say it had been a mistake, beg them to stop. Nothing came out. His jaw was clamped shut in fear and he could only inch backward in hope of the dancers changing their minds. When they got no more than a few feet away, they stretched their mouths open into grins, revealing rows of yellow fangs. The pleasant smell of perfume and flowers turned rotten, like a bucket of dead fish. He must have been facing demons because no beast could unhinge its jaw the way those things did as they jumped and tackled him. Rows of serpentine teeth protruded from their mouth and they salivated over their fresh meal. Thick, scratched-up fingernails grabbed at him from all directions. Koschei would have wept, if not for the horror gripping him by the throat.

A woman's voice was all it took to bring everything to a dead halt. The music, the dancers—even the fear. Everything froze in place. Koschei on his back, the nightmares straddling him. Then, as if in a trance, the demons got up, turned around and walked back into position, and the music continued, and they danced. Koschei stayed on the floor. *If this is a nightmare*, he thought, *I'll never fucking sleep again.*

"It's not a nightmare," he heard the playful female voice say, "nor a dream. Stand up, Tripetovich."

He obeyed. From a balcony above the dance floor, a woman stared at him. She wasn't wearing a mask. The voice he'd heard was much closer than that balcony, but he was done questioning logic. The lady walked across the balcony to a door on her left and glanced at him before closing it behind her. Koschei looked at the giant entrance, then back at the door on the balcony above. *Ah, plague on the whole damn thing.* He weaved among the dancers, climbed up the polished, solid wood stairs, and paused at the door at the balcony. He looked back to the exit once more, separated from him by a sea of dancing strangers. He sighed.

When he opened the door, he saw the lady sitting on the windowsill, talking to the little girl that had led him here. The child was playing on the ground, and as Koschei stood like a mute idiot at the doorstep, the lady smiled and told the girl to go play elsewhere. She giggled and ran past the duke, mocking him one last time.

The lady wore a slim black dress, pearly earrings, and a gold necklace resting on her exposed collarbone. She'd tied her black hair into a low, braided bun, but had no makeup on, which was unusual for a wealthy woman. The most peculiar thing was her pale skin, which Koschei could only compare to that of a corpse. He knew that much from experience.

She broke the silence. "You didn't turn away."

"You know my name," Koschei said. "And my thoughts."

The lady walked over to a table stacked with food and drink. She poured red wine from a decanter into two silver chalices. "You are Koschei the Traitor," she said. "Everyone knows your name. As for thoughts, well... men aren't terribly difficult to read."

Her voice was smooth and dignified. It demanded attention.

"Why did you bring me here?"

"I brought nothing—" she handed him a chalice "—you came on your own. And for that, you have my consideration."

"What do you want?" He tried to sound commanding.

The lady chuckled and took a sip, then approached him. "My, you are the right one indeed."

Koschei hesitated. "Right for what?"

She looked at him with big, black eyes. "Don't you remember?"

Oh, he did. His vision flashed like he'd gotten thwacked with a club. The dark hair, the eyes, the wine. Rot and winter dancing with flowers and music. Cruel beauty and comforting blight. The palace of mirrors. Kalinov bridge. The White Death. He fell to one knee and looked up at her.

"Lady Misery," he muttered.

She smirked. "I prefer Morana. Rise, Koschei, I can't talk to you like that."

He did. *Good thing I don't feel anything*, he thought. *The nausea would kill me.*

"You're welcome," she said.

He remembered the rose he'd concealed in his cloak. He took it out and presented it to Morana. The petals were smashed and the stalk crooked.

Morana looked shocked. "What is that?"

"A gift," he said. "Guests must bring gifts."

She blinked, took the flower and thanked him. When their fingers touched, Koschei could feel the terrifying cold of her skin. It was the first thing he'd felt that evening. The numbness had slowly begun fading.

The duke gulped. "Am I...?"

"Dead? For now," she said. "But that is negotiable." She put the rose in a vase packed with withered plants.

He raised an eyebrow. "Pardon my asking, lady—uh... Morana—" he checked for approval, which she gave with a nod "—but what could goddess death want with a mortal like myself?"

She drank from her cup and wiped a dark red drop from her blue lips with her thumb. "Let me get to the point," she said. "The Korgyran rebellion is the stuff of legend. The viciousness of your people is feared across the continent. And as far as I understand it, you are not in good relations with Perun."

He gulped. Until then, the thought of the God-king's retribution had been an abstract concept to him. Morana sat on a velvet-covered sofa framed with ornate wood.

"But I wouldn't worry about that," she continued. "He is only one god, after all." There was a sly tone to her statement.

Koschei had, by then, gathered himself enough to find the situation less uncomfortable. Bizarre as it was, she respected him and he knew it. His strung-up shoulders relaxed and he stepped closer to the sofa.

"And what do you mean by that?" he asked.

"That we can come to a mutual benefit, you and I." She fidgeted with her hands. "As you know, the God-king and I are not in good relations, either. Not since he arranged for me to marry that jovial moron, Yarilo."

"I thought you loved each other," Koschei said. "People sing songs about your affection. The power you hold together is monumental, Spring and Winter united. And arranged marriages are a good way to forgo the annoyances of courting. Excuse me if I find no reason for you to be so offended."

She snorted. "If only it were that easy... This charming spirit of spring you people love to worship is a power-hungry, cheating son of a whore. I care no more for him than you do for the rot. Our marriage is a strictly political one, and the politics have since become redundant."

Koschei stayed silent.

"The balance between spring and winter," she said, putting her cup down on a small table in front of the sofa, "fertility and death, sun and night, is a delicate one. If he prefers going out to disrupt that harmony by... *courting*, then let him have it. The balance will be no more." Her dark eyes turned evil in an instant, becoming of Death itself. "But rest assured, dear Koschei, winter will not be the one losing."

The duke froze. *'Dear' Koschei?* Morana turned her gaze back to the chalice, from which she took another swig.

"How do I benefit your situation, Morana?" he asked in a low voice.

She cleared her throat. "You are a warlord, Koschei. You bring death. And with immense purpose and success, at that. I represent death. Therefore, the better you act, the bigger an advantage we have over Yarilo and Perun's side of the table. The deeper we wedge you into the conflict, the more power they lose. They become weaker, like a candle covered by a cup. Eventually, they get snuffed out. And we..." She smirked again. "Well, you get to be proclaimed King. Your people thrive in the new age of winter, and you are unmatched as Warlord of the continent. And I get to be free to do as I please."

He thought on her words, downed the rest of his wine and put the empty chalice next to Morana's. Then permitted himself to sit close to her on the sofa. "Helping Lady Misery reign free over the world... I can have no guarantee you would do as you say."

"You came with a gift," she said, looking at the rose. "All anyone else has brought to this house was fear and sorrow. But you took the time to show kindness. You can say you've gained favor with me."

"I'm honored," he said. "But favor is not enough."

"You don't trust me?"

"No."

"I can send you to Veles and let your bones burrow themselves where they lay."

They locked eyes and squinted at each other.

"Do it, then," he said, "if it means my people are free."

"How do you know I won't enslave them regardless?"

"Because you invited me here for a reason."

They leaned toward one another as they talked.

"And you came for a reason," she said.

"I did."

"Say yes."

They leaned closer.

"I'll consider it."

"Say yes."

"Maybe."

"Say yes."

They kissed. Her blue lips felt like snow on his. Her hair smelled of lavender. Koschei propped himself up on the sofa with his knee and they embraced, bodies squeezed together.

"Yes," he said.

Then he woke up.

He could hear men shuffling around him in the snow, though he could not see much with his head against the ground. His limbs were burning cold, bones frozen solid. He tried to move his arm around to push himself up, but the attempt shot bolts of pain down his back, forcing him to utter a painful groan.

"Hey!"someone said. "It's the duke!"

"What in a thousand hells," someone else stammered.

They lifted him from the snow-covered ground, trying not to hurt him and failing. As they carried him back to the camp, he asked only about Luka. Their hesitation was answer enough. Sobbing made his ribs hurt, so he just let tears stream down his swollen cheeks in silence. He remembered the strange dream he'd had while he was out.

What a morbid thing to hallucinate. He could not, however, explain the sour aftertaste of wine in his mouth.

Weeks had passed, and the Duke had almost recovered, save for a limp in his left knee and blindness in the right eye. Consequences which, healers reminded him, are a divine marvel, considering the punishment he'd suffered in battle. They told him how the enemy had fled after a freak blizzard followed their arrow barrage.

The soldiers noticed he became more withdrawn, rarely accompanying them to fireside feasts. His conversations were dry and his appetite low. Their Duke could have eaten a boar by himself, given the right conditions. Some theorized that Koschei Tripetovich had died in battle, and a demon had taken over the body when he rose. They would often catch him standing at the edge of the cliff, looking out into the valley for some time, and then going back to his tent. The Duke had had the spirit of the steward of the universe, and now his world became small, reduced to the hill and his quarters.

From his secluded spot atop the hill, he commanded battle after battle, never joining as he did before. His streak went undefeated, even with more questionable strategies. Some instance of luck would turn the tide in their favor, and they'd chase Ivan's forces further back into the unknown. They were winning, but they weren't sure it was for the right reasons.

After another successful charge, Koschei was sure Ivan's forces were stretched thin, close to utter annihilation. The thought made him feel indifferent, and he could not understand why. Was victory no longer exciting? I am acting like a spoilt child. Times are good and I should be grateful.

He saw the sun dip beyond the horizon, so he went back into his warm tent.

The sight made him smile reflexively, for the first time in a while.

"So it was no dream after all," Koschei said.

A slender figure with dark hair and corpse-white skin sat in his chair.

"Koschei the Immortal," she said. "A fine reputation you have for yourself."

"They call me that," he said, "yet I feel no better than a carcass."

She looked at the map on his desk. "You've grown sloppy. What's the matter with you?"

"I've been winning."

"Because of me."

He shook his head. "My people are the ones with the swords."

"Your people—" she shot up from the chair "—would have died without me. This was not the deal—"

"Don't tell me how to fight my damn wars!" He hammer-fisted his desk. The figurines on the map toppled. He rubbed his forehead above his blind eye. "I'm sorry. I shouldn't have yelled."

"Where is your saber?" she asked, slowly.

"Stored away, with the rest of my gear." He pointed to the chest. "Not much use to a cripple."

She looked down and said nothing.

"Why did you come here?"

"Because your strategies—"

"Stop," he said. "You don't have to lie to me."

She fidgeted with her hands. "I was worried. You look gaunt. Is everything alright?"

"Thanks for the compliments," he snorted, "but I'm doing fine."

She put her hand on his chest. "You don't have to lie to me."

He slapped her hand away. "If you cared, you wouldn't have waited this long."

Morana frowned. "I've had my business to take care of, too, I was—"

"Busy fucking Yarilo, the jovial moron?"

She slapped him so hard he went temporarily deaf in one ear.

"How dare you use that language on me." Her voice grew deeper and louder. "I am your patron goddess, Queen Winter, the White Death." The words seemed to be splitting into five different tones at once, her eyes turning white, and a wind picked up inside the tent. The battle map flew into the canvas wall of the tent. An armor stand by the chest rattled and Koschei was reminded of his locked away weapons. His chest swelled with the heartbeat of a strange newfound excitement. "I should have you gutted open and hung for decoration, handed over to Ivan's—"

Koschei bent down and kissed her, holding her by her shoulders. She hesitated, but gave in and kissed back. When she seemed to have caught herself running her fingers through his hair, she pushed away.

"I hate it when you interrupt me," she said. "Never do it again."

"Never."

She put her finger on his lips. "And if you ever talk like that again..." She leaned forward and whispered something into the ear she'd slapped a second ago, so he couldn't hear much. He did catch the word "balls" somewhere in the sentence and deduced it would be best to apologize.

She kissed him then, and slid her hand up his neck. He grabbed her by the waist, lifted her, and limped over to his bedding, which he threw her down upon before settling on top of her. She giggled while he kissed her cold neck, chest, and collarbone. He grabbed the top of her dress' sleeve.

"You have more of these, don't you?" he asked.

"Mhm."

He squeezed the sleeve and ripped it off, then proceeded to do the same to the whole thing. Before long, both of them were down to their bare skin, rolling over soft animal hide until she locked her legs around his hips. Koschei felt dizzy as he had when he'd first visited her. Only, he knew, this time it was real. She ran her blue lips up his neck and bit his ear. He heard the wonderful music from the palace once more. She coiled her hips against his. They interlocked fingers, and so began a delightfully sleepless night.

The guards outside stood dumbfounded. How has anyone snuck in? What if somebody's in trouble? They shrugged at each other and went back to the fire and beer with their friends. Let the duke be happy for a night, they thought.

It was near dawn, and still they lay in Kochei's bed of animal skins and wool. He admired Morana's lavender-scented hair, spilled over his pillow, as he ran his finger up and down her spine. She snuggled up to him where he lay on his side. He was happy.

After some time, he felt obliged to break the illusion. "Morana..."

She beamed at him. "I like that," she said. "The way you say my name. Nobody uses my full name anymore. Always Misery or Mara or Death..."

Koschei smiled, but not with his eyes. "Listen—"

"Don't," she said. "Not yet."

"I have to."

She held herself as if paralyzed, her breath reduced to nothing.

"When can I see you again?" he asked.

"I don't know," she said, twirling her hair.

"What's the problem?"

"You know what it is."

"Yarilo? I can kill him. Wasn't that the plan? Don't use him as an excuse."

She drew back to herself. He stroked her cheek.

"I didn't mean to be crude," he said. "You make me happy. I'd lost that for some time now. You understand that, don't you?"

She didn't reply.

"Marry me, Morana."

He could see something unspoken caught in her throat. Her eyes sparkled. Had Koschei known no better, he might have assumed those were tears.

"That's not going to happen," she said.

Koschei frowned. "Why not?"

"I'm a goddess, Koschei," she said. "I represent natural forces that could destroy the world at the slightest mistake. I'll live to see myself make those mistakes, in thousands of years from now. Maybe I'll be here to see the mountains crumble and blow away in the wind. And after that, who knows? You are an admirable one, Tripetovich." She looked at him. "But you are a man. Nothing more."

Koschei went numb. All the joy of the night before abandoned him in an instant, and he fell to his back, a wave of exhaustion washing over him. *Of course.* He rubbed his eyes.

She placed her hand on his chest. "Sleep, sweet Koschei," she said. "Forget all this. Sleep."

She rose, and out of a shadow, a slim black dress materialized around her body.

"Morana," he said, dozing off. "What was that music they played in your palace?"

"It's called a waltz," she said. "Maybe I'll teach it to you someday."

She kissed him on the forehead and he slept like a cannon.

She was gone long before he woke, and he knew it. From outside he heard the gentle crackle of flame and a pleasant smell of roasted meat. His people were out by the fires, gathering for lunch. Koschei could not remember the last time he'd felt so rested. He fumbled into his clothes, wrapped himself in his cloak, and limped out of the tent, where he was met by whispers and laughs and giggles.

"Sleep well, my lord?" one of his captains asked, handing him a slice of slow-roasted lamb. They'd been there long enough to secure a supply of their favorite meat, and had apparently decided it was the right day to prepare some. Koschei returned a groggy grunt and looked at the meat, which made him sick. He took a bite anyway, grease dripping down his mustache. He swallowed and composed himself.

"My brothers and sisters," he said. The commotion of his people stopped, and they all stared at him. This was the first public address their duke had made in months. Koschei felt somewhat shaky, but nevertheless, he started. "You've been nothing but brave and faithful, and I have done nothing to reward it. Following such a successful streak—" he gulped, remembering the bodies they'd buried for that streak "—a celebration is due. My command to you until further notice is to rest, dance, eat, sing, fuck, and whatever else you might desire, so long as it does not infringe on the desires of another."

They watched him in silence, exhausted in their own right. Koschei could read they were not yet ready for festivities, but he'd concluded it must be better than spending days mourning. They gave him a half-assed cheer, and Koschei was off.

He sat at his desk, staring at the map. He pondered Morana's words from the night before. Goddess, he thought. Forces of nature, thousands of years... And just a man? He drummed the arm of his chair with nails, grown long in the meanwhile, biting bit the inside of his mouth and rubbing his temples with his other hand. *Am I desperate enough?*

He stood up and approached the large chest, bolted shut by his desk. Rummaging through it, he pulled out his saber and set it back in his belt.

He then left camp without explanation. His people were merry with songs and cheers and shouts, and they paid him no attention.

It took Koschei two days to negotiate the treacherous paths of the forests and the hills with his limp. He carried no food, for he would not need it. His only concern was his blind eye, since he could not see incoming threats from the right.

Heaving through snow and wet dirt had become much more tiresome, but he did not waver. When he saw it, he was certain it was the right spot, and he exhaled with relief. Facing him was a house made of rotten wood, orange light emanating from the inside. Haunting shadows danced in the windows, creaks and cackles and cracks accompanying them from the run-down place. That, and the house stood on two enormous chicken-like legs. Tracks as big as men were tall were stamped into the earth behind the four-toed feet. Dark feelings gripped him, and one last doubt tried to tell him to turn back. *Risk your life for the return trip*, it said. *There are worse things than death.*

Koschei did not listen. The door of the chicken-legged house slammed open, and at its entrance stood an ugly, hunched woman with unnaturally gray skin and bony fingers clutching a broom. It was too late to run now.

"My, my," the woman croaked, "the Korgyran smell was never heard of nor caught sight of here, but it has come by itself. Are you here of your own free will or by compulsion, my good youth?"

IVAN BOTICA

Koschei clutched his throbbing leg which was shooting pain up his thigh after the long walk. "Baba Yaga," he said. "I need your help."

When the duke returned in the early morning, the few that had not drunk their minds to oblivion were concerned. First, with the fact that no one seemed to have noticed that their leader had gone. Second, because he seemed not to be the Duke anymore. In his stead walked something not recognized by any. Something not human. Whereas he had been gaunt, he was now bone-thin. Faded pale flesh was strung over his skeleton, his eyes sunk deep into his skull, and his skin would have better fit a cadaver. His thick hair had grown sparse, and his menacing stature bent forward. Yet, the Duke's cloak was around the man, and his saber swung from its hip.

"My lord," the man named Toma said. Koschei looked at him with terrifying eyes. For a moment, Toma thought he saw them twinkle bright green. He refrained from saying anything else, and his commander went on into his tent.

Koschei sat behind his desk and waited. He knew she'd come this time. The entrance flapped open and blew a gust of snow in. He shielded his eyes with an emaciated hand, and when he lowered it, the familiar slender shape with charcoal locks stood before him. He gleamed and expected the same in return. It did not happen. It was not his Morana, the snow-cold lover, that had entered the tent. It was Lady Misery, the White Death. Her neck showed veins Koschei had not seen before. Koschei could almost feel the murderous pressure pent up in her head.

"Tell me it's not true," she said.

"Depends on what you're referring to," he said.

160

He blinked and she was three strides closer, almost touching the edge of the desk. He felt a cold tingle crawl up his back, and a fog began rising at his mouth. Ice started crawling over the desk like an infection, spreading outwards from one point until it enveloped the desk entirely. Then the ice exploded up and out, leaving Koschei's desk as no more than a heap of frost-covered splinters. Morana approached him through the gap.

"Did you ask a favor of Baba Yaga?" she said.

The duke, even with his newfound powers, felt smaller and more fragile than when he'd opposed rows of men in the field.

"I did, darling," he said, "but I did it—"

A spike of ice formed in the air and shot toward him, stopping short of his good eye.

"Never call me that again," she said. Koschei could have sworn that, once again, there was a tear building up above her cheeks. The spike dropped. She covered her face with one hand and shuddered.

Koschei rose from his chair and embraced her. "It was not vanity," he said. "You know this. I can be here for you now, see those mistakes you'll make, and we'll work together to fix them. You don't have to worry."

She pushed away from his chest but lowered her voice. "You are stupider than I thought."

Koschei grew more confused by the second, and she seemed to notice it.

"Your favor," she said, "separated you from Death."

He felt his eyes stretch open.

"Permanently," she continued, making sure he understood.

"I-I...thought—" he mumbled.

"You," she said with a sneer, "thought nothing. Had you done any thinking, you would have known that unnatural pacts are never a worthwhile venture." She turned her back to him and started walking out of the tent. "I am sorry. It could have been good," she added and left.

Koschei did not move for what felt like hours. Could he have been that stupid, to overlook something so obvious? No, he was better than that. No, if she could visit him, there is no reason for... No, none of it made sense... Yes, it was her fault. She'd tricked him into this. She'd planned this. She'd wanted him to do this, to be forever tormented for what she called *sins*. Use him as a murder weapon and a fuck toy and leave. And she thinks she'll get away with it?

But what if it was his fault? But how could it be? It was all because of her, which means... The weight of an eternity in this hell crashed down on him.

If they won't be together in love, Koschei would make damn sure they shared their pain.

Years passed. Ivan's forces were now no more than a few men scampering about in the mountains. Bounties were offered for their heads, land and title as reward. Koschei's war room was now made of brick and mortar, instead of sticks and canvas. Bronze braziers hung with burning coals from the walls. From his window, he looked out at his soldiers down by the bonfires, gutting traitors and deserters. A crown sat tight on his head, golden spikes rising from his skull like tiny stalagmites adorned with sapphires, rubies and onyx.

Behind him, a towering man in armor two fingers thick, brandishing an orange beard, spoke with a booming voice. "Koschei," he said. "Please test my patience no longer. Will you accept these terms as your penance and reward?"

Hunting and killing was his profession, after all. Killing gods would prove much easier with help. Koschei looked over his shoulder. Yes, lord Svarog."

Svarog held a scabbard out to him. Koschei snaked his fingers around the leather grip of the sword. He squeezed and pulled the golden pommel toward himself. As soon as the blade had left its sheathe, it sparked and hissed as flames danced around it.

"With this, you may kill anything with a soul. The thing ceases to exist entirely once you strike it down."

"What's stopping me from using it on you?" Koschei asked.

Svarog scoffed. "You find me foolish enough not to have set fail-safes?"

"Very well." Koschei grinned, revealing a row of paradoxically white teeth from beneath his grim visage. "I look forward to our cooperation."

Svarog grimaced and grunted in agreement. Then, enveloped in a ball of fire with no obvious point of origin, he was gone.

King Koschei walked through his war room to his throne, amid a great hall with velvet carpets. Music played in the place, a sweet cadence, swaying back and forth like a dance.

"For the living know that they shall die," he thought, *"but the dead know not any thing, neither have they any more a reward; for the memory of them is forgotten..."* He made his way up the steps and sat on his throne. *Except for me.*

Koschei the Hateful, they called him. Koschei the Traitor. Koschei the Tormentor.

Koschei the Deathless.

KRESNIK AND ZLATOROG

ROBERT NOROK

Dawn was breaking in the Trenta valley. Even though it was getting brighter by the minute, it would still be a few hours before the sun climbed from behind the mountains. Branimir was still lying in bed, listening to the chirping of birds, when he heard a knock on the door. He slipped into some clothes to retain the warmth from under the blankets, created flames in the fireplace with a wave of his hand, and made for the entrance.

On the other side of the heavy door stood a woman. He had seen her before but didn't know her name. She was breathing fast, her breath visible in the morning air.

"Are you the kresnik?" she asked him. No greetings, no good mornings. People from the village still distrusted him, as he was younger than the previous kresnik of their village. He hadn't had much work in the four months he had been there to prove himself a worthy successor.

"I am. What can I do for you?" He motioned her inside, away from the cold morning air, but she stayed at the door.

"My neighbor's son. He's missing. Come with me." She stared at him as if expecting him to follow her as he was.

Branimir suppressed a sigh, faked a smile and excused himself for a moment. He retreated back inside to put on some warmer clothes and his woolen coat. He put out the fire and told the lady to lead the way.

This time of year the sun only shone for a couple of hours in the narrow valley and wasn't yet able to melt all the snow.

Even though their destination was a thirty-minute walk away, they only passed by five other houses. The local people called this place a village, but to Branimir, it seemed more like a collection of scattered houses.

The woman led Branimir up the outside staircase and into the house. The air inside was heavy with smoke and the walls black with soot. It was too cold outside to open the small windows and let the smoke out, lest they lost the precious heat as well.

A younger woman greeted them and introduced herself as Dana. She showed Branimir to her son's bed and explained that it had been empty when she woke up and she couldn't find him around the house. Since he was nowhere to be found, she'd asked her neighbor to fetch the village's kresnik.

Branimir was unsure how to proceed. He thought the boy had probably gone for a walk, exploring the forest. He'd be back when he got hungry. Still, Dana expected him to do something, so he started by checking the bed. There was something hard under the covers. He removed them to reveal an axe.

"Why is there an axe in your son's bed?" Branimir asked as he started examining it.

"I don't know," Dana said and moved closer to inspect it. "It's not even one of ours."

They stood motionless as the realization slowly crept into his mind.

"A perta," they exclaimed at the same time.

Dana started sobbing and the older woman tried consoling her. Branimir had never had to deal with a perta before. He had heard the stories from his father, a kresnik like him, and from people in the inns. The pertas came in the night to take away misbehaving children, or so the tales went. Branimir had always thought it was a scary story to make children do as they were told.

A scared mother stood in front of him. She was looking at him, the local kresnik, the one who can control the elements and fight with spirits. Her only hope in finding her son.

He had to put on an air of confidence to reassure her. Truth was, even though he was able to track a perta, he had no idea if he could save the boy, or if he was even still alive. He left that last part out when he told them he'd do anything in his power to get the boy safely back home. He took Dana's nod while sobbing as a sign that she heard him and he let himself out the door.

Outside, he pulled power from his beech staff and concentrated. It was like listening for a whisper, except he felt it with his whole body. When magical creatures passed by, they left a trace that dissipated with time. Each creature had their own signature and, with time, he could learn to distinguish them one from another, but at the time he only felt that something had indeed stopped by the house during the night. Even though Branimir didn't know what it was, he knew the direction it had gone.

Once he was locked in on the trace, it was easier to follow it and stay concentrated. The trace led him further up the valley, away from the main road and down smaller paths, away from the houses. Branimir had no idea if the perta would ever stop, so he sped up his pace, hoping to eventually reach her and the child. The trail led him further away from the village and into a smaller and narrower valley, Zadnjica.

"Excuse me, sir?"

Branimir held back a scream and took a step backwards as he broke from his trance. He had failed to notice a young woman standing by the path. She introduced herself as Jerca, a young shepherdess from the Trenta valley.

"Are you going up the mountain?" she asked.

"I don't know yet." The path the perta took with the boy led to the mountains, but there was no telling how far it would lead him.

"Please, sir, if you see my friend, could you tell him to come back? Or at least let me know that he is well." She looked towards the mountains for a few moments, then back at Branimir. "He left to hunt a few days ago. He has never been gone for so long." She clutched her chest and looked back to the mountains.

Branimir's first worry was the child. Still, he'd keep an eye out for the missing hunter. "If I see him, I'll let him know you are waiting for him."

She sighed without moving her gaze away from the mountains.

Branimir excused himself and searched for the trace again.

On his right, a stream gurgled down stones and rocks as he continued following the perta. He was keeping a fast pace and was starting to breathe heavily. The path he was on was mostly used by hunters and woodcutters, which meant that he was among the first humans to use the path since fall.

Judging by the light, he had been following the trail for over an hour and it had brought him close to the end of the valley. The trace became stronger. He crouched behind a tree and started looking around. Up ahead, among the trees across a snowy field, he noticed an old woman with long white hair, draped in white fabric. Had she been in the snow, she would be impossible to spot.

Then Branimir saw a child running around the old woman. The child seemed unharmed and enjoying himself. Branimir concentrated and felt the trace coming from her, confirming his suspicion that she was the perta. He started looking around from his hiding point and coming up with an attack plan to bring the child back to his mother. He had never fought against a perta before and didn't know what to expect. The pertas were known to use their axes and this one had left hers in the boy's bed. This gave him a boost of confidence.

But why would she leave her axe behind?

Branimir dismissed the thought and concentrated on the battle ahead. He took a few deep breaths to calm himself and prepared to leap across the field.

Before he could attack, he felt a hand on his shoulder and as he turned, he saw a female face smiling at him. She was the prettiest woman he had ever seen. Her long black hair fell past her shoulders and rested on her white gown. He barely heard her whispered command to follow her as she took his hand.

She led him across the snowy field, the snow crunching under his boots. Everything was peaceful as they walked. He looked around at the quiet forest. In the snow, he could only see their footprints, one facing in their direction, the other facing away. A squirrel was running up a tree.

Something didn't feel right.

There was an old woman playing with a young boy up ahead. Branimir had a feeling they were important, but he didn't care at the moment. He felt warmth in his hand from the beautiful woman and cold in his feet from the snow.

Snow.

Footprints in the snow.

One in their direction, the other away.

Branimir felt as if a fog lifted from his mind. He remembered stories about beautiful women up in the mountains that help people by guiding them to safety. Sometimes they warned them about bad weather. He snatched back his hand. Something all the tales agreed was their physical characteristic that gave them their name: their feet were backwards. "You are a krivopeta!"

As he said the words, the air around them changed. The temperature dropped, the colors were less vibrant. The woman, while still beautiful, had an angry expression on her face. "You shouldn't call us that."

In a moment, everything went back to normal. Not the vibrant world, not the cold one; plain normal. Branimir had heard a gossip in an inn that a man had married a krivopeta once and she stayed with him until one day, when he called her krivopeta. She left him and he died of sadness not long after.

Her face was calm. She continued in a neutral tone. "I'm sorry for my outburst. We need your help, follow me." This time, she didn't take him by the hand. From the other side of the field, the perta was looking at them.

Branimir's plan for a surprise attack was busted and he was outnumbered. He could try running away, but that would mean abandoning the boy to whatever cruel fate they had in store for him. Fighting them there put him at a disadvantage. In the end, he decided to follow her without a word to where the perta and the boy were. The krivopeta nodded at the perta as they passed by and stopped a short distance further as she motioned to Branimir to sit on a stump.

"We need your help," the krivopeta said again, still standing. "Up in the mountains, someone has bound the Zlatorog."

Branimir had heard stories of the Zlatorog, the Goldhorn. The white mountain goat whose golden horns were said to unlock incredible riches. He was supposed to be immortal. Was someone actually foolish enough to try and get the riches?

"Why didn't you come for me yourself?"

"With the Zlatorog bound, my sisters and I are unable to move far. We ran into the perta and asked her to get you. We need you to free him."

"What's in it for me?"

The krivopeta studied him for a moment. "We'll let the child go. Isn't it your job to help the people from the village?"

Branimir felt his hands starting to shake. He crossed them and stood up in an attempt to fake confidence. "Why should I go up in the mountains when I can defeat the two of you?"

She walked around him and whispered in his ear, "Maybe you can take the two of us, that's true. But can you defeat my sisters hidden in the forest and get the child safely home? There are dozens of us."

Branimir couldn't see nor hear anyone else in the forest, but he wasn't willing to test whether she was bluffing. The child seemed safe and the krivopetas were known to help people, not harm them. He sighed and chose what he deemed the best option for him and the child. "Fine, I'll do it."

She smiled.

"Where should I go?"

After getting a general direction where to look for the Zlatorog, Branimir followed a path through the forest. Occasionally he caught some movement out of the corner of his eye, but ultimately couldn't decide whether the krivopeta was bluffing or not. He got to a large path that took him to the end of the narrow valley. As he walked, the steep slopes closed in around him.

When the path took a sharp turn to the right, he continued on a barely visible trail used by hunters that cut steeply into the mountain. Branimir soon found himself panting, grasping for air. He was gaining altitude fast, following a dry riverbed, occasionally climbing over small stone walls. It wasn't long before the forest was behind him and the trees made way for small shrubs.

Further up the steep slopes, he could see his destination up ahead and kept ascending. Underneath him, he could see the path he had walked so far. The view almost made him dizzy, so he kept his eyes up the mountain. Soon he was more climbing than walking and had to fasten his staff to his back as he needed both hands free. The bitter cold accentuated every sharp edge he found with his fingers to push himself higher. He wondered whether he was still on the right track and occasionally saw signs that people had passed by before him.

When he couldn't get further up, he crossed on a narrow ledge that cuts the mountain wall. He kept his gaze ahead, away from the bottomless pit on his left. He went slow, mindful of the small stones beneath his feet.

The sun was already high in the sky when he made it to the other side of the wall. The terrain leveled out and grass and shrubs grew around him again, making the trail visible once more. According to the directions given him by the krivopeta, he was near the area where the Zlatorog was being held captive.

He walked towards a saddle between mountains. On both sides, steep rocky slopes climbed upwards. Near the saddle, once the path started sloping down again, there was a small hut, used by hunters to rest and occasionally spend the night in. He entered and took a short break to catch his breath and get his bearings.

He closed his eyes and concentrated, drawing power from his staff. He started searching for magical beings and immediately sensed something powerful in close proximity. He focused on the feeling and followed it. The trace led him down the other side of the saddle, and once the path started moving away from the source, he started climbing up the left slope, following a trail.

After the final climb, he felt the source of the powerful energy from across a green meadow, dotted with colorful flowers. A giant black snake, its scales reflecting the sun in all directions, was slithering across a motionless white animal. The white animal was lying down with one hoof on the ground, as if trying to fight the snake to get up. When the snake's head perked up and looked towards Branimir, it revealed the white animal's head and his golden horns glistening in the sun. Branimir wondered what kind of powerful snake that was to be able to stop the Zlatorog. He had heard stories of magical snakes, his father liked to say he'd encountered some of them himself. The most powerful one would be Veles himself, the shapeshifting god of the underworld. But why would a god bind the Zlatorog?

The snake hissed and squeezed its prey. The Zlatorog let out a scream that echoed across the mountains. Branimir felt as if it were his bones being crunched under pressure, his eyes watering. The snake, keeping its gaze upon Branimir, slowly unwound from around the Zlatorog, leaving it to collapse on the ground. As soon as the scream subdued, so did Branimir's pain. Then the long scaly creature started to shorten and rise. Its features began to change; arms were growing from its body and its tail split into two legs. In a matter of moments, a hooded man stood in front of the Zlatorog. Branimir thought he recognized the man, but was unable to put a name to the face.

A shapeshifter, possibly even a vedomec. Branimir focused on the magical traces for a moment. Since the two weren't intertwined anymore, he realized that the strong presence he'd felt before was a combination of two powerful, yet distinct sources. He swallowed hard. He was expecting a strong opponent, but not another wizard.

"Go away!" the other wizard yelled across the plateau. "His treasure will be mine and mine alone!"

"I don't want his treasure, I'm here to help."

The vedomec stared at Branimir for a few long moments. "I've seen you around," he finally said. "You are the kresnik from the Trenta valley. Of course, you are supposed to help the people from the village. Together we can make him show us where his treasure is and then she'll finally love me."

Things clicked into place for Branimir at last. "You are the hunter from Trenta! You don't need to worry about love. I saw your girl earlier and she's eager for you to return."

A smile split the hunter's face.

"Leave the Zlatorog be, come back to the valley with me. Jerca is waiting for you down there."

The vedomec's smile left his face as fast as it appeared. "Jerca? The shepherdess? The only one I care about is Ančca, from the inn. She said she'd be with me if I brought back his treasures." The hunter grabbed one of Zlatorog's golden horns and tossed him aside. The Zlatorog barely responded, only letting out a small whimper. The hunter shook his head. "No matter. You're supposed to help me, so get over here."

Branimir clenched his teeth. "Actually, my duty is to protect the balance of nature. In this case, I have to help the Zlatorog."

"Then you are a fool." The vedomec raised his arms, his palms facing Branimir, and a gust of wind swept across the meadow, hitting Branimir in the chest. He planted his staff in the ground and gritted his teeth. It took all of his strength not to fall.

When the gust subsided, Branimir called forth a bolt of lightning to strike the vedomec, but he transformed into a snake and slithered away. Branimir needed a few moments before he could summon a new lightning bolt, but his opponent was faster each time.

Branimir moved towards the Zlatorog, but halfway across the plateau, a thick fog enveloped him. He called forth heat, but it only dispersed a small circle of fog around him. He could hear slithering around him, he knew the vedomec was preparing his attack, and he in turn prepared to strike the snake as soon as he saw him. Then he heard hooves hitting the ground behind him, and as he turned, a bull charged him, sending him flying through the air.

His body hit the ground, but his head hit something soft. He felt fur under the back of his head. He looked to the right and was face to face with the Zlatorog.

"Go away now, little kresnik, if you want to live," a voice bellowed from the fog. "You are no match for me." Branimir knew the vedomec was right. He fought at full power, yet couldn't land a hit on his opponent. He looked into the Zlatorog's eyes.

Branimir sighed. He still had a duty to protect the protector of the mountains.

"Don't worry," Branimir whispered. "I'll distract him and you get away." He tried to stand up but his strength betrayed him.

The Zlatorog nudged his head towards Branimir's belt. Branimir searched it for what the Zlatorog wanted from him. He found his knife and took it in his hand.

"Do you want me to fight him with a knife? I doubt it will work."

The Zlatorog shook his head. He took Branimir's arm in his muzzle and moved it so the blade touched his leg above the hoof and made a cutting motion.

"You want me to cut you?"

The Zlatorog increased the pressure of Branimir's blade. Then Branimir remembered another part of the Zlatorog legend, his healing abilities. His blade pierced the white animal's skin and Branimir watched blood gather in the wound. The blood welled up and started to leave a red trail in the white fur. When the Zlatorog's blood touched the ground, a beautiful red flower sprouted, the triglavska roža.

Branimir understood that the Zlatorog intended for him to eat the flower to regain his strength. He plucked a flower and started chewing it. His mouth exploded with sweetness. He saw his wounds close and his bruises heal. Each time he swallowed he felt a wave of heat wash over his body. He felt his strength return and with it a power like he'd never felt before. Branimir rose up and looked around. The thick fog still engulfed the meadow. He closed his eyes and tried to call forth heat. A fire was roaring within him, stronger than he ever felt, even with the help of his staff. He opened his eyes and the fog retreated in an expanding circle around him. The vedomec was again in his human form, standing with his eyes wide and mouth open. "How is that possible? Your power was too weak!"

Instead of answering, Branimir charged towards the vedomec, running like never before. The sound of his hooves beating on the ground echoed through the mountains, his tail flailed behind him. He hit the vedomec in the chest, this time sending him flying through the air. Branimir reared on his hind legs and for the first time realized he had turned into a bull.

He was standing on his two legs again when the vedomec summoned a new gust of winds. The winds were blowing harder and longer than before, but they didn't affect Branimir. He felt tingles in his fingers and the hair on his body rising. He summoned lightning to strike at his opponent. Bits of stone flew in the air as the lightning struck ground, but the vedomec managed to dodge it, transforming into a snake again.

This time, Branimir didn't have to wait to strike. Powerful thunderbolts appeared at his command, leaving a trail of scorched grass behind the vedomec. They were moving fast towards the valley, almost as if backtracking Branimir's journey to the meadow. Branimir noticed a pattern to the other man's movement and anticipated his opponent's next move. A bolt of lightning finally landed on the scaly body, flinging him across the air. The attack made the vedomec change back into his human form. He stood motionless at the edge of the precipice, high above the valley.

Before Branimir could offer the vedomec a chance to surrender, he heard the thundering of hooves on stone from behind. A glint of light blinded him temporarily as the Zlatorog charged by. His golden horns struck the vedomec in the chest, pushing him over the edge.

With a yell, Branimir ran over, only to see a black figure plummet down the mountain and land on the bottom of the precipice.

"Why did you do that? He was already beaten."

But the Zlatorog didn't wait or give an answer. Instead, he reared and let out a roar full of anger, or at least that's what Branimir felt as the sound hit him. The Zlatorog charged back towards the alpine meadow, grass and earth flying around him, leaving barren rocks behind.

"He is angry. We will have to calm him down," a gentle voice said behind Branimir. He turned and saw the krivopeta from before.

Before he could ask her when she got here, he noticed other women, other krivopetas, around, looking down at where the vedomec's body lay. They started singing in unison. He couldn't understand the words but still felt the sadness in them. He turned back to the krivopeta beside him and noticed tears in her eyes.

"Why are you sad? I thought you wanted the Zlatorog freed and his captor dealt with."

"I did. We did." She paused for a moment. "That vedomec was the son of one of our sisters. We always loved and cherished him, helped him hunt in the mountains. A few days ago he was determined to get the Zlatorog's treasure, to make a girl love him. Foolishness. We begged him not to. We warned him not to. But ultimately, our duty is to the Zlatorog and his mountains. We had to free him." She looked to the bottom of the cliff before continuing. "Still, we mourn the loss of our son."

They stood in silence for some time, listening to the sorrowful song with the echoes of the Zlatorog's rampage in the background.

"What about the boy?"

"We sent him back to his mother as soon as you left."

Branimir wanted to know more about the vedomec, but before he could ask her more questions, she turned to him. "You should go now; the weather is about to turn."

Branimir looked to the sky and saw dark clouds gathering. He did not look forward to making the climb down in the rain.

As if sensing his concern, the krivopeta shook his arm. "You are a kresnik with the power of a triglavska roža in you. Turn into a bird and you'll be back in the valley in no time!"

She was right, Branimir knew that, but he had shapeshifted for the first time mere minutes ago, without intending to. He had been running and changed into a bull. Was he supposed to throw himself into the emptiness and hope for the best? Should he start swinging his arms to trigger the change?

"Well done," said the krivopeta, who towered above him. "Now flap those wings and go home."

He did it again. He transformed without realizing it. He stretched his black wings, walked to the edge, and jumped off. Flying came easy to him. He could feel the wind beneath his wings, adjusting his feathers ever so slightly to allow him to soar through the sky.

He flew up, carried by the winds, with almost no need to flap his wings. He wanted to explore the mountains, but a low rumbling of thunder from the distance changed his mind. He searched for the valley he'd made his home and dove towards it.

As Branimir was nearing the valley, he had a harder time riding the air currents and felt like he stumbled in the wind.

He chose a clearing near some house to land on and he was beating his wings in order to reach it. He fell to the ground and rolled in the dirt, ending on all fours. He stood up and dusted off his coat, then looked around to check whether anyone had seen his ungraceful landing.

He tried to summon heat like before, up in the mountains, but he managed to increase the temperature around him only slightly. He sighed as he realized that his hope that the power gained from the triglavska roža would be permanent turned out to be nothing more than wishful thinking.

He went by the young woman's house to check if her son had really returned home. She was outside, getting ready for the rain, when she spotted him.

"I'm sorry to have bothered you," she said. "Looks like we didn't need your services after all. My son returned home after you left. I guess he went to play in the forest." She took a look at Branimir and frowned. "Where have you been? You look terrible."

Branimir nodded and waved her goodbye. He wondered whether she'd forgotten about the axe in the boy's bed or was trying to.

He tightened his cloak around him as he felt the first drops of rain on his head. A cold wind pushed him towards his home, where wood was already waiting in the fireplace.

FROM THE SWAMPS

MIHA TROCHAEL

I HAVE LIVED HERE for a long time. I remember the three oak forests that have decayed and the three new forests that have grown upon them. I have seen many people crossing the roots and witnessed their stories unfold. Happy, sad, gorgeous, and terrifying. Some of them live forever in people's memories—famous fights, broken hearts, and acquired treasures. Others are forgotten, only the earth under your feet guarding them deep down. It is one of these stories that I would like to tell you today. So sit comfortably, my dear child, and allow me to carry you back to the time of the old gods, before they were banished by the sound of church bells.

This is not an ordinary story; not the type often exchanged during long winter nights over hot flames, when waters are locked behind threefold ice and dangerous *bieses* loom through the woods. There is no Jarilo to steal his wife from the horrific *zmij*, no Perun chasing Chernoglov around until the latter finds safe shelter under a rock. Who we have here is a young woman named Jaroslava, after her grandmother. She is not threatened by an evil stepmother; no divine path toward marriage with a wealthy lad awaits her. But she is not dull either. Her family is known by every man, every woman, and child on this beautiful island, her homeland Ruja, as well as on both sides of Pjena, the Foam river. The Swantevic or

Svantovit's family became famous among Slavic tribes a lot of summers before their king Vartislav climbed up the King's Chair and way before the name of the Rujan god from Jarkun gained its greatest fame. Yet you might have never heard of them, have you? It is, after all, natural that the shine of gods cast shadows over their servants.

Still, the family's role was essential for many. As time went by, leaders of all tribes in the Lutician union headed to the Svantovit's homestead in the times of need. The guests left rich offerings in the nearby grove, where a huge stone Svantovit stood. In return, they acquired a marvelous white horse. That was Jaroslava's family's vocation for as far as their ancestors' memory reached. They were always settled there, always taking care of the sixty-headed herd of oracles. Until the horses shed their dark fur, the family trained them. Afterward, the best stallions left to serve their divine master at his temples. Thanks to that, Jaroslava lived in affluence and no one expected anything but a bright future for her children's children as well.

However, the gold thread of life is often tangled in unexpected knots. One can never fully predict what fibers get spun into their yarn.

Our tale started one late afternoon, shortly before the great spring celebration. Back then, it was a day full of work because no cleaning, baking or noisy labors were allowed the day after, and the fields should not be touched at all. Everyone knew their task. Year by year, these little rituals of Svantovite's servants to honor him and his mother Earth were repeated. Jaroslava's brothers woke up the fruit trees, shaking them for the fine crop. Since early morning, her mother baked honey buns shaped like a knotted rope to trap all upcoming danger in those loops and her father made sure that every single one of their horses got a bite alongside the human members of their family. Jaroslava's sister planted peas that day for them to grow well, with no fungus or pests destroying them. Meanwhile, Jaroslava had to clean Svantovit's statue and the whole sacred grove from old dead leaves that would be burned at dawn, as well as collect fresh young herbs for a special soup that would be prepared later.

If snow fell that day, that would indicate a hot summer awaiting us. However, the sun was shining bright; not a single snowflake occurred. The warm breath of the awakening spring actually brought Jaroslava joy after she had finally finished her tasks in the grove. With a wide smile, she walked alongside the corral when she noticed a foal on the wrong side of it. The horses, particularly the young ones, often desired to explore surrounding fields. People in the area knew to whom they belonged, and it had been long since the last sighting of a wolf. Still, the island was full of swamps where no helpful ear would hear a soul scream...

Jaroslava dropped the basket with herbs from her arms and rushed forward to the mischievous animal. She could already see the wild sparkle in the foal's eye as he turned around and fled.

"Stop!" Jaroslava yelled, but she kept smiling as she hurried after the joyfully scampering colt. For him, it was merely a game; he never ran too far and was always checking whether she still followed. Jaroslava, too, enjoyed this little distraction. And so, she playfully chased the colt, until they reached the first trees of the Ljutosh swamps.

Then the fun ended.

The wetland in front of them was no less hungry than others around the island. It waited, patiently, for unwary travelers to lose their life in favor of the dark ghosts living there. Jaroslava leaned against the nearest tree trunk and called the foal to return. She should have realized earlier what a dangerous place they were rushing towards. The animal ignored her completely. He stayed several steps ahead, carelessly grazing on early spring grass. Jaroslava slowly approached, and the colt remained calm. Apparently, the game was over for them both. But once her fingertips brushed over his butt, the foal neighed and bolted away. His hooves led him unerringly closer to the inscrutable morass hidden in the forest. Jaroslava knew the safe path through, but this poor foal had never set foot on it.

"Stop right there, you silly horse!" she yelled in desperation. Unlike before, the foal did not slow down to check on her. The red glow of the setting sun colored the trees the foal's tail flicked among in the distance. After she lost sight of the colt and could not even hear his hooves anymore, the time came for Jaroslava herself to stop. Above the tree canopies she could see the sky turning dark blue. The night was about to fall soon. The moon had been reborn just yesterday, and she had already strayed too deep into the forest. With a long sigh, she headed back.

"May the *vily* take good care of you..." she whispered. But three paces later, a terrible roar arose behind her. As if a harmed animal called for help. Or a drowning one.

Without a second thought, Jaroslava ran towards the scream. The sound stabbed her heart; she could not let the colt suffer, no matter the peril. Jaroslava stopped only as the darkness surrounded her completely, and the roar silenced. She was left alone, with just the chirping crickets and croaking frogs who kept disturbing the peaceful night. She turned around straight away, but no clear path back awaited her. Carefully, she tried to walk ahead, but it seemed the morass encircled her. She had no idea what part of the forest she had ended up in after the senseless run. With each step away from the piece of solid ground around, the earth under her feet wiggled and wobbled back and forth, threatening to devour her. Jaroslava decided she should not leave the swamps tonight. She was sure, more than ever, that she had crossed paths with a *bludni koren*, the mischievous wayward root waiting for travelers on the forest trails. It would be foolish to move now and get lost even further. People do not say for nothing that morning brings clarity to evening's opacity.

As the temperature started dropping, her breath turned into white clouds and her lips quivered. The early spring nights were still cold. It took her a while to blindly collect dry remains of last year's grass and suitable wood to start a fire. After creating a little pile in the middle of her safe piece of solid land, she dug into the soil under her feet. Their island was full of fire stones, so she quickly unearthed two gray pieces perfect for the job.

She shielded the pile with her body, bowed over it, and crashed the stones together. A few small sparks popped up and died immediately. Starting a fire this way was not easy, but with no other means, she had to at least try. A few times she even hit her own finger, splitting its nail. She bit her lip to to maintain silence. It was hard to swallow her pain, however, she worried to attract *corne zimenik* or other dangerous beings by letting the screams out. Still, Jaroslava felt so close to uttering a desperate cry. That night, she was supposed to meet other girls and young women for the spinning of the last yarn; the powerful thread able to protect from Perun's rage as well as Chernoglov's chorts or other bieses. Her tools should have been a spindle and distaff, not these stones. She should be sitting with her friends, having a lively conversation, not in this lonely place of death...

Thankfully, her effort was rewarded once a small flame began dancing over the hay. Smiling wide, Jaroslava cupped it with her palms and breathed in more life. She continued until the fire bit into the wood. That was the moment she let down her arms, straightened her back; and then jumped up with a high-pitched yell.

"*Kurva*," she cursed.

Right there, curled near the improvised firepit, a huge snake lay. Not far from where Jaroslava's hands used to be, its head rose from the ground, staring directly into her eyes. Jaroslava had never before seen such an animal. It was at least as thick as her own forearm, and its scales glowed like gold in the unsteady light. Although scared at first, Jaroslava soon calmed enough to notice the flames reaching dangerously close towards the snake. She grabbed the serpent and dropped it at a safe distance.

"Careful, little one!" she said, despite the animal's enormous size. It looked into her eyes again, as if saying *Thanks*. Or was it trying to tell her something else? Jaroslava could not break away from the stare until the snake turned its head. Jaroslava followed the motion. Suddenly, a wide path appeared right there, among the spiny bushes and wrinkled tree trunks. How did she not notice it earlier? It might lead her home, or to the foal... Should she try her luck one last time? The snake hissed and slowly slithered in that direction, beyond the reach of the amber fire.

"Wait!" She decided to follow the guide whose life she had sort of saved. After all, maybe the path led nowhere, and she would be returning to her firepit soon. The flames seemed strong now, so she needed to gather more wood anyway. Jaroslava grabbed a burning stick from the fire and rushed to catch up with the snake. When her look fell on its tail again, it was already beyond a curve. Like the colt earlier, the snake waited for her.

"Will you show me the way out of here?" Jaroslava whispered, a little bit nervous. Her guide, obviously, did not respond. Instead, a strong gust of wind wrapped around Jaroslava and her torch died off.

"Not again!" Once more, Jaroslava found herself in complete darkness. Or was it, really? Somewhere far ahead, she could make out a bluish glow among the trees. *Maybe someone's built a house here?* Or maybe the snake had led her farther than she had thought, towards the neighboring village?

But deep inside she knew what this meant. It could always be dangerous to lurk around a swamp, lake, or thick forest during the night, but particularly at the times when the earthy gates gaped open. Like tonight, on the last spinning day.

Being in service of Svantovit, the light god, Jaroslava used to be discouraged from the dark ways of Chernoglov's followers, those who knew how to see the future in the water's surface or find lost treasures buried in the ground. They were taught how to manage the dangerous powers to their advantage, while she has been instructed to avoid such practices. Yet, or maybe especially for that reason, she could not stop herself. It is not easy to always be a good girl.

"You're not leading me home, are you...?" It was not much of a question. And whatever the answer, she would not be able to return, because the path behind her had disappeared. No remains of her own fire provided guidance anymore. She gathered all her courage to keep walking.

Eventually, she found the bluish light source. It shone from within an ancient tomb, too old for Jaroslava's tribe to fully remember the ancestors who lay inside. She knew them only as *ljudki*, the little people, who were watching over treasures in their stone houses. And, according to the old teachings, exactly this type of light should be visible over hidden treasures. Jaroslava imagined the fuss that would rise if she strayed from the path in the woods and then returned home with arms full of gold... No one would be angry about her disappearance then!

The glow lost a bit of its intensity and supernatural coloring as she stopped in front of the entrance. More than anything, it now seemed as if somewhere deep down in there the ljudki sat around a big, warm fire. She even heard echoes of muffled voices. The snake crawled inside, leaving

Jaroslava alone with her conflicting thoughts.

But surely you know that she decided to go. After all, any other choice would bring the end to our story prematurely. She took a hesitant step forward before she frantically started looking for something among the folds of her dress. With relief, Jaroslava finally revealed a four-leaf clover she had stumbled upon that afternoon. She had taken it for good luck, a little blessing from her god after cleansing his grove. But now it should also protect her from whatever dangers or vicissitudes might possibly await her.

Carefully, she put it into her shoe before bowing to the low roof stone and stepping inside. The tombs were never too deep, but this one's corridor seemed nearly endless. The air around felt moist and heavy. Squinting her eyes, Jaroslava used her fingers to curiously trace deep damp cracks between huge stone blocks that were encircling the hallway from all sides. The farther she went, the louder the sounds of muffled voices grew and the more intense the light appeared. Originally it resembled a honeycomb held against the noon sun but now only the brightness of the sun remained. At one point Jaroslava had to shield her eyes, until she felt the space around her widen, and the glow gained back its pleasant firelight color. The voices were not as close as she had thought, but now came across as panicked, scared.

Jaroslava tried to whisper: "Don't worry, good ljudki, I'm not here to cause harm. I'm just seeking shelter from the cold." Her own words sounded a bit hoarse and her whole body trembled. But no one answered, only the smell of smoke encircled her. It remained up to her to make the first move and fully uncover her eyes.

She found herself in a wooden room, not a stone one anymore. She was, indeed, alone. Not even the snake was waiting for her. The light of the fire and the dense smoke, as well as the voices, were all coming from somewhere else.

But the room had immediately revealed its secrets, wrapped in shadows, and Jaroslava forgot everything else. Never had she seen so much gold and silver in one place yet, such a huge treasure. It looked exactly like the old tales promised. However, the same tales also delivered a warning. She had to remember to flee before the roosters start crowing, or she might stay trapped in there forever. But how could she take it all in such a short time, how could she leave so much behind?

Quickly, she knelt in front of the closest chest, full of silver cups. It had surely taken forever to create these, all with the perfect ornamentation. Looking around to ensure she was alone, Jaroslava dared to touch one of them. Nothing happened, no bad omen, and no one tried to stop her. *Why hesitate anymore?* She made a makeshift holdall using the long length of her skirt and started putting the cups inside.

But what was that? What changed, in her mind, as she reached for the gold bowl decorated with little birds?

Her mind, previously fogged by the glamorous view, warned her. After all, she had heard enough stories to know better. The ljudki were mischievous creatures; because of their trickery she might well bring home nothing but a dirty skirt filled with horse manure.

No, she decided not to risk that and be smart about this. She returned the cups and let go of her skirt. Then she found the biggest gold bowl in the room—to keep at least something, if the treasure was not just an illusion. However, she did not fill it with coins or jewelry. Instead, she swept dust, old spiderwebs, and dry leaves out of the room's corners with her bare hands. Because what seems useless to humans is often the most valuable thing in the netherworld.

It took a while to fill the bowl with the debris. As she finished, the whole place was so thick with smoke that she could barely breathe. Coughing, she sought a way out. The brightest light was coming from behind a heavy purple curtain on her right, so she pushed through it. What she saw on the other side made her drop her loot.

There, directly in front of her, stood a huge statue. It was much higher than any human and it watched her with one of its four pairs of eyes. Jaroslava knew the statue; she was used to seeing it regularly during annual celebrations and events, although never from this close. It was almost fully carved out of one very enormous beech trunk, crafted in the times before the crow had dropped Jaroslava, maybe before her parents and their parents, too. However, the statue should not be down here with Jaroslava, but in its own temple, just as Jaroslava should not be here with the statue. *How would that happen*, right?

And yet, as she forced herself to look away from Svantovit's four heads, she discovered his saddle and bridle hung on a nearby wall. Her heart began to beat faster. This was bad, much worse than looting in the ljudki's cave. She knew that if someone found out what she had done, the punishment could easily be death. All the smoke and voices coming through the temple's door... *Maybe the people outside have already known what she's done, and that was why they sounded so distraught?* At this point, she had no choice but to accept the consequences. Penitently, Jaroslava bent her head and went to face the crowd.

And once again, no one paid her any attention.

It only took a few blinks through the grease-filled smoke to understand why. The whole stronghold she had suddenly found herself in appeared to be on fire. The sun was high in the sky but nearly invisible behind the gray haze. The screams Jaroslava had heard and ignored before belonged to the people desperately running for more water. Some aimed to appease the blaze by pouring goat milk into the flames, to little effect. Whoever kept feeding the fire from the other side of the ramparts was doing a great job. It had already devoured the gate tower and taken several lives, while others fell victim to the enemy's arrows.

"This must be just a terrible nightmare!" Jaroslava blurted out. She even tried to pinch herself, but that did not wake her up. Instead, she felt the pain, and *one should never feel pain in dreams.* "How's this real? It can't be, it can't!" she screamed so loud that a few people glanced in her direction. But no one cared; they were risking lives to save their people's pride and dignity, their freedom. Who could possibly attack them this fast and this effectively without Jaroslavas family hearing a single word about it? Her head was spinning. She needed to figure out at least something, so she moved a little closer to the fires, trying to see the foe's banners, ignoring the increased danger she put herself in.

"Who did this? Who's attacking us?" she roared, running around with cheeks stained by ashen tears. "Help, anyone, help me, this can't be happening!" She wondered whether it could be her fault—her god's punishment for breaking the rules, entering his temple, and stealing his treasures... And then all thoughts left her mind as she bumped into someone. She had simply missed him, standing still in the smoke right in front of her, until she ended up in his arms. Whoever it was, his clothes were clean and did not smell of the omnipresent destruction. He hugged her and she cried into the bright yellow and gold cloth covering his chest.

"What's happening?! I wanna wake up! Wake me up! Please..." she sobbed while the day kept passing around them. A bit later she finally had no more tears to shed. She raised her face and noticed that the stranger could not be from the Rujan kingdom. His cheeks were covered with a black beard and long, no less black hair grew on his head. Upon it sat a hat with a red feather. Only the priests here did not shave their beards nor cut their hair. Although clearly a wealthy man, Jaroslava knew for sure that he was no priest.

"Who are you?" she wanted to know, feeling a bit dizzy.

Then she looked around and discovered that it was night again. No more fighting could be seen, only the dying snakes of the white smoke silently rising to the sky from the burned ramparts. Many people slept on the ground near the temple's entrance, cuddled in each others' arms, just as she was in the arms of this stranger until now.

"You saved me..." Jaroslava realized as she observed the smoldering ruins and dead bodies. Were it not for him, she would still be running around like a decapitated chicken or killed by a flaming arrow. Did she fall asleep in his embrace? *Where did the whole day go?* "Thank you." She shook her head, still confused.

"No, you saved me, actually." He grinned. "And this is your reward." He put a hat similar to his own on her tresses.

"Um, thanks... But I don't understand anything. What's happening here, I beg you, tell me!?" Jaroslava asked despite her suspicions that the answer would not please her.

"The mighty Jarkun fell." He looked at the temple. Right in front of their eyes, the night around them turned into a white day. Speechless, Jaroslava stared at foreign warriors walking into the temple and listened to wailing people and the sound of axes. Then a wall of the building got torn down so they were able to pull out Svantovit's statue. Jaroslava could not believe her own eyes, to see all of that occurring so shortly after she was worried about merely touching a few cups!

"Farewell, old adversary..." the stranger whispered, barely audibly, with a smile. Jaroslava did not notice it, nor did she see how his red tongue clicked against dangerously sharp teeth.

"What dark magic and lies are you showing me?!" Her sight could clearly not be trusted. Everyone knew that Jarkun was unconquerable. Not waiting for a response, she turned her back to the desecrated temple and ran directly towards the gate. After rushing through piles of ash, mass of sods, and charred oak columns, she stopped to stare at the enemy collecting their hostages. While she breathed heavily with anger, another night slowly fell upon them. Among the sleeping troops, in their firepits, the last remains of the wooden statue burned. She was so heartbroken that not even the touch on her shoulder startled her. Somehow, Jaroslava instantly knew it was no one else but the man she had tried to escape.

"Why didn't the reinforcement arrive from Korenica?" She kept trying so hard to wrap her mind around it, to make out any sense of what she had seen... He did not mock her as he might have. Instead, his hand reached out, and within the blink of an eye, a beautiful white stallion came to nuzzle against it. Jaroslava immediately noticed that the horse wore the bridle and saddle she saw recently (or *days ago?*) in the temple. Even without these, however, she would know to whom the animal belonged.

"There's nothing easier than to go, and see for yourself what happened with the famous Rujan troops." He patted the horse's neck and brushed blood from the white fur. Where the idea itself would have seemed stupid to anyone else, in Jaroslava's ire and misery, she did not think about it. "But I'm not allowed to ride Svantovit's stallion," was her only objection.

"Nonsense. He's from your family's herd. Today, he's here just for you!" The man stepped back slightly, and the horse hurried to bump his nose against Jaroslava's cheek. He pawed the ground thrice with his left hoof as if saying *Please*. Jaroslava knew she should not do it, but still, she jumped into the saddle. The man slapped the stallion's butt, and a moment later, the horse and Jaroslava were gone like the wind. They flew over the tops of trees, through the white clouds, and scared flocks of birds. This way the stallion brought her swiftly to the other stronghold that was usually many hours in the saddle away.

She found herself in the middle of Korenica, surrounded by plenty of people, more than she had ever seen in one place. Most of them were warriors ready for a fight. And yet, no help had arrived... As she got off the horse, the horns sounded and excited voices arose.

"A messenger from Jarkun! Granza has returned with news!" cried out the guards at the gate. Jaroslava walked there to see what was happening. A couple of people had brought a man with a bleeding arm and tired face through the main gate. Promptly, they led him to the biggest building in the stronghold. The commotion in front of it made one of its inhabitants come out even before anyone called for him.

The messenger Granza bowed briefly, just a quick move, no doubt to avoid pain, and pushed words through his sore throat: "Jaromir, we must act fast. Jarkun needs our help immediately. I saw the Danish army and we are strong enough in number to gain the victory."

"Is that all you're bringing to me?" the man called Jaromir asked.

"Also this, from their king's advisor, who truly leads the troops." Granza handed over a scroll.

Jaromir smiled, swiftly broke the seal, and started reading its foreign letters.

"I got out only thanks to a trick... What I've told them will divide their forces and send a part of their fleet to us." Granza puffed up his chest. He seemed proud of himself for, as he believed, outsmarting the enemy.

"Hmmm," Jaromir grunted in disinterest. "Come, let's go inside and talk about everything with my brother." Then he added, to the people listening to them eagerly: "Soon we'll announce our decision, be patient!"

Jaroslava, who had been listening in on the discussion,

decided to wait together with the others. She was excited to be here and see all these strong warriors finally move to crush their foes. When the time came, Granza, Jaromir, and one more man came out of the house. Granza seemed especially sullen and the newcomer somber, while Jaromir took the lead. He began explaining how Jarkun was gone, talking about how they no longer had the favor of their old gods, and how they must think of the people still alive, not lives or ground lost...

"What? Who are the two with Granza, anyway?!" Jaroslava growled. An explanation was not expected, yet her unwanted companion was suddenly standing right next to her, instead of the horse which had vanished. And she could not miss the hoof that now stood at the bottom of his leg, replacing his foot. But Jaroslava said nothing; it would be dangerous to make him aware that she had noticed.

"Don't you recognize your own kings?" her guide asked. Hearing him, she frowned. These men were surely not her kings. "Tetislav and his younger brother Jaromir, grandsons of Vartislav," he added.

How many years had actually passed since she had chased the foal?

"Then what is Jaromir talking about? It's not time for words..."

Her companion sneered. "I think they're surrendering."

She swiftly shook her head. "Never. No Rujan king would ever bow in front of a Christian—or a Dane."

"Indeed, Tetislav doesn't seem very happy about that." He tilted his neck slightly as the older royal brother agreed abruptly with what had been said. "But it is how it is..."

"I will no longer listen to this!" Jaroslava turned around and headed straight for the gate, towards a safe ford through the marshes protecting Korenica from all sides. With her first step on the footpath, thousands of other people were rushing in the same direction.

The Korenican men who by kings' order could not protect their stronghold anymore were plunging tips of their weapons into the soil on both sides of the path to seal their loss. Together with the roosters, they welcomed an unhappy morning. The Danes had already emerged from the port and Jaromir led them safely through the dangerous bogs and pools encircling the stronghold. Unlike the ashamed warriors, Jaroslava refused to be defeated without a struggle. Hearing the familiar sound, she asked her companion promptly:

"Don't you hear the red chanticleer crow?"

He only smirked, not worried at all. "That must be his last song of glory for the times that will come no more." With these words, he looked up, over the walls of Korenica, at the three columns of smoke which stained the blue sky right above the places where the three local temples used to be.

Jaroslava's shoulders dropped. "Why are you doing this to me? Just take me home!" she begged.

Remarkably, he nodded. "My pleasure, hop on!" He turned around, but Jaroslava was not excited enough to do such a move recklessly.

"You must swear that you'll take me to my home and nowhere else!"

"I'll do as you wish." He took Jaroslava on his back. She grabbed his shoulders and pressed her thighs against his waist so as not to fall, yet she didn't feel very safe. Shortly after they flew through the air, no slower than she had gone earlier, in the white horse's saddle. This time, however, they hardly went close to the heavenly heights. Her legs often tangled in long weeds, wattles, or sharp rosehip thorns.

"What do you have in your shoe, Jaroslava?" he called over his shoulder as another twig lashed against her calf.

"It's nothing, just a little leaf from Svantovit's grove..."

"Cast it away, it's heavy like a stone and it's slowing us down."

His deep growling voice gave her no choice so she tried to reach her foot. "I can't do it unless you stop, or I will fall!" she yelled into his ear.

He took her shoe himself and tossed it away. Right after that, they gained height. Only the branches of the tall trees kept whipping her as a storm roared over their heads. Before they reached the destination, she lost her second shoe, too.

She was foolish to hope for a peaceful landing. As they were flying over her home's roof, he threw them right into the chimney. How was that even possible, through such a tiny hole? Jaroslava had no time to think about it. She only saw a light at the end of the dark tunnel. Then, suddenly, she stood inside of the house. Black clouds lifted all around the room and blinded Jaroslava's senses for several eyeblinks. She coughed and coughed even after the ashes settled.

Then she finally saw the familiar walls but could hardly recognize the house's furniture. And she stood there alone; neither her parents, siblings, nor her worrisome companion was around. She hoped to find someone outside. However, after running out of the door, she did not see even the horses in their corral.

"Show yourself, you shameful trickster, I have not asked for this!"

As she finished the sentence, he hobbled from behind the building. He was hunched, and his long, cow-like tail was whipping around angrily.

"Oh, uh, you're heavier than you seem. You've ruined my back," he complained, but Jaroslava could not bring herself to care.

"What happened to the herd, where are our horses?!"

"Priests of the Christian god took them." He shrugged.

"Are they dead?"

He straightened his spine, the bones cracking ominously. "They were sold to foreign places, faraway..."

Well, at least they survived, she thought. "And where's my family?! Where's everyone?!" With a loud laugh, he disappeared. Then a whisper reached her ear:

"I've heard some voices from the swamps..."

Jaroslava jumped like a startled frog under the touch of his cold breath. She did not even look backward as she hurried to where all her troubles had begun. Soon, she noticed a bunch of people moving something heavy towards the deepest part of the bog. But they resembled no one she had ever known. Once she got closer, Jaroslava stopped among the trees, terrified. The thing they were dragging through the mud? It turned out to be the stone statue of Svantovit from their sacred grove.

"This can't be...!" With horror in her eyes, she approached the group and tried to remove the ropes tightly secured around the statue. They had made the knots strong, yet she succeeded with one.

The men swore.

"Damn, tie it properly so it won't slip out again!" one of them yelled at the rest of the workers. Neither of them had seen Jaroslava unraveling their loops. She would hardly be able to escape if they knew. But at some point, she had to accept that it was not in her power to save the statue.

Staring at her bare feet, she walked back to the grove—only to find a wooden chapel in the place of her dear Svantovit. *When did the foreigners have the time to build this?* Jaroslava wondered, full of grief. She needed to see a familiar face, anyone but the bies who had brought her here. Maybe her mom or dad had returned? She went home with hope.

And indeed, she recognized the man who stood there, knocking at the door. Although, she had only gotten to know him just recently. It was the older of the two brother kings, Tetislav. He had arrived with his retinue and cart. Jaroslava frowned; these kings had not won her sympathies so far.

"*What are you doing here!?*" she mumbled. Then the door opened, and a young woman asked him exactly the same. That put a smile upon Jaroslava's face.

"You have every right to send me away, just hear my words before I go," he pleaded, and the woman agreed to listen. "I've repurchased each piece of your former land from the Christians. You needn't worry about your home anymore. I'm also bringing gifts. The rest of my bounty from Pomorsko as well as the stones saved from Jarkun's graveyard and temple." His arm waved towards the cart. "The choice is yours. But personally—" he winked at her "—I think it's time to get the Danish shrine built in your grove razed..."

While they talked some more, Jaroslava, hoping she was still invisible, dared to go closer and look at the great stones. Most of them were simply regular and could be brought here from anywhere. But one she recognized. It depicted a one-headed Svantovit holding a huge horn in his hands. Four of these, each slightly different, used to be in front of the main temple, as she remembered. With sadness, her fingers brushed over the sacred *kamen*.

"Nonsense!" The joyful female voice from the door distracted Jaroslava again. "Stay however long you want. You are our king who has brought pride back to my family! You and your men, come in!"

The men in question laughed and hurried inside even before Tetislav moved. One of them patted his back, whispering:

"I told you so. Just leave your shame at the doorstep. She's beautiful, and I bet she has no husband yet..."

"Shut up, you fool!" Tetislav punched him in the shoulder, but he did not appear really upset. They all seemed tired and so did their steeds.

Later, the same woman came out to take care of them. Tetislav joined her, while his men ate and drank with her family.

"I couldn't bring back the herd, my deepest apologies,"

he said, helping her with the buckets of water. She nodded silently, her cheeks turning a little red. Jaroslava found peace in watching the two dancing around his party's brown mounts and asking one another's forgiveness for only half-unwanted touches. Until the night fell over, and they disappeared back inside, Jaroslava kept her eyes on them. She actually considered going with them, too. But a loud sound, as if thunder struck out of the blue, drew her attention away.

She looked around and noticed a blaze flaming in the swamps. Despite the thing seemed to be getting closer, for a while yet she could not recognize it. The night fully darkened before she finally figured it out. A burning barrel was rolling right towards her. She tried to jump aside from its path, but it changed direction to follow her.

"Dammit!" With the flames at her heels, she ran into the darkness. A lone, rocky path led Jaroslava to the unknown. Deep in her throat, she felt the muddy taste of blood. Although she stepped on a few sharp stones, she could not slow down, or the blaze would devour her. She had stopped looking over her shoulder a long time ago and saw nothing in front of her until a huge, red brick building appeared. She rushed in and slammed the heavy wooden door closed right before she heard the sound of the barrel crushing against the wall.

This building was bigger than anything she had ever seen. In some spots, she did not even catch a glimpse of the ceiling. No light shone inside, and the moon revealed just a little bit of her surroundings to her. However, she felt like she should not be there. Something was off, she did not belong. She searched for another door that might let her out. The stone floor tiles became stained with blood from her sore feet as she passed over them. Instead of escaping, she entered a significantly smaller room. *Maybe one more door*, she thought as she reached for the next knob.

Before she managed to push it, someone knocked from the other side.

Tap, tap, tap.

"Jaaa-rooo-slaaa-vaaa," called a voice.

"Enough already!" she screamed and swung the door open. No one was standing there; only the moon was present, lighting up the narrow room. Thanks to that, she noticed the Svantovit's stone from Tetislav's cart. Although she had seen it in front of her own house just moments ago, it got visibly older, the depiction on it more dingy or faded. It appeared lodged deep in the wall, the legs of the depicted figure pointing north and its head turned southwards.

"What? Why is it here like this, why didn't they leave it in the grove?" She furrowed her brows.

Her companion lazily leaned against the red brick wall nearby. "It's lying here as the king beneath it lies, lulled to sleep in Morana's embrace..."

"I just saw him doing all fine, what are you talking about, you liar?" She rushed out, and despite each step causing her pain, she did not stop.

"Where are we going?" His curious voice would not allow her to escape.

"You go wherever you want, to Nava, perhaps, who cares! I'm going to Jas, to Chernoglov's stronghold. His sorcerers surely know a trick to get me out of this misery!"

"Do they?" her companion sang skittishly. "Let me help!" Waiting for nothing, he pushed her so hard she fell.

Instead of hitting the grass, Jaroslava ended up in water, facing downwards. She panicked and swallowed some of the liquid involuntarily. Despite that she managed to pop her head above the surface just in time, before losing her breath forever. Wet hair sticked to her face. She tried to remove them from her eyes and her fingers ended up wrapped in smelly green slime. Soon Jaroslava noticed that all her hair and shoulders were full of frog scum.

"Are you trying to kill me?!" She lashed out at the man grinning from the bank of the pond she had ended up in. For a second, Jaroslava forgot who he was and regretted her question almost immediately. Thankfully, he said not a word about that. Looking around, she recognized an old forest and a bog. Jas had always been the wettest part of the Rujan kingdom...

"So, where's the stronghold?" she wondered aloud. His sight turned left, and she found nothing there, only a tall hill with young trees. "Wait..." Finally, it clicked. They were viewing the remains of a fortification. Jaroslava crawled up the hill, unsure of what she hoped to see behind it. What she actually saw was a rye field.

"Did you forget? The old times are gone..." His voice carried a trace of mockery. Jaroslava's knees buckled, and she just crumpled onto the grass.

"There's no escape, right?" She gestured helplessly with her hands.

"If you are tired, maybe we can rest in the hut over there," he offered. She was honestly worried to glance where he pointed to. But she did and noticed only a little cozy hut. One that probably never existed in Jaroslava's time. What bad thing could she possibly encounter in such a place?

"Fine!" She raised herself from the ground. "Please, let me rest."

"Nothing is certain in our world," he purred. "But why not give it a chance...?" And so they moved forward. Before they reached the building, the abandoned stronghold disappeared in the distance. He stepped aside for Jaroslava to open the door. The inside of the hut felt warm; Jaroslava might easily fall asleep here.

"There's a bed in the backroom," he offered again. She should have known immediately that it would not be this easy if her companion suggested it. Still, she followed. And indeed, the bed was not empty. An old woman lay in it, she seemed sick.

"Is she okay?" Jaroslava asked, worried for the hut owner.

"Will be soon," he promised, then added promptly: "She's very ill, actually." The woman lay asleep but woke up as she sensed them in the room.

"Why did you want me here? Who is she?" He must have had a motive, another way to torture her, Jaroslava knew it for sure. He took his time with the reply. First, he reclaimed the hat he had given Jaroslava in Jarkun. She had fully forgotten about it. Only thanks to a little miracle she had not lost the hat during everything. Once he had it back, he said:

"Ask her yourself."

How, she won't see me like everyone else, Jaroslava thought. But after she eyed the woman, Jaroslava realized she was looking directly at her. So, Jaroslava tried:

"*Dobre jutro. Koto jis?*" 'Good morning. Who are you?'

"*Joz jis Gülicyna, kåtü töjis?*" 'I'm Gülicyna, what about you?'

"*Jaz jism nikoto, babka, kaba vot stareg caso.*" 'I'm no one, grandma, a ghost of the old time.'

Despite Jaroslava's rather creepy answer, Gülicyna's face lit up like the sun that had begun hesitantly peeking in through a small window. There were almost tears of joy in her eyes. Jaroslava wanted to ask so many questions, but she noticed her worrisome companion move to stand at the head of the bed. He reached for Gülicyna's hair and started caressing her with his claws. Unable to see him, Gülicyna must have believed the wind was touching her. But Jaroslava saw his hungry smile clearly. It did not change for a while, not even after the voice of a rooster from the backyard filled the room.

Jaroslava piped up harshly:

"Don't you hear the white chanticleer crow?!"

Her companion nodded slowly, saying: "That must be his swan song for a people who will talk no more..."

"Wha—?" She did not have to finish the question. As her eyes dropped from him, back to Gülicyna, Jaroslava noticed the change. The grandmother had passed away, and Jaroslava sobbed. "Why was she so happy to see me?"

"Not to see you but to hear you. She'd had no one to speak with, not in the language of her childhood, for so long. Poor Gülicyna... Everyone else who spoke it has died before her."

Jaroslava blinked in surprise. *Which language do the Rujans speak, then? People can forget their gods, even their past, but how would they lose their voice?* "You lie! And it's your fault that she died, what did you do?!"

"I swear I've done her no harm. Her time has simply passed. And so did ours. Let's leave before her daughter finds the body."

Knowing that he was probably right, Jaroslava walked out of the door. In front of the hut, a woman holding an older man's horse noticed her.

"*Wölkeen büst du un wat maakst du hier?*" she asked, visibly disturbed. But Jaroslava understood nothing. Did she recognize a Saxon dialect in the words? Hopelessly, she looked at her companion. All he had to say was:

"We should run!" And so they ran.

The woman yelled something after them, but she had just brought a doctor for her old mom. She could not leave to chase after a possible thief. But Jaroslava did not know this. And regardless, she felt as if someone was chasing her. She stopped only after she had no strength to keep going anymore. The *bies*, however, kept on her heels without trouble.

"What do you want from me, you *chjudac*?!"

"I want your hand, my dear sunshine!" He guffawed. In a single move, he grabbed her hand and twirled her around nine times, as if they were dancing. Jaroslava's vision blurred, she could barely catch her breath. Once it came to an end, the night ruled again.

They stood in a cold, wet forest, snow falling, and her toes sank into the mud.

She decided to trick him because she saw no other way back.

"If you wish me to stay with you, we must first return to where we met. I left the flames burning, let me put them out before every tree catches fire."

He pointed to the left. "Then go!" Wayward lights rose out of the swamps around her and shone the path. She did not believe him, though. *How can it suddenly be so easy?*

Hesitantly, she shifted her weight from foot to foot.

"Unless you choose to join me, of course..." he said seductively. "All it takes is a few steps forward. It's nice on my side, calm. Your heart is good, but a terrible future awaits your bloodline... Follow me one more time, and you can avoid it."

Jaroslava wrinkled her nose. She had not thought the choice would be hers. "You showed me all this hoping to break me? That I would give up and leave with you? So powerful and still so ignorant... You understood nothing about me and my people, did you?" She felt proud, not crushed as he wished for. "We are always willing to die resisting, rather than submit to servitude. Even if the chances are low, we refuse to go without fighting. And now, the tears are already shed! I know what to expect, thanks." She granted him the stare of a shrewd fox. "I'm going to make sure that my children and the children of their children will never conceive a hatred for our land, whatever the land brings to us. Besides—" She overheard a distant sound of freedom and stopped. "Don't you hear the black chanticleer crow?"

"That must be his farewell song for me... We'll meet again one day. Til the time comes." He doffed his hat. As he bowed, Jaroslava noticed two horns in his dark curls.

Afterward, he crawled into a nearby hollow willow. Only two yellow eyes still watched her as she slowly walked away.

Back on the path where she had chased the foal, no remains of her firepit awaited Jaroslava, but the lights led her through the swampy forest until she reached its edge.

The new morning was just starting to emerge from the east. In the distance, she could see the corral full of horses and her home. Something still felt odd, but she was back.

The family welcomed her with tears streaming down their cheeks. As it turned out, a year and a day had passed since the muddy foal returned from the swamps. However, their beloved daughter had disappeared without a trace. They worried that she had died, but kept leaving sacrifices to Svantovit for her safe return.

Jaroslava apologized from the depths of her heart for the distress. She had also tried to explain the smelly frog scum in her hair, but instead of it, she had realized her shoulders were full of gold scales, no bigger than duckweed leaves.

That year's summer was unusually warm. And Jaroslava never stopped seeing those two yellow eyes in her dreams.

I have lived here for a long time. I remember the three oak forests that have decayed and the three new forests that have grown upon them. I will be here to see three more, but through all of the epochs, I have witnessed only a few stories like the one of the Rujan kingdom. Great heroes, as well as traitors, and great sorrow are always born in great battles.

While people die and nations disappear, I persist and see them repeat their old mistakes. Sometimes the small, brave ones resist, hold their ground against the big, smug ones; and it is beautiful, although no less sad. In the name of faith, the blood of millions quenches my thirst and their meat feeds my hunger as my children fight over my body. One day, even I will lie as still as the dead under the roots.

But who will remain to remember that?

TRAVELING SPRING
LIDIANA BUNDA

Sunday, February 16th, 2048 - Ukraine, Zaporizhzhia

MY FATHER ALWAYS TOLD me to write out my dreams to figure out what they mean and what our subconscious is trying to tell us so we can better prepare for future circumstances. He tells me that my dreams are both my subconscious and the world trying to get me to understand patterns that need to be changed or predict things to happen and correct them to make that change. Our dreams are magical, they allow our subconscious and intuition to speak. Here I'm starting a separate journal than from my regular journal so that I can compare the vividness of the dreams I've been having lately that I think are interlinked and connected but don't know how yet. Both my dreams and intuition tell me that they are and that they're trying to tell me something, so in this journal I'm going to try to figure out what exactly they're trying to communicate to me.

I'll write out my daily journal entry here as well to see how my dreams may intertwine with my daily life, and I'll start with today. Because we move often and the position of the stars always affects future outcomes and guides our dreams, I'll also give our location and note down when it's the first night we slept somewhere, because my mother always said the dreams you have when sleeping the first night in a new place are significant and prophetic. So here's the dream I had the previous night. Continuing on, I'll add everything in chronological order.

I'm cleaning and preparing the house for visitors. I feel so absolutely preoccupied and worried about my mother-in-law judging my house that I need it to be spotless, even if that means not sleeping and cleaning through the night. I'm older in my dream, I'm no longer 16 but now 21. The window is open, letting the cool spring air come in and dry off the floor that I had just washed. The sunlight that gets brighter each day comes in through the window and I know that by the time it reaches my husband's eyes in bed he'll be awake.

All of a sudden, I glance up from my cleaning and see the weather change outside the window. Not a slight change but a significant one. It moves from snow to rain to sun and as the clouds graze across the sky it changes each time. I'm frozen in place, confused and not sure whether to go outside to check it out.

The unpredictability of the weather eventually leads me to the window to look up at the sky. And outside, in the sky, I see the snow and the sun battle each other as if they're in a tournament ring with the clouds as their referees. The warmth and the cold clash against each other, simultaneously creating and melting frost on the flowers here at my feet. Finally, though, in the end, the warmth and the sun cross the center and defeat the cold and the snow, creating a new constant rhythm of sun and warmth with the cold gone.

Confused, I go back inside. I see my husband rubbing his eyes awake and asking me to come back to bed and sleep with him. Because I'm already up, I make an excuse that I need to go plant seeds outside, now that the weather is consistently going to stay warm.

I go outside now, forgetting about my chores, and each seed I plant feels like a deep spiritual or sacred connection, as if what I'm doing in this moment will affect the outcomes of the future. And I belive it will. What I plant now will create an abundant harvest for us in the future, the true wealth of a good life.

The holiness of this moment between me and the earth fills my heart with hope and happiness as I wish each of the seeds a healthy and prosperous year ahead. My mind drifts to the circle of life that seeds have each year and my own connection with them and how I aid to their own life and they do to mine. It feels that, just like the earth has its own circle of life, we have ours, and we're both born from each other and die from each other. Life is at the center of everything, both living and giving life.

I continue to prepare for my mother-in-law. And before I know it, it's tomorrow already and she's here. She immediately makes her way into the kitchen to start unloading her bags of ingredients that she brought to make pancakes. We spend the day in the kitchen, cooking with each other as relatives make their way in and out of the house. This is happiness to me, having all those I love come to see me and spend quality time with me. A few people parade in the streets, but mostly spend their time with their families.

It immediately jumps to the next day where the streets are full of young people having fun, playing games, courting each other. I observe all the men searching for wives and I think back to this same time three years ago, when my husband did the same with me. I hear the whisperings of mothers planning their sons' and daughters' weddings to come in the spring, and I see the streets are filled with colored ribbons, beads, food, plates, drinks, and desserts, and happiness fills the air of this youthful day.

Then the next day arrives just as quickly as the previous one did. My husband and I are packing up a bag of food to bring over to my parents' house. We're soon on our way and we pass other young couples in the streets, also on their way to visit their parents and in-laws. My mind immediately drifts to each of them, wondering if they're excited or nervous, or if they're expecting their parents to continuously ask when they'll have a baby, just like mine always do. And because it's not far, we shortly arrive and start eating breakfast together and chatting.

My parents have invited others over and in no time at all there's a small party happening in their house. As soon as my mother asks my husband about grandchildren and when she'll get them, my embarrassment ends this day in my dream.

I then wake up into the next day of the week, sitting up in bed. My husband is already up and putting on his snow clothes. He's so excited and can't wait, it's absolutely adorable. He asks if I want to join him, and even though I hate the snow, I say yes. We head out in our warmest clothes to join the village at the top of the hill where everyone is sledding. I only go down the hill twice before I'm winded from continuously climbing up and I decide to head back. On my way back to our house, I see and hear all the children throwing snowballs at each other and playing with their snow castles with their older brothers and sisters.

The days continue to come and go as I fall asleep and wake up the next day within my dream.

The next day comes around and again it's another full day of visiting family. We all share times of hurt with each other, and continue to eat pancakes together, and most importantly, we spend time listening to each other and forgiving each other any hurt or pain we've caused. It's a day of new beginnings. And as I look up at the hill, where we'd sled down a few days ago, I see the snow melt, and I glance over at my seedlings, and I see small green sprouts poking out of the ground.

Time for some dream reflection now. I know that family was the biggest theme in my dream. Family is absolutely everything to me. I don't know where I would be in life without them. And the setting was definitely where we are located now, Zaporizhzhia. And I think, maybe because we don't have family here, and I'm so excited to finally see my family again in the next few weeks, my dream is centered around the theme of family. I don't know, though, I'll ask my dad again because he always knows everything.

Monday, February 17th, 2048 - Ukraine, Zaporizhzhia

My dream last night was the exact same again. Not a single detail changed, which makes me feel like it must mean something. I just don't know what.

Today we're spending the day with acquaintances, all my parents' friends and their children. None of them I'm really close with, though, so I'm just spending the day observing everyone's interactions and in my own thoughts. I'm excited to see my cousins again when we move. I've missed them a lot and the approaching spring always reminds me of how close I am to seeing them.

This place is new to me, not just where we're staying, but the whole town. I haven't been here before but my parents have and they're at least familiar with the setting and some of the people. The most noticeable thing is that people are preparing for some kind of week-long spring festival. Their preparations are unfamiliar to me but I find them quite intriguing and I'm at least a little bit curious about the festival, the traditions, and the folklore that they have here.

I follow my dad to the village today, where he sells fur coats that he's made. This in between season of the end of winter and the beginning of spring is warm. People used to call it "unusually warm" each year, but now they've acknowledged the warmth and the dryness that exist as a normality. With my father being a tanner and making fur coats out of animals to sell, the shortening winters have hurt our family a lot, and caused us to migrate more than usual these past ten years or so. When I was little, we would stay in about 3 places a year, and now we're moving almost every month just trying to chase the winter so people would buy from us.

But it's not all bad, because the weather will hit one area very hard and give it extreme snow for a prolonged period of time, and that's when I know we'll be moving there and staying a little while longer than normal.

But today, in the market with my dad, we didn't sell a single coat.

Tuesday, February 18th, 2048 - Ukraine, Zaporizhzhia

Same dream again, this time I do remember one single difference. The weather in my dream stopped changing and instead stayed the same in the beginning, when I was cleaning the house. Also, the seeds that I planted never grew, and the snow disappeared. Instead, people were playing in the sand as if it were snow on the one day we went sledding. And it felt natural in my dream, but thinking about it now, it sounds weird.

But the same routine repeats today as it did the past few days. I go with my dad, I observe, we come back home, and we sleep.

At dinner I hear my parents talking about moving up the date to leave here and that gets me excited because then I'll be able to see my favorite cousin, Valeria, even sooner! They said that it could be as soon as within the next two weeks!

I can't fall asleep tonight because I'm too excited to leave here and I don't end up dreaming again for a while.

Sunday, March 1st, 2048 - Romania/Serbia, Vladimirovac

The ground has a light fog covering the dewy grass. The air, still cold, wraps around my body as the bright rays of the sun begin to rise from behind the mountain. I don't recognize where I am, but I know it's my home and I'm sitting in front of the house, looking up at the mountain. The warmth of the sun warms my cheeks as its morning rays hit me. The smoke from the chimney behind me then warms my back. Down the dirt path that leads away from my home, towards the river and the mountain, I see a man walking in my direction. Again, I don't recognize him but I know he's my son. I look down at my body and realize I'm now older again, no longer the teenager I am in real life, or 21 years old like from my previous dreams.

From behind him a woman appears and takes his hand as they leave the path and walk through the dewy wet grass towards my cottage. With each step closer they take to my house the air becomes warmer and the grass greener. I stay seated, waiting for their arrival, excited to greet my son. My face cracks into a smile filled with warmth and happiness as I open the door to let them in. In the light, I now see the woman clearly. My son doesn't say a single word but I automatically know what has happened. My son married a woman without telling me or even inviting me to the wedding. With the realization of the situation, and the ways that my son has shut me out of his life, my smile starts to disappear and a scowl forms that chills the once warm air.

My new daughter-in-law realizes now, too, that my son didn't tell me they were getting married, and she tries to start explaining the situation, and she asks me if there's anything or any chores she can do to help while I talk with my son. I return her offer with silence and go towards my bed, at the foot of which there is a large wooden chest, with golden carvings of flowers on the top and across the front. I open it and pull out fabrics and textiles that each tell a unique story with the embroidery on them, until I reach one at the bottom. It's a large, body-length shawl made of sheep's wool in black. I carefully place the textiles back in the chest and close it before bringing the black wool over to my new daughter in law. If she wants to help with cleaning, then I'm going to have her clean.

I instruct her to go to the river nearby and wash the black out of the wool to make it white again. She takes the wool, almost afraid of me, and doesn't ask any follow-up questions before she turns to leave the cottage and head out to the river to start washing the wool.

In that moment as she leaves my home, my spirit leaves my body and follows her to the river and watches her wash the

211

wool. Her frustration with her inability to wash the wool to white turns to crying. I start to feel bad for a moment before realizing that this is my son I am saving from her. My spirit then returns home.

After some time, though, she comes back to the house and is carrying white wool. My first thought is that she traded it with someone, but who could she possibly trade with here? We're all alone here in the valley. No one is within walking distance of us. So my second instinct is to take it as a sign. I don't know what the sign is, but I know that the wool is blessed and that I must take a journey to thank the Earth for this sign.

I say goodbye to my son and pack my bags with my nine wool coats, including the newly cleaned one, to head with my flock to the mountain top. Each night I camp with my flock and the nights become warmer and warmer. And so each morning I leave one wool coat to lighten my load during my journey, thinking I'll pick it back up on my return home.

On the ninth day of the trip, we almost reach the summit, my own personal place of spirituality and reflection. I wake up feeling cold and suddenly regret not bringing all my coats with me despite the heaviness they imposed on the trip. My mind panics as I see my breath and those of my sheep. The journey continues and the cold doesn't end. My body rests from being so weary and weak, and I wake up from my dream only after my body freezes alongside the frozen sheep of my flock.

Yeah, I have no idea what my dream could possibly mean, but it did spook me a little bit when I woke up alive after dying in my dream. But today was a normal day. We're in a small town called Vladimirovac that some of my cousins live in, so I'm quite excited to see them. Because we just arrived yesterday late at night, we ate so much food that I slept in all morning and missed everyone else getting up.

We spend the day greeting each other, catching up, and telling stories while the town around us revolves around celebrations of red and white, celebrations of welcoming the spring and bidding farewell to the winter. Decorations are happening, but the only thing that matters to me is getting to see my cousin Valeria again. My little sister and cousins follow Valeria and I around like little ducklings and we keep trying to ditch them throughout the village, but because there's so many of them, one of them always finds us and the others are quick to catch up.

Valeria and I spend the entire day around the pond gossiping about boys. She told me she had her first kiss and that she has a new boyfriend, who's in the military. Valeria is 17, so just one year older than me, but I'm already insanely jealous because we move so often that I don't know any boys and don't have the time to be in a relationship with one.

At the pond, Valeria and I spend the day weaving the bracelets together of red and white strings, to give to each other and our friends and family later this week for the Martisor holiday. This is one of my favorite holidays of the year because it always makes me excited for the warmer weather to come. So I feel lucky that I get to spend it here with Valeria.

When we get back to our parents, once the sun starts to set over the pond, they surprise us with matching outfits with embroidered flowers all over them. We all try them on and look at ourselves in the mirrors. We look like a complete family together in our new, clean, matching clothing that fits each of us so perfectly because it was tailored specifically for us.

Both of our moms gush over us and make us pose for hundreds of photos and I just can't wait until all this embarrassment is done and everyone goes to sleep so Valeria and I can sneak out and meet her new boyfriend later this evening.

Monday, March 2nd, 2048 - Romania/Serbia, Vladimirovac

Again, same dream as last night. There was just one change this time. At the end, when I went up the mountain, I made it without freezing and without my coats because the weather was so warm that I didn't need them. But also, my herd couldn't make the journey alongside me because they ended up overheating under the sun's direct warmth. I'm so excited about today, though, that I can't even think about what my dream means.

Today, Valeria and I woke up earlier and ditched our families before they could even catch us. I know my dad was either going to make me help him with work, or my mom was going to try to do the same or have me do some chores. We ran out to a small, abandoned barn that Valeria has been using to meet her new boyfriend. Inside it was decorated with small things: a rug on the ground, a sleeping bag, a few candles, and some wooden chairs. Not quite homey, but it's getting somewhere.

Spending the day in the barn, I told Valeria about my dream and she reminded me that if I dreamt that on my first night here, it's prophetic. So maybe, since I dreamt I was a mother in my dream, it's trying to tell me that this is what it'll be like when I'm an older mother?

The day ended too quickly. On our way back from the barn, we saw Valeria's and my siblings riding their bikes, taking turns since there were only two bikes, and chickens just running around everywhere, pecking at the dirt. I always love visiting Valeria and my family here because they have so much land and space that they make me feel safe and settled whenever I'm here.

When we got back, Valeria's dad and grandfather were roasting a lamb to celebrate our family being reunited for the year, so we spent the whole night near the fire, eating and drinking.

Tuesday, March 3rd, 2048 - Romania/Serbia, Vladimirovac

Same dream as the previous two nights yet again, but this time I did realize some changes that were quite significant. As I climbed up the mountain with my herd at the end of the dream, the weather was so cold this time that I kept all my coats with me, in preparation to stay warm, but my herd, who each only had one coat of fur and warmth, all died during the journey to the top.

But today my parents broke the horrible news to us that we're moving on already. We'd only been here for THREE days! This was the shortest amount of time we've ever spent here. They kept saying that we're coming back and that it's temporary, but I don't believe them. What could possibly make us move already after just three days with family?

My mom kept trying to tell me that we're moving on to see our other family, that the incoming weather isn't so good here, and it's best to move ahead and beat the weather, rather than stay and wait. When I was little, she used to tell me that we chased the good weather and always left the bad weather behind. But I don't believe her anymore, especially since we're always chasing snow storms now.

Packing took me a lot longer than normal because I had settled myself here and was ready to stay forever. I give Valeria my martisor for her before we leave and I keep the others to give to my other cousins that we'll see in Saedinenie. And again, tonight I can't sleep because I'm so upset, and who knows if I'm going to dream tonight.

Wednesday, March 4th, 2048 - Bulgaria, Saedinenie

I'm with two of my many brothers, but they're not my siblings in real life. These are new brothers for me, each a little bit older than me. But I look at them, and then down at my hands, and recognize that we've aged. We're now old, about the same age as my grandparents.

We're fighting and arguing over something that I can't even remember. There's 12 of us in total here, and I'm the third eldest. All 12 of us are siblings and each has a very different personality. My sister who's one year younger than me joins in on the argument to back me up on some points but then quickly disappears as soon as she's appeared.

We live in the clouds above the Earth, just like I always imagined Greek gods do. Each of us has a specific weather pattern that we bestow to the earth below that matches our personalities. Mine is the coming warmth that breaks through the winter and gives hope to the people for the approaching spring season.

I'm tired of arguing with my brothers about the cold they've been placing on the earth during my turn of sending warmth and spring, cool breezes, and sunny days; dewy grass, and the smell of fresh flowers popping out of the earth.

I leave the argument to follow my sister into her room and try on all her clothes. I notice her entire closet collection is set for the spring season without any winter wear at all. Very dissimilar to mine. My closet contains mixes of spring and winter clothing, as I'm prepared for any season that hits me with change.

After I pick an outfit to wear from her closet for this warm, early spring day, we all go down to the earth together to plant seeds, to start planning all the crops for spring. I love touching my hands to the earth and feeling its warmth as it begins to defrost between my fingers and the wetness of the dew that washes the dirt from each hand. Together all 12 of my siblings and I thank the earth for our crops and continue planting the seedlings.

Today makes me smile and makes the sun shine above us all. My mother, even older than myself in this dream, approaches me and tells me that my smile brings the sun but my frowns brings the clouds, which explains the clouds earlier, when

I was arguing with my brothers.

Finally, we return to our house in the clouds. Everyone starts cleaning their rooms now that my smile makes the sun shine and warmth enters the homes. I look below and the people on Earth are doing the same, emptying their homes, cleaning out every part so that the bright sun can dry the water from the newly cleaned home. This makes me smile even more, and the last bits of snow that had remained from the morning grayness of the clouds finally melt.

But soon enough, my brothers come back and they spill wine in my room, staining the floor and furniture, and that further infuriates me. Just as quickly as the clouds had disappeared, they come back again. My younger sister comes in and tells me to stop my mood swings. I start arguing with her, too, because I can't help it if all my siblings are playing with my feelings and doing things to anger me. My sister then sends a part of her warm and calming personality down to Earth to make the weather clear and warm for those who were cleaning their homes.

We arrive in another one of my family's villages, or rather, a village where a lot of my family lives. As we unpack I ask my dad about my dreams. He asks me again if I've been recording them and so I read out my journal to him while he carries things around. He tells me to recognize the repetition between each of the dreams to know what's speaking to me, and also that nobody but myself can interpret my dreams for me.

I find that vague and annoying and I wish Valeria had been more helpful with the advice about my dreams when we were together. Although I do have family and cousins in this village, unfortunately, all my cousins here are younger than me and wouldn't understand.

But I do recognize the repetition of two things: the familial relationships and the changing weather. I don't have the energy to work out what those could mean now, so I'll just remember to think about it later.

After lots of food and greetings, as always, I spend the day with my cousins and one of my uncles collecting bugs in the woods and fields. A cat follows us that we've named Simba and I'm dearly attached to him. He's an orange cat that looks high off of catnip all the time.

The people here in the village are planning for their spring holiday as well. We continue to see the red and white strings everywhere as we walk. When I look down at my bracelet on my wrist it reminds me of Valeria and it makes me miss her.

My siblings and cousins end up trying to climb some trees and mountains, but they soon give up and head back. All day I feel like I'm just babysitting and I wish Valeria were here with us so we could talk more.

We all stay up late, talking to each other, eating, drinking, and I soon become so exhausted, sitting on the couch, that I'm the first in the family to excuse themselves to go to bed.

Thursday, March 5th, 2048 - Bulgaria, Saedinenie

Yup, you guessed it. Same dream as last night again. It makes me think how chaotic it would be to have 12 siblings, though. I'm now happy with just my two siblings.

So I guess my dream did lead me to appreciate that, because we don't fight much, or argue, except when we use each other's things.

Today I'm working with my mom, and my cousins spend the day with us, too, to catch up. I guess it wasn't as bad as I expected because I did miss my cousins here a lot, too, even though we're not as close to each other because we see each other less often and there's a greater age difference between us.

We joke around all day and teach each other new words and slang from the places we've been to since both our families travel often. Today just feels cozy while we're inside and bonding with each other.

Our dads go to the market while my mom teaches each of us how to make jewelry by using minerals from the earth. She shows us first how to make simple earrings and then we move on to bracelets and necklaces. By the end of the day, we're all covered with new sparkles that my mom will probably take to sell in the market tomorrow.

As we make jewelry together, my mom and aunties tell us the story of Baba Marta Day and the martenitsas that we wear with our little charms. I've heard the story a million times before though so it doesn't really sound like anything new to me. The story about the holiday is different everywhere, but here we tell stories of an old Grandmother March that brings the changing weather. There's another version, too, where siblings represent the months of the year and therefore have different personalities based on the seasons they have in their month.

In the evening, our dads return home with news that we did just escape the storm and it was good that we left when we did because most everything in the village is ruined and the storm has still not yet stopped. My mind raced to Valeria, wondering if she was safe. I talked to my dad about it and he assured me that their family was prepared too and had moved on, like us, before the storm hit the village.

I look outside to check the weather and I'm grateful that it's warm and sunny where we are. No cold, no rain, no clouds, no storm in sight. I thought back to Valeria and wondered if she was seeing or feeling the same sun I am right now.

We stay up later than usual tonight, hanging out and talking, and I'm quite tired, but I don't want to be the first person to go to sleep two nights in a row, even before my younger siblings and cousins. So I do get a little bit grumpy as the evening grows late, but I eventually crawl up into the bed and fall asleep.

Friday, March 6th, 2048 - Bulgaria, Saedinenie

I think my grumpy mood carried into my dreams last night because I dreamt of fighting with my siblings. In my dream I had 11 brothers and sisters again. Maybe we're representing the 12 zodiac signs? But that wouldn't make sense for mine, then, because in my dream it wasn't my personality or my horoscope personality. Anyway, my dream was the same, except this time, my arguing with my two brothers continued and didn't stop. My smile was gone, the clouds remained, and the snow continued to remain on the ground against my will and my attempts to get rid of it. The climate was totally different, and the remaining snow and cold and clouds left me feeling depressed, both in my dream and when I woke up.

After getting up, I wandered around for a bit and realized I was right about today. My mother went to the market early this morning to sell the jewelry we spent the day making yesterday. I don't really know what to do today because everyone is out working, so I just spend the morning roaming the village, learning where everything is, and then come back and nap in the early afternoon.

My siblings and cousins arrive home from school. I have no idea how they were able to fall asleep after me and yet wake up before me to go to school. They go outside to play with bugs again and I decide to join them. None of them are squeamish with the bugs but I definitely am, so I just keep a bit of distance.

The day just seems to drag on with nothing really happening at all, so I get to spend it with my thoughts in the field among the herds and my family, just thinking. I wish I had brought a book with me, but I'll remember to do so for tomorrow.

We head back for dinner and the routine continues with eating late and staying up late, and again I'm grumpy and I can't fall asleep. If I do end up dreaming tonight, I hope to remember to write about it tomorrow.

Monday, March 9th, 2048 - Bulgaria, Saedinenie

I haven't dreamt in a while now and I now miss my dreams. The comfort of the repetition soothed me, and felt like a puzzle that my brain was trying to piece together in my sleep. The geography of my dreams and reality changed along with the versions of the stories, showing me a map of tales as we traveled. I note that down, draw a map of our travels, and try to draw out pictures from the dreams using my terrible drawing skills. Now I don't know if I'm not dreaming at all or if I'm just forgetting my dreams each morning, which would be very unusual for me.

My parents say the storm is coming this way, so it's time for us to move again. But this time my cousins and aunts and uncles are going to go with us, which will be nice.

My dad says there are no reports of snow or winter anywhere, leaving him out of work and unsure of where to move next. We decide as a family to follow the spring. So wherever the sunshine, cool breeze, and good weather are, we will follow until snow returns.

WHERE THE BIRCH
TREES SING

GREG GAJEK

"YOUR FINGERS ARE COLD," Letka whispered.

There was no answer.

Letka wearily opened her eyes, her eyelids heavy, and only then understood that the sweet caress upon her face was not the touch of her lover but that of a cold, slender birch twig.

It should be warm in the birchwood, she thought sleepily.

"I'm not cold," Bośka said, and Letka, hearing the voice of the other girl—her love, her betrothed friend—stirred, her mind clearing a little. "You can get used to it, I reckon'... D'you know? In fact, it's not cold at all."

They were sitting together in the snow, in a birchwood, somewhere deep in the wilderness, far from their home, their *opole* community, their tribe, far from the caring protection of their ancestors. Though maybe not so far, after all. The wind—fierce Świst and kindly Poświst—seemed to be carrying voices, familiar though ethereal.

Why did you run away? Don't fall asleep. To sleep is to die. You cannot feel the cold, for the warmth is already draining from your hearts.

It should be warm in the birchwood, Letka told herself again, stubbornly.

Only then did she realize that she wasn't thinking of this birchwood, nor just any birchwood, but *their* birchwood.

She could almost smell the sweetly scented smoke of the bonfires. That, however, had been an age, an entire lifetime ago—last spring. Winter had gone by quickly, and before anyone in Rybnica knew, they were burning Marzanna to welcome spring. Then the birches began to bud. The women of the *opole* waited for the first full moon—a time when their goddess gazed benevolently upon them from the starry heavens—and left their homes in a procession headed for the holy grove. And then there was singing and spell-weaving and all the breathless revels of a night most holy.

That last spring, as they were walking toward the holy grove for the birch festival, Bośka was clearly nervous. Her hand—small, rough and damp—twitched in Letka'slike a fish. It was to be Bośka's first birch festival, even though she had just entered the fifteenth spring of her life. She had bled for the first time only this past winter and had been mortified by it. Entering womanhood at the age of fifteen seemed like a reminder from the gods that she was not part of the tribe; Bośka was, after all, the daughter of a freedman, a Piaszczan taken into captivity during one of the many tribal raids.

Letka had been bleeding for a long time and not once had she been ashamed of it. On her first day of womanhood, she'd proudly gone to face her mother, who had scowled at her as if she had seen something wicked.

"Foolish thing," mother had said. "You still have the hips of a boy."

Mother had never enjoyed the birch festival much. She usually sat aside from the others and drank mead from a pitcher that a serving wench carried after her, to remind all the other women that she was the wife of a wealthy *gospodyn*, a clan chieftain. And as she drank, she grew steadily redder in the face and kept lowering her eyes as if willing the world to go away.

Now, she strode haughtily at the front of the procession, never sparing a glance at the women behind her, nor the pack of girls loitering at the back.

"Gives you the chills, doesn't it?" Bośka whispered as they entered the grove and saw a circle of wispy birch trees, silvery-blue and ghostlike in the light of the full moon.

Letka squeezed her friend's hand in response.

The women huddled together and a hum of excited voices rose above their heads.

"Silence!" ordered Lubomiła, the wife of another *gospodyn*. There was something solemn about her voice, and yet it also had an undercurrent to it, like barely suppressed laughter. "Let us lay down our offerings to the goddess Mokosh."

Lubomiła and two other women squatted amidst the sparse woodland grass of the grove. By torchlight, with their bare hands, they slowly, reverently, dug a shallow pit in the ground, put an egg in it and covered it with dirt.

Then Lubomiła named all the children that had been born over the past year, as well as the ones who had died. She asked the gods to grant their souls—cleansed in the flames of the funeral pyres—quick passage to the heavenly lands of Viray, so that they need not wander the realms of mortals like the spirits of those who were buried in the cold earth.

"Holy Mother, take pity on us wretched womenfolk," Lubomiła finally said and there definitely was a mischievous note in her voice now. "And next year, please grant us bountiful crops, healthy bairns, and make it so that our no-good husbands keep their britches on more often than not."

Somebody hooted her assent, somebody else laughed.

Lubomiła got to her feet and clapped her hands. "Come, sisters! Let's light the fires for Chors, goddess of the moon! Now ain't she lovely in the sky! Light the fires! May the sparks carry our prayers to her silver chariot!"

There was commotion in the grove. The bonfires were lighted and a thin mist of incense – smelling heavily of angelica and dried hemlock leaves – filled the birchwood, as the dazed women nestled in their chosen spots,, laughing and chattering, undoing their braids, pulling off their headscarves and wimples. Baskets of food were set out, all containing the traditional offerings for the moon goddess: boiled eggs and bowls of *kasha* and barley flatbreads. Wineskins of light beer mixed with birch juice were passed around.

Letka pulled Bośka away from the others, towards a smaller fire at the edge of the clearing, where they could be alone. She made Bośka drink a cup of birch beer in one go, and then, giggling, stuffed a whole boiled egg in her friend's mouth.

"Ee ood 'are," Bośka spluttered with her mouth full.

But Letka paid her no heed, already biting into a flatbread, her head a-hum with excitement.

They drank another cup of birch beer each.

Bośka hiccoughed and blushed. "Tastes awful," she complained. "All watery and bitter. Wouldn't it be better to have wheat beer with honey, like rich folk do? Now there's a proper feast."

"One shouldn't be too fond of sweetness," Letka said. "Sweet things make your mouth taste bitter, while bitter things make it taste sweet. You'd know that if you knew how to kiss."

The blush on Bośka's face deepened. "I know how to kiss," she said.

Letka snorted with laughter, but then fell silent as another woman joined them by the fire. Aunt Bogna was raw-boned and drawn, her delicate, willowy hands all red and chafed from work. Only her eyes were beautiful; neither gray nor brown, by the light of the fire they seemed the color of gold.

"Would you share your *kasha* with me, girls?" she asked

in a voice that was musical and soft, and yet seemed strained somehow, as if it could instantly turn into a wail.

"Here you go, auntie," Letka said.

Letka felt uncomfortable. Everyone felt uncomfortable around Bogna. "Poor thing..." they'd sigh, whenever she was mentioned. She'd probably be expecting again soon, Letka thought.

The older woman turned her golden gaze to Bośka. "How're things at home? How's your *tata*?"

"Oh, you know. He keeps complaining about that leg of his. It's the damp, you know. But it'll be getting warmer soon, and he'll be off to Borki or Krosno, fixing roofs and fences, carrying goods to the market. He just needs to go out a bit more, see some people, is all. He's a good man, my *tata*, only, the winter, it gets to him, makes him all sore and grumpy..."

For some reason, Bośka's chattering was getting on Letka's nerves, as were Bogna's sad little smiles and knowing nods. Letka couldn't wait to free herself of the woman's gloomy presence and was delighted to see Lubomiła rise to speak again.

"Well, sisters," Lubomiła slurred, her voice already thick from the drink. "The time has come. Go forth and weave thine wreaths! Who'll be the first? Huh? Whatcha waitin' for, girls?"

"Come on!" Letka hissed, pulling Bośka to her feet.

Somewhat breathlessly, they ran into the middle of the clearing. Lubomila clapped her hands, beaming. Letka's mother, who sat apart from the other women, stared fixedly into her cup of mead.

"Right now, off you go!" Lubomiła said, shooing the two girls towards the trees. "Find yourselves a juicy young birch!"

Letka and Bośka hurried off into the birchwood. At first, still blinded by the firelight, they bumbled about like a pair of moths. Then, as their eyes grew accustomed to the dark, they were amazed to find that the whole grove was flooded with silvery light. High above, beyond the haze of thin, almost ghostlike branches, the giant eye of the moon shone brightly.

"Slow down!" Bośka said. "You'll pull my arm right out!"

Letka kept pointing at different trees, "How's this one? Or that one?"

Finally, they stopped beneath a young birch with a slender, leaning trunk and outstretched branches that gave an impression of contained movement, as if the tree had been caught off-guard, ready to pounce.

"Perfect," Letka said.

She let go of her friend's hand, pulled a pair of iron shears out of her pouch and began to cut long, thin twigs from the birch tree's lower branches.

Bośka, meanwhile, put her hands on her hips, panting. "We're gonna use 'em for wreaths?"

"A wreath. One for both of us."

They were quiet for a little while, then Bośka looked back towards the heart of the holy grove where other women could be heard giggling and leaving the bonfires to wander the birchwood in pairs. "Poor Bogna..."

"What?" snapped Letka, bewildered. "Why?"

"Have you seen how pale she is, poor thing? So thin, it's almost like she's... oh, I dunno... not there at all."

"Get off it. She's been like that for years."

"You can be so mean sometimes, Letka. You know full well that it hasn't even been a month since the last time she was... taken ill. And before the men go on another raid, she'll probably be with child again. He doesn't have a heart, that man of hers. Couldn't he just let her be? She's borne him two sons already; they're almost grown up. The older one not too hard on the eyes, either."

"I don't know what you could possibly see in him, the fat lump. Just a kid, really".

"Alright, no need to get all cross," Bośka muttered. "I'm just saying Bogna hasn't had it easy, is all. How'd you feel, if you'd keep losing one baby after another?"

"Well, I don't intend to have any babies."

"Oh, you don't? And how're you gonna get out of it?"

Letka's eyes twinkled in the moonlight. "With a spell," she said. "Right, I think we've got enough twigs. Now help me weave."

They squatted down, the earth soft and bursting with the freshness of spring under their feet, and started working on the wreath, twisting and bending the twigs which seemed to dance to their touch.. Bośka seemed to ponder her friend's words for a while, before asking, "You really wouldn't want any kids of your own?"

"No, I wouldn't."

"Well, *I* would. Only... D'you think there's a spell that lets you have a baby without having to marry a man?"

"Sure there is. It's called shagging a perfect stranger who'll then bugger off into the sunset."

"Oh, you know what I mean." Bośka sounded exasperated. "If I had a baby now, tata would have to take it into his household, wouldn't he? And father can't afford another mouth to feed. So he'd have to marry me off to some man who'd take in another's child, or give it away to the gods.I meant a spell that would allow me to have a baby all of my own."

"What a silly goose you are," Letka murmured, but she said it lovingly.

Bośka laughed and elbowed the other girl in the side. "We're both silly, aren't we? Unless you're serious about that spell of yours."

"We'll have to see. Chors has her eye on us tonight, and she knows a great deal about spells."

Soon enough the wreath was done. Letka rose to her feet, slowly turning it in her fingers.

Bośka got up, too. "So, what do we do now?" she asked.

"Now we make our vows," Letka said. "But first you need to grip the wreath with your left hand and place your right hand on the side of the birch tree."

Letka, who was holding the wreath in her right hand, waited for Bośka to follow her instructions, then touched the tree with her own left hand, the bark under her fingertips as smooth as skin. She took a deep breath. How fresh the night air smelled. And, oh, how the birch trees sang in the soft wind.

"What do we vow?" Bośka asked.

"Whatever you wish. Some vow eternal friendship. Some vow maidenhood. Some vow to speak nothing but the truth to each other."

"And what will *you* vow?"

"To never have children. And to never marry a man."

"I'll never marry, either," Bośka declared in a tight voice.

"Good. I also vow that I'll love you forever. Till death do us part. And then some."

"And I'll love you."

They fell silent. The birch trees sang. Two hearts fluttered.

"Is that it?" Bośka whispered. "Is it done?"

"No," Letka said, also in a whisper. "Now we kiss through the wreath... But we don't have to, if you don't want to," she added quickly.

"I do."

They leaned towards each other. Letka instinctively shut her eyes, but then opened them wide. As she inhaled, she was enveloped by a mixture of scents—the cool scent of night breeze and dew, the sour smell of birch beer and sweat, the sweet, strong smell of desire. Before she could exhale, she felt the touch of Bośka's lips—neither cold nor hot, dry. She froze. Her breath mixed with the breath of her beloved—her betrothed friend, as of now. She gently sought out Bośka's tongue with her own.

"I feely a little... dizzy," Bośka said. And burst out laughing. "Sorry!"

"I feel a little dizzy myself."

They were both laughing now. They kissed again, through the wreath, gently caressing the bark of the birch tree with their fingers.

"And what now?" Bośka asked.

"I dunno." Letka grinned. "We can go look for the fern flower, if you wish."

Bośka giggled. "Are you thinking dirty thoughts, Letka?"

Because *looking for the fern flower* was what boys used during Kupala Night, the summer solstice festival, as an excuse to be alone with girls.

"Aren't you?"

"I might be."

They found a cozy clearing.

"Will this do?" Boshka asked.

"It'll do perfectly."

Bośka gave a wobbly curtsy, her eyes shining from all the beer she had drunk. She kicked off her clogs, then threw her cloak down on the ground and tried to spread it out over the dewy carpet of moss. But the damned thing just wouldn't lie still. Its edge caught on a nearby raspberry bush, and the cloak got all bundled.

"Leave it, silly!" Letka laughed. "Let me!"

"I've got this!" Bośka said. "Gimme your cloak. We'll use it as a blanket, see? To cover ourselves from the chill, and the... Oof, my moss is so wet. I mean, *the* moss is so wet."

"Oh, *your* moss is so wet?" Letka said, and she started to

laugh so hard, she couldn't contain herself. "Let me!" she snorted again through tears of laughter, pointlessly pulling on her friend's cloak to straighten it out.

And before they knew, they were both rolling in the moss, revelling in its lush dampness, their skin cool against the other's touch, their breath hot against the other's skin, panting, laughing, their hair tangling, their cloaks bunching up over them, covering them, so that only their feet – pink and cold – stuck out.

"Oi! Oi!" Bośka said. "Your fingers are cold."

"My fingers, love?" Letka giggled. "My fingers? How about my toes?"

"Oh, no, no, the toes are much worse!"

"And how about you? Aren't you cold at all?"

"No. I feel hot all over," Bośka said, her voice thick and throaty and shy.

Letka stopped tickling her. She looked into Bośka's eyes, dark and opaque in the eerie moonlight. Your nose is cold," Letka said serenely and kissed her beloved on the nose. "And how about the ears? Warm. And the neck? Cool. And the shoulders... Oh, my. They're frozen stiff."

"No, they're not."

"Oh, yes, they are. And the arms and the hands and the fingers... all cold. Let me warm them for you. Give them here."

"Oh, honey, but you're wrong. I'm not cold at all."

"Your sides are warm enough," Letka said, continuing her inspection, her voice now muffled by the bundled cloaks. "Belly... warm. Thighs... cool. Knees, calves, ankles, toes..." She emerged suddenly from beneath the cloaks as if surfacing from underwater. "The toes are damn near frozen off."

"You're wrong, honey. I feel all warm now."

"Here?" Letka asked, touching her. "Are you warm here?"

GREG GAJEK

"Yes," Bośka gasped, shivering slightly.

"And here?"

"Yes... and in... inside..."

And so they passed the night on the damp moss, breathing in the scent of the singing birch trees, salty and sweet. And for a time they felt hot. But as the day neared it got so cold that they shook the dew out of their hair and their clothes and sprinted back towards the heart of the holy grove, where they hoped to warm themselves by the dying bonfires.

As they got there, they saw that most of the women had fallen asleep in the arms of their friends, some still clutching birch wreaths between them. Letka and Bośka settled down on their previous spot; the embers of the bonfire still ticked and glowed slightly amongst the ashes. The girls covered themselves with their cloaks and a wool blanket, and soon enough Bośka fell asleep with her head in Letka's lap.

Letka smiled to herself and looked up. And as she did so, she encountered the gaze of aunt Bogna, who sat huddled on the other side of the firepit. The woman had seemed asleep, but now she studied the girls carefully through half-closed eyelids.

Unable to think of anything better to say, Letka asked, "Aren't you sleeping, auntie?"

"No. Sorry. It's just so nice to look at you two."

"Oh."

"You made your vows, didn't you? You're sisters now."

Letka felt uncomfortable again. Yes, we made our vows," she said, somewhat defiantly, for some reason thinking of her mother.

"Good. On this holy night, under the eye of Chors, vows have a special power. You'll always love each other now."

"We'll always be together."

Bogna hesitated, then said, "You'll love each other. And that's important: knowing that someone, somewhere, loves you. Without love one can find it quite... difficult... to carry on. Motherhood can be a source of solace, of course. Sometimes. Not for every one of us. A child's love is something else entirely, you see..."

"I'm not sure I'm following, auntie. Or maybe all this smoke has made me stupid."

Bogna gave Letka a rather sharp look. "Oh, you're anything but stupid, Letka. You know precisely what I mean."

"No, I don't."

"From now on, Bośka and you will always be sisters, you'll always love one another. There are some things no spell can change, however. One day, both of you will get married and have children. And when you do, and you fall on bad days, as we are all bound to, seek solace in the memory of this night." Bogna leaned forward over the firepit, her face oddly hazy in the predawn gloom and the faint glow of the dying embers. "Solace, nothing more."

"Poor, poor Bogna..." Bośka muttered. "It ain't right, what happened to her... An end like that... Plain cruel, it was."

Letka gave a little start, shaking off the memories of last spring and the birch festival. She had heard a peculiar sound, like the rustle of worn leather. Suddenly, she found herself alert and small against the swaying, babbling vastness of the snow-covered forest, a tiny girl with a tiny heart beating painfully against the ribs of a tiny, constricted chest.

"Hush," Letka hissed at her friend. "Don't you talk about that, lest something evil come this way."

"Like what? The wind's died down, wicked old thing. He won't come bitin' at as no more. And it's so warm under the snow..."

Letka scrambled up from the cold ground and tried to pull Bośka to her feet, and—gods!—what a scare she got, for her friend felt as heavy as a corpse.

"Get up," Letka said, barely containing the scream that was bubbling up in her throat.

"Just lemme rest a teensy bit..."

"Get up!"

A loud slap echoed through the birchwood, and only after a while did Letka realise that it was she who had slapped Bośka. Her friend was staring at her now, startled and awake.

"See what you made me do?" Letka hissed, afraid that her outburst might draw the attention of... something. "Hush now. Hush."

Bośka staggered to her feet and leaned on Letka, who drew her friend close and, instinctively, kissed her neck.

The birchwood slowly settled. The unpleasant, wet rustle of snow sliding down branches died away. The trees quietened down. The two winds, Świst and Poświst, fell silent. Then, among the trees, the faintest of murmurs rose, like the breathing of some vast being. The air thickened with snow-dust—glittering brightly in the moonlight—and beyond this sparkling veil a shape could be seen, the shape of something tall and lithe, man-like in stature, yet alien, with thin, long horns on its head.

"Leszy," Bośka said, breathlessly.

Letka shook her head. She didn't know what the thing was—she wasn't even sure if it was really there—but there seemed to be something distinctly out of place about it. From old folk tales, she knew that before her tribe had come and laid its gods on the banks of the Wełna, the Warta and Gopło Lake, a different people had inhabited these lands and worshipped a horned deity. Near her home village of Rybnica, on Perginia Hill, idols of that ancient god could still be found. Lightning often struck around them in the summer.

Letka shook herself out of her awed reverie. That faint murmur that had risen among the trees was now worming its way into her mouth and nose, thundering in her ears; it seemed it was no longer the air shimmering with snow-dust but her own eyes filling with tiny shards of ice. She knew she had to get them moving, and yet there was danger in movement, too; for she felt that, should she start running, she wouldn't be able to stop.

Letka forced her left foot to slide forward. Then her right. She tried to drag her friend behind her, but Bośka wouldn't budge. "Come on."

"I don't want to," Bośka said in a flat voice. "I just want this to end."

"Come. On."

And Bośka went. But it was no good. It was exactly as Letka had feared. As soon as they turned their backs on the thing which perhaps wasn't even there, they felt something rising within them, pushing them forward, faster, faster. Their steamy breaths mixed in the cold night air. Through the skin of their tightly clutched hands, they could feel each other's pulse, racing unevenly as if one heart were trying to keep up with the other. Before they knew it, they were running, like that night in the birch grove, only this time it was fear goading them onwards.

We shouldn't be going this way, Letka thought. *If we're already beyond Perginia Hill... Marshlands lie this way... the graves of the old folk...*

Wham! She felt herself bounce off something. In the dark, she had hit a tree. She staggered, too dazed to feel any pain. And then, solid ground slid from under her feet. For a heartbeat, she was gliding.

They had run onto ice, a frozen-over marsh, perhaps.

There was a loud crack, a moan. Letka slid forwards, pulling Bośka after her. They skidded and swirled. The thin film of ice didn't break as much as collapse inwards like a sheet of cloth, and the girls were engulfed by black, numbingly-cold marsh water.

At first, Letka didn't feel the cold. Quite the opposite, she was enveloped by a sensation of warm effervescence. She reached out with her hands, groping for the bottom, trying to work out which way lay solid ground. And then she felt it. Somebody's touch.

Your fingers are cold, she thought, as a thin, almost fleshless hand—sheathed in skin as slick and tight as a leather glove—gripped her wrist. Only then did the cold finally hit her.

Bośka screamed. Thrashing about in the icy, foul-smelling sludge, she wallowed out of the water.

Letka pulled her hand free of the cold grip and, surfacing too, followed in her friend's wake. They huddled together, shivering, among the gnarled roots of an old willow. The bark of the tree was rough, and their skin felt raw, and the dead grass crunched unpleasantly under the soles of their shoes, but at least it was dry.

"Who... Who was that?" Bośka asked.

"Shush, love. There's no one there. Just weed, is all."

"Our folk wouldn't try to pull us under, would they? Our folk are cozy and snug in Wyraj, feasting on bird milk. Let's give them some kasza. Whaddya think, Letka? A bit of *kasza*, if they're angry..."

"We don't have any *kasza*, love, remember? We lost it with the basket."

Bośka seemed not to hear. "It's too early for our folk to wander the lands of the living, isn't it? And, besides, they'll find plenty of offerings back home. Yes. Let's tell them to go to Rybnica. Father always leaves a bowl of *kasza* on the doorstep. And some curdled milk, if we have any. But them dead folk can't be our folk. Our folk wouldn't scare us like that, would they?"

She shivered from the cold and from fright as the chattering of Bośka's teeth drove her near mad.

"There's no one there," Letka forced herself to say. "Come. We need to try and stay warm."

"Oh, why did we ever come here, Letka? Why did we ever run away from home? It ain't our land, and it ain't our folk who lie in it."

"Hush, now, honey. What do you mean, not our land? We're barely two days away from Rybnica. Maybe less, we probably backtracked, when the blizzard hit."

"Well, it's easy for you to say. All land's your land, to you," Bośka said, incoherently. Words were flying from her lips in little gasps of steam. "You're the daughter of a wealthy *gospodyn*. Husbandmen bow to you. Boys would kill to marry you. And me? A freedman's daughter! A Piaszczan! A stranger! When I die, you lot'll prob'ly chuck me in the bog. Or bury me in the dirt, like a dead cow, like the old folk did. Why waste all that firewood on a *slave* girl! Cos' that's what you think of me, ain't it? There's no place for the likes of me in Wyraj!"

Letka should have been hurt by her friend's ramblings. But all she felt was weary. And that was a very bad sign. Don't say that," she said, softly. "You're being silly. The old folk were a wild, uncouth people who knew neither gods nor custom. You were born here, in this land. This is where the ashes of your mother were laid to rest. You're no Piaszczan. You're one of us."

"Well, they should've left, then," Bośka declared. For a moment, Letka had no idea who she meant. "They should've left, shouldn't they? The old folk. Their gods ain't around no more. Our gods are. And our dead."

"There's no one there. Hush, now, please. What if something hears us?"

"But it has. Letka, it has. Oh, we shouldn't have run away!"

Something in Bośka's voice made the hairs on Letka's neck rise. She looked around.

On the edge of the murky water, a warrior was kneeling. His helm was cracked and eaten through with rust, his sword broken in half, and he carried a tall, oddly shaped shield that seemed to be made not of leather and wicker like the shields of her people, but entirely of metal. His empty eye sockets gleamed faintly—like rotten wood.

Aunt Bogna died in the middle of winter, just after the winter solstice festival of Szczodre Gody. Letka visited her for the last time in the morning. It seemed that all the other women in the village had come by, too, a procession of mourners mourning one who yet lived. Her and the dead child she carried in her womb. A few days earlier, Bogna had bled a bit, and the child had stopped stirring; some said that a zmora had strangled it.

As Letka got up to leaveBogna—who was lying on a simple straw mattress, buried in furs and blankets, shrunken and pale—caught her by the hand and said, "Come see me in the evening, would you? I'm sure I'll feel stronger by then."

"I will," Letka said, but Bogna still clutched her hand tightly, pleadingly.

"Your fingers are cold," Bogna said. "You should take better care of yourself. The days are so cold now... Barely any sun left in the sky. Dress warmly, dear, and bring us some of your mother's broth when you come by later."

"I will, auntie."

That was the last time they talked. When Letka came again, in the evening, Lubomiła told her Bogna was dead.

Letka knelt down by her aunt's unmoving figure. She thought of taking Bogna's hand, but didn't dare to. It was not the first time she had seen death, but only now had she realized how strange it was to keep vigil by a body in which a living soul still dreamed its last mortal dreams—and would dream them, until set free by the cleansing flames of a funeral pyre.

"May Mother Mokosz accept you into her womb," Letka whispered. "The earth has borne you, the earth has fed you, with earth you shall now become one."

And suddenly, she felt ashamed of these old, ritual words. They seemed to her a false kind of comfort.

So she said goodbye to Lubomiła and went away to look for Bośka. And a strange thing happened. For as Letka was leaving Bogna's house, she was still a child, and yet, by the time she had joined her friend, she was all grown up.

"What's up with you?" Bośka asked, seeing the odd look on Letka's face.

"Nothing. Bogna's dead. Did you know?"

Bośka shook her head and gave the other girl a curious look. "I thought you didn't like her."

Letka shrugged. "I didn't. Mother told me to go pay her a visit. Come on, I feel like taking a walk."

So they went down to the bank of the Wełna, and as they were making their way through the brambles by the water's edge, Letka took her betrothed friend by the hand. Bośka said nothing. She pulled her cloak tighter around her shoulders and pressed Letka's small, cold hand against her hip.

Finally, they saw the river. The water seemed heavy and thick, rolling lazily as it slowly turned to ice.

"Letka? What is it, love? You crying?"

Letka hastily brushed the tears away. "Have you ever seen me cry?"

"Well... no."

"Oh, what a fool she was. Bogna. How could she let her man do that to her?"

Bośka nervously shuffled her feet. "Darlin'... What could she have possibly done?"

"She should've run away," Letka said, sternly. "As should we. In the spring, as soon as it gets warmer, before the next birch festival. We'll take our wreath and run away."

"Letka!"

"What?"

"Well, we can't just... I mean... It's dangerous to travel during springtime. Before the spring Dziady, the forest can be... spooky. And there could be rain or even snow. And then, I mean, we can't just leave everyone behind. What about my *tata*? And your parents? It just ain't right."

"Why not? Will your *tata* starve, if you go away? Will the other menfolk starve? I think *all* the women should just up and leave Rybnica."

"But... It ain't right!" Bośka repeated, stubbornly.

"Why? What's keeping us? Is there a spell binding us to this land? You think we wouldn't be able to make it on our own? Well, perhaps you wouldn't. But you'll be fine, as long as you're with me."

"Oh, I don't know, Letka!" Bośka threw her arms up in exasperation. Words tumbled out of her mouth, chaotically. "The children need the women to take care of 'em, don't they? And the women need each other, and all of us need the men, sometimes, I think, and then... everything's... right. Everything's as should be. And maybe it's not always good, but it's not always bad, either, is it? Things are the way they are for a reason. The gods must've wanted 'em this way or otherwise they wouldn't've made 'em so."

"And you're sure it was gods, not men, who made the world as it is?" Letka said. "Not husbands and fathers and brothers? From the day we're born, we're told things are organised in a certain way, because it's the *only* way. But what if it isn't?"

"I dunno, Letka. You're making this too complicated for me."

"Alright, let me put it to you plainly, then. If I run away, will you go with me?"

"You know I will," Bośka said. "We made a vow. It's only that... I'm scared, what might come of it."

As Letka backed away, the warrior slowly faded into the gloom—unmoving—until all that remained of him were two bright points where his eyes should have been. But Letka soon realized that more flickers of phosphorescence were blinking at her from the dark. She froze in place as she imagined a whole host of men rising from the marshes. Then, in the distance, she saw that same shimmer she had seen before, when the horned thing had come out of the woods. And a strange thought entered her mind: she imagined it was eyes, hundreds of them, glittering in the dark, staring, staring, staring—at her.

Bośka shuddered in Letka's embrace, then gave a great sigh and suddenly went still.

"Don't fall asleep," Letka whispered. Her arms and legs shivered from the exertion of supporting Bośka's weight. "You hear me?"

"I'm not sleeping," the other girl mumbled. "You know, there *is* something binding us to this land... Holding us... The earth's holding us..."

A cold lump formed in Letka's stomach as she heard these seemingly disconnected words. She felt dizzy and, oh, so dreadfully tired that it wouldn't have even mattered if all the eyes in the world were watching her.

Setting her teeth, she tried to shake Bośka awake. "Don't fall asleep. Fall asleep, and I'll leave you," she hissed, forcing her legs to keep moving.

"You crying, Letka?"

"No. Come on. Get up. Get moving."

"I don't want to go looking for the fern flower. I feel warm here. And here. Inside."

"Shut up!" Letka snarled, shaking her betrothed friend again. "Please, get up. Please. I can't drag you like this much longer."

Bośka swayed and tried to stand, but it was no good. Their feet got tangled. Letka slipped, struggled to keep her balance, then fell. For a moment, she felt as if she were gliding through the air, still holding Bośka in her arms. Then, they landed on something surprisingly warm and soft, like a mattress filled with fresh hay. *No*, Letka thought defiantly. *I'll die, if I fall asleep.*

At the same instant, Letka heard a rustle. Snow crackling. Twigs crunching. It seemed to her that the whole grove was coming to life, whirling.

They're coming for me, she thought.

Something loped out of the nearby shrubs and started circling the two girls. It was moving lithely, with its nose to the ground. At first, Letka thought it was a wolf. Then she realised it was a giant dog, poking at her with his wet, friendly muzzle.

She was too exhausted to feel surprised. Hugging Bośka tightly to her chest, she sat up—and heard somebody whistle. The dog tilted his head, spun around and bounded back into the trees, just as someone emerged from among them.

In the gloom, the newcomer's face was a silvery blur, yet his gait and silhouette betrayed a tall young man. His mere presence was enough to make Letka's earlier fear of ghosts and *upirs* seem silly and unreal.

Seeing the two girls, the man stopped dead and stared.

Thoughts were spinning drunkenly in Letka's head now. She ought to have said something, but her chin was shaking and her tongue was numb. "What're you doing here?" she finally managed; it was the first coherent thought she could grasp.

"Beaver trapping," the man said. His voice was not unpleasant, a bit rough from the cold perhaps. "I always check the traps before dawn. It'll be daylight soon."

Letka thought that it couldn't be right, that surely it was the middle of the night. When she looked around, though, she realized that the forest was already full of that cold, blueish light that precedes dawn. And that predawn glow reminded her of the old tales about the god Veles who was said to sometimes visit the dwellings of man. In these stories, he would always come in the small hours between nighttime and daytime—or perhaps it was his coming that marked the boundary between one and the other.

"Are you a god?" Letka asked, with one corner of her mouth curling into a wry half-smile.

The man didn't answer. He stepped forward and crouched beside the two girls. "Ran away from home, have you?"

"You can tell, huh?"

The man reached out a hand and touched Letka's hair, the hem of her cloak. Normally, Letka would probably flinch away, but she was too tired to care.

"You're soaked through," the stranger said. "You'll catch your death, like that."

"Could you, perhaps, lend us a cloak? And a place beside the fire? Do you live far from here?"

"No. Quite close, actually. Only you won't find any fire there."

At this, fear crept into Letka's heart. Some inner voice warned her to be wary; but her head felt as if it were full of wool. She didn't know what she should fear, and what she shouldn't, anymore. "Why isn't there any fire?"

"Touch your friend's face," the man said, ignoring Letka's question. "Can you feel how cold it is?"

"I can't feel anything. As if we're not even here."

"See if she's breathing."

Letka bent over Bośka. She felt the touch of chapped lips, but only a faint suggestion of breath washed over her skin.

"She's breathing," Letka said, then added, in a voice that didn't sound like her own, "Please, you're frightening me. And I've had quite a scare already. They chased us through the woods."

The stranger nodded. "You're right to be afraid. They have been dreaming in this cold earth for ages. Dreams that would drive a man mad."

"You're frightening me," Letka said again, softly this time, almost in a whisper.

"Fear is necessary. It strengthens the community. Serves as a reminder of duty. The gods did not create fear without reason. Had you been more afraid, you wouldn't have gone into the woods before the spring Dziady festival. You would've known that this is a time when the forces of life and death still struggle against each other, and snow may yet fall."

A small ember of anger lit up deep within Letka. In its warmth, she could once again feel her feet, hands, chest, head—blood pumping through her veins.

"One cannot spend their whole life in fear," she said, glaring at the man. "If you're not going to help, leave us be."

"But I do mean to help you. Why, that's why I've come here. That's why we have come here. We've eaten the *kasza* left as an offering by your kin, and set out to look for you."

"And the price?" Letka asked, suspiciously.

"Oh, it's nothing much. You'll go back home, get married, bear children. And when the time comes, you'll die in this land, and your ashes will be buried in it. As will the ashes of your offspring. Many would consider it a gift."

"A gift?" Letka almost choked on the word. A cold kind of laughter was rising in her chest. "You're calling this a gift?

A small price to pay?" Her voice was trembling now, the laughter dissipating in a powerless rage. "What you're asking is that we give our very selves away."

"Let me guess. You'd rather die?"

"Yes. If I can't be my own, I'd rather die."

In the faint light, Letka saw the stranger smile. He raised his hand and brushed his thumb over Bośka's forehead. The girl's eyelids fluttered; she stared at Letka, her eyes as wide and black as a corpse's.

"*You think we wouldn't be able to make it on our own?*" Bośka muttered, repeating what Letka had said to her a long time ago. "*Well, perhaps you wouldn't. But you'll be fine, as long as you're with me.*"

Letka swallowed back tears. "It's vile, cruel, what you're doing..." she said, not meeting the man's eye.

"You must understand that you were never your own to begin with," the stranger said. He was still smiling, his tone conversational. He casually flicked back a strand of hair that had gotten into his eyes. "So, what's it going to be?"

"I don't have any choice, do I? If it were just me, I'd send you to—"

"I know".

Letka swallowed hard. How will you do it? Will you conjure food, a fire?"

The stranger got to his feet, brushing the snow off his knees.

"So we have an accord," he said. "Take your shears out of your pouch and draw a drop of blood with them to seal it. As for food and fire—oh, it's much simpler than magic, you'll see."

Letka did as she was told. And for a brief moment, she felt as if all the spirits in the forest had rushed forward to suck out the few droplets of blood that had fallen onto the snow. When she raised her eyes, though, the ghosts were gone. As was the stranger.

Dawn was breaking.

Something stirred in the nearby shrubs, and the dog came out of them again. At first light, he didn't seem as big as before. His ribs were showing as if he hadn't eaten for a very long time, but he was wagging his tail in a friendly manner.

Letka shook her betrothed friend by the shoulders. "Wake up, Bośka. Please, try to stay awake just a little longer."

"I'm not sleeping. I'm just... so warm..."

"Come on. We'll rest in a little bit."

"Alright, love. Just let me rest my eyes a spell. Just a spell."

Letka pinched Bośka's thigh. She started to pat the other girl's arms and sides and legs to get the blood flowing. Bośka protested, meekly, but finally, leaning heavily on her friend, she managed to get to her feet.

Seeing that, the dog turned around and trotted off into the shrubs. They followed. Bośka's legs were still wobbly, she stumbled more than she walked, but Letka was determined to get her betrothed friend to safety, even if it meant dragging Bośka through the woods.

Thankfully, they didn't have far to go. The dog led them into a grove, another birch grove, where, in a small glade, stood three pit-houses. Judging by the big firepits nearby, coalmen must've lived here once. It seemed that most of them had gone away before the start of winter and only one had intended to stay—the dog's owner, apparently. His skeleton was still sitting under a split birch tree, mummified by frost, but practically untouched by wildlife.

The dog lay down by his master's body, staring pleadingly at Letka.

"Later," Letka told him, softly. "I promise."

Then she dragged Bośka to one of the houses, pulled down the planks and pine branches meant to keep snow out of the house, and climbed down a few broad, roughly hewn steps. Inside, the air was stuffy, but not altogether unpleasant. It smelled of earth and old smoke that had bitten deep into the wood over the years, and of the animal furs with which the earthen floor was covered.

Letka laid Bośka down by the hearth and rummaged around. She found a pile of firewood wrapped in oilskin and some additional furs that could serve as blankets—smelly and frayed, but warm nonetheless. With shivering hands, she built a fire, and as it danced and crackled, she first undressed Bośka, then herself, and stretched their wet clothes over the entranceway to dry. There was no door, so their woollen cloaks would keep at least some of the cold out.

Finally, the two of them snuggled together under the furs, buried themselves deep in their musty, scratchy warmth. The small space warmed up quickly, and the pithouse filled with the ticking of drying wood and the sweet scent of sap.

Letka woke up—startled to find that she had fallen asleep. Blood rushed to her temples, her heart began to pound. She hurriedly checked if Bośka was still alive. She was. Her breathing was somewhat labored but regular. A deep, red flush covered the girl's face.

Letka sighed with relief and waited for the pounding in her chest to die down. Then she propped herself on her elbow to look around.

Little mots of sunlight were dancing on the earthen floor of the hut, having squeezed their way between the clothes covering the entryway. Somewhere in the distance, a faint murmur of dripping water could be heard. Letka leaned forward, pulled the hanging clothes aside and gazed out of the pit-house. She was surprised to see that not a trace of snow was left anywhere. A delicate golden mist covered the birchwood.

The dog barked, his voice ringing in the fresh, spring air.

Letka bundled herself in one of the furs and climbed out of the hut. The wet grass tickled her feet. She nearly burst with laughter, seeing how pink they were.

Her stomach rumbled. She drew in a deep breath and realized that, in the birchwood, the morning dew smelled of tears.

The dog barked again and ran up to her. He sat down at her side, whimpering softly.

Letka looked around. Well rested and in full daylight, she recognized the glade. It was a common haunt of the coalmen from Borki, a village belonging to the same opole as Rybnitza. It would probably take less than an afternoon to reach the settlement.

"Well, we haven't made it very far," Letka said, ruffling the dog's ears absentmindedly. "I'll go to the village to get help. I'm sure they'll build a proper pyre for your master." The dog just stared at her with his big eyes. "Don't be sad. If the gods willed it so, there was nothing you could've done to save him."

The wind rose slightly and the birch trees began to sing. And Letka thought that, perhaps, one could defy the gods, for what were gods if not the shadows of men, long-armed and horrible in the cold of the night. Still, the price of such defiance would be steep. Oh, how steep. After all, it is a hard thing to fight against the order of the world.

She shivered. "There's one more thing I need to do, before I set off," she told the dog.

She pulled a pair of iron shears out of her pouch, walked up to the nearest birch tree and, as it sang its sorrowful song, began to cut long, thin twigs off its branches. She was making a new wreath.

Bogna had told her to seek solace in her love and in the birchsong of the spring festival.

There's no solace in this, Letka thought fiercely. But there is pride. There is pride.

AUTHOR BIOS

A professional author since 2007, **Josh Reynolds** has over thirty novels to his name, as well as numerous short stories, novellas and audio scripts. Born and raised in South Carolina, he now resides in Sheffield with his wife and daughter, as well as a highly excitable dog and something he hopes is a cat. A complete list of his work can be found at joshuamreynolds.co.uk.

Petra Rapaić is someone who likes reading and writing, and occasionally some of the writings turn out just fine. As long as the readers are happy, Petra is happy too.

Srebrenka Peregrin is a storyteller, translator, and educator. She is also an award-winning author of short stories, which deal with intimate relationships, mental health, history, myths, and women's rights. She enjoys therapeutic use and modern retellings of folk and fairy tales, performing them in libraries, schools, museums, and at SF&F conventions. She has co-authored three collections of fairy tales from around the world: Bajkarice, Bajkari, and Bajkarenje. Srebrenka works with grown-ups, and children of all ages, teaching English and the art of storytelling in Croatia.

Ivana Geček is a visual artist and cartoonist based in Zagreb, Croatia. Her interests lie in various types of storytelling, with themes ranging from slice of life to horror. Her comics have been published in Croatia and Sweden. In her spare time she likes to read, paint and watch good and bad horror movies.

Petra Valković (1983) was born in Pula, where she now lives and works. She has a degree in History and Croatian language and literature. She began writing in her early high school years and never stopped since. Six of her short stories, as well as a few history articles, were published in various collections. Her first novel Zaboravljeni (The Forgotten, 2022) is available through Naklada Cranium. She loves all things SF- and fantasy-related, and her other interests include photography, exploring old historical sites, and all sorts of creative things. Music is her main fuel and inspiration.

Laura J. Veligor grew up in a house on the edge of the woods just outside the area known for the historic Salem Witchcraft Trials. Currently residing in Cambridge, Massachusetts, she works at a local non-profit healthcare organization by day and writes stories of the folk horror and gothic fiction variety by night. Laura's writing is influenced by a love of all things spooky and strange, with a particular interest in myths, folklore, and the supernatural. She can often be found writing poetry, painting, and getting lost in a good book—all with her beloved cat, Hazel, by her side.

Ivan Botica was your average fantasy nut who had an itch for telling stories. While studying business, he decided to test his writing mettle and take a shot at publishing. Once Upon a Winter is now his debut, in proud collaboration with Shtriga.

Robert Norok is a computer scientist and educator from Slovenia. He can usually be found near the Slovenia-Italy border, where he is from, or in the capital, Ljubljana, where he works. When he is not coding, Robert crafts stories for younger audiences, as well as fantasy and sci-fi adventures for older readers. Chief among his interests is Slavic mythology, especially tales from his home country, which he loves to include in his stories.

Born at the end of 1992, just in time to see her old country fall apart and to start growing up together with the new one, the Czech writer **Miha Trochael** has always been interested in supernatural themes. The "dark side" has especially captured her curiosity, which has influenced her stories ever since. Eventually her interests guided her to the Slavic roots, our gods, all the creatures of our mythology, and beyond.

Lidiana Bunda graduated with an MA in Geography with a focus on refugee resettlement and refugee camps. She organizes locally for Palestine, the decriminalization of sex work, and reproductive rights in the US. Published in academic anthologies, this is Lidiana's first fictional published piece. For questions or inquiries you can contact Lidiana Bunda at bundalidiana@gmail.com.

Life according to **Greg Gajek** begins in the summer of 1987. And it is a simple life, a life of books. Of reading them, translating them and writing them. Greg is the author of ten novels, many of which were inspired by Slavics myths, culture and history. He lives in Warsaw, Poland, with his wife and a wizened old rabbit.

OTHER CONTRIBUTORS

Vesna Kurilić is a historical fantasy writer and werewolf-loving, skirt-making librarian. Her main literary focus is reclaiming local history on behalf of non-binary, queer folks like herself, and making it accessible and relatable to readers. A native and resident of Rijeka, Croatia, she's recently discovered a passion for paying forward what the Croatian fandom had given her—a chance to tell the stories she wants to read, while building a friendly and welcoming community.

Antonija Mežnarić is a Croatian writer, editor, podcaster and cosplayer. She writes queer horror and fantasy, mostly inspired by South Slavic folklore which is evident in her collection of folk horror stories *Mistress of Geese*, two published horror novellas (in English) and one novel (in Croatian). You can follow her book ramblings on hauntednarratives.com or on Instagram and Twitter @antonijamezni.

Karmen Fodrek is a graphic designer and fantasy lover. She's a host of the podcast Mythoslavic, dedicated to the Slavic mythology and folk tales. Follow her on her epic journey to unearth the secrets Slavic cultures hide by listening to Mythoslavic on Apple Podcast, Spotify, and other places you listen to your podcasts.

Antonio Filipović is an illustrator and a comic book artist from Rijeka, where he studies Visual Communications and Graphic Design. In his comics he likes to focus on LGBTIQ+ themes, explored through genres of mythology, surrealism and fantasy. He creates his illustrations by mixing traditional and digital media, with the focus on atmosphere and mood. And when he's not writing or illustrating, he's probably somewhere reading about obscure historical moments, or maniacally worldbuilding fantasy settings.

ABOUT SHTRIGA

Hidden Stories In Your Pocket.
Scifi, fantasy and horror on the go. Publishing your daily dose of speculative fiction since 2020.

Visit us at
www.shtriga.com
@shtrigabooks
(Facebook, Instagram, Twitter)

OTHER BOOKS:

Ranger Paraversum series by Vesna Kurilić:
Johnny's Girls
Girls in Black
Girls Back Home
Girls Across Worlds
Freddie and Ivan Go Ice Skating Together

Igor Rendić:
A Town Called River

Antonija Mežnarić:
What Do Nightmares Dream of
Mistress of Geese
It Eats Us From the Inside
Od kolijevke pa do groba

Printed in the USA
CPSIA information can be obtained
at www.ICGtesting.com
LVHW012154141123
763978LV00031B/686